Get Your
Coventry Romances
Home Subscription NOW

And Get These
4 Best-Selling Novels
FREE:

LACEY
by Claudette Williams

THE ROMANTIC WIDOW
by Mollie Chappell

HELENE
by Leonora Blythe

THE HEARTBREAK TRIANGLE
by Nora Hampton

A Home Subscription! It's the easiest and most convenient way to get every one of the exciting Coventry Romance Novels! ...And you get 4 of them FREE!

You pay nothing extra for this convenience: there are no additional charges...you don't even pay for postage! Fill out and send us the handy coupon now. and we'll send you 4 exciting Coventry Romance novels absolutely FREE!

SEND NO MONEY, GET THESE
FOUR BOOKS FREE!

THE COVINGTON INHERITANCE

Barbara Hazard

FAWCETT COVENTRY • NEW YORK

THE COVINGTON INHERITANCE

Published by Fawcett Coventry Books, CBS Educational and Professional Publishing, a division of CBS Inc.

ISBN: 0-449-50267-8

Printed in the United States of America

First Fawcett Coventry printing: February 1982

10 9 8 7 6 5 4 3 2 1

THE
COVINGTON
INHERITANCE

PROLOGUE

THE CANDLES WERE burning low and it was very late when at last the old woman straightened up and, laying down her quill, gratefully massaged her twisted, tired fingers. As she did so, she stared at the letters she had spent all evening writing, a wicked smile of satisfaction creeping over her wrinkled face, and she laughed out loud, a raucous chuckle of complete enjoyment. The old bulldog, obese and almost blind, who was sleeping at her feet gave a snort of alarm before he settled his head back on his paws and began to snore again.

"Do be quiet, Excalibur!" she said tartly, pushing him a little with her foot to reinforce her command. The dog paid no attention to her, but then he had been her constant companion for so many years he knew instinctively this was an order he did not have to obey. Of the two of them, it was hard to tell which was the more decrepit. The woman, although she was still as slender as a girl, appeared to be of a great age. The powdered wig of an earlier time, with its high pompadour and dangling curls over each ear, that she wore on her head did nothing to enhance her lined face and sunken lips. She wore a man's dressing gown of moth-eaten scarlet velvet and a worn fur collar that had belonged to her father, and on her fingers and wrists, at her throat and set in her earlobes, were all manner of jewels. They had not been cleaned in some time, but still they twinkled in the light of the candelabra that was set on the writing desk. One candle sputtered, and as she reached out to extinguish it, a huge ruby solitaire sparkled in the light.

The room she was in was no less incredible than she was herself. It was very large and was filled with all manner of furniture, placed with complete disregard for period or style, so that priceless antiques sat next to coarse country pieces of rough construction. Although it appeared to be a drawing room from its size and the length of the many windows set along one side wall, one end was dominated by a huge four-poster bed, draped in faded purple hangings heavy with tarnished gold braid. In addition to the bed, there were sofas and chairs and stools, as well as tables and étagères filled with the bric-à-brac of many generations. Every surface seemed to be covered; on one large table of Queen Anne style was placed a pair of ancient dueling pistols, several books and papers, two fragile French figurines and an irreplaceable Chinese porcelain bowl in which reposed a large and moldy stuffed owl. The floors of the apartment were covered with several carpets, laid one over the other. Some were priceless orientals, some worn drugget more suitable to the servants' quarters. The mantel over the huge fireplace held still more ornaments, and occupying a position of honor on the center of the wall above it was a dark oil-painting of an elderly man dressed in the clothes of the middle 1700s. There was a distinct family resemblance between the old lady and the gentleman in the portrait. Perhaps it was the deep set of the dark eyes under their bushy brows, perhaps the arrogant beak of a nose, or perhaps the haughty expression of the aristocrat who bowed to no man save his king. On a wing chair near the fire, several gowns had been thrown carelessly, as if the lady had had trouble deciding what to wear before she put on the velvet robe for warmth and comfort. In spite of the drafts that occasionally stirred the drapes and curtains, and the fierce wind that could be heard moaning outside the windows, the room was very hot, so hot that one wondered why such a garment was necessary.

The old woman picked up the last letter she had written and read it through again, nodding her head in satisfaction and tapping one finger on the desk as she read. "Yes, that will fetch 'em!" she muttered to herself, and as the old dog pricked up his ears, she added, "And then we shall see! Oh yes, Excalibur, than we shall see!"

She rose unsteadily from the writing desk and held onto it tightly for a moment until she was sure of her balance, and then, picking up an ebony cane with a chased silver head, she moved slowly towards the fire and a table which held several decanters and glasses that was placed conveniently near the faded wing chair. She poured herself a glass of wine and held it up to the firelight, admiring the ruby color, so like so many of her jewels. Father had been fond of rubies. With the tip of her cane she pushed the discarded gowns to the floor and sank into the chair to stare at the dying fire. She wondered if it were worthwhile to summon Crowell to build it up again, for she knew it was very late. She should sleep, but sleep came hard these days. Some nights she did not even close her eyes at all, but wandered aimlessly around the room, picking up and admiring her bibelots with all the memories they held, and sipping the wine that her doctor had forbidden her to touch anymore. When he had made that pronouncement, she had scowled at him and he had flushed before he said, "Yes, but it will kill you, Lady Cecily, I warn you! No more wine, nor brandy, nor spirits of any kind or I cannot be responsible for the consequences!"

At that she retorted, "And if I abstain, dear Dr.

9

Ward, you will promise me a complete recovery from all my maladies and a chance to live for many more years?"

The doctor did not reply, and she shrugged her shoulders. "Let us be honest and admit I have but little time left. I am, as well you know, almost eighty and I have lived hard. What good can it possibly do to give up the few comforts I have left to me in my remaining days? Besides, it eases the pain."

Matthew Ward shook his head, but he did not attempt to reason with her. He had been her personal physician for only a few years since he had taken over the practice when the old doctor died, but he knew full well that neither he nor any man alive could make her change her mind. There had been only one man who could control her, he had heard, and he had been in his grave these forty years.

Now she sipped her wine and smiled. Yes, she had very little time left. She had known it for weeks, and that was the reason she had spent the evening painfully writing her seven letters. Spenser could address them in the morning, but she had not cared to dictate the contents to her long-suffering secretary-companion. This was to be her secret, and she wished to relish it alone. She chuckled again, and then she put her empty glass down with a snap. No more wine tonight, she told herself. It was a little late to begin obeying her doctor, but until she had finished the task she had set for herself, she would be careful, no matter how her body cried out for the cessation of pain the liquor always provided. What she was about to do was so very important, and it promised to be the most entertaining enterprise she had undertaken for many a year as well. And when she had reached a successful conclusion, why, then she would be grateful to go to her grave, and peace at last.

She struggled to her feet and for a moment stood looking up at the harsh face in the portrait above. Then, nodding her head, she prepared for bed. When she was under the covers, she closed her eyes and sighed, and, as if the letter writing had eased her spirits and her pain for this evening at least, she slipped easily into deep slumber. In a short time, both Lady Cecily and Excalibur were snoring gently. The fire died down, and the only other sounds to be heard were those of the wind which continued to moan around the house, and the incessant reverberation of the breakers as they crashed against the rocks far below.

CHAPTER 1

"I SAY! WHAT a singular thing!"

Mrs. Covington looked up, startled, from her breakfast plate to see her normally good-natured husband indignantly frowning over a letter he had received in the morning post. His face, always a bit florid, was now even more highly colored, and his lips were set in a most uncharacteristic frown. Quickly in her mind Mrs. Covington reviewed her latest expenditures. Of course it was probably a bill, it always seemed to be a bill, she thought, but for the life of her she could not remember spending any extraordinary amount of money these past few weeks. Perhaps Caroline . . .? No, not Caroline. It had to be Gregory again. Whatever had he been up to in London *this* time?

Breaking into her revery, her husband shook the letter impatiently, and said, "I have never heard such impertinence! How *dare* she? Here, Janet, just listen to this!"

He read the letter aloud in a still disbelieving voice, and Mrs. Covington put down her coffee cup and so far forgot herself as to sit with her mouth open in amazement. When he had finished and thrown down the letter in disgust, she could not even attempt to speak. Indeed, it would have been impossible in any case, for her husband had risen and was pacing the breakfast room in agitation, muttering to himself.

"Bad lot indeed! Not worthy of her money! I don't know how she can judge whether we are a bad lot or not; she hasn't had anything to do with us for years! Buried up there in that ancient pile of stone my grandfather so foolishly left her, along with most of his fortune, never answering letters or inquiries about her health, nor even replying to Christmas greetings! Why, you remember, Janet, only last year I sent her twelve bottles of an excellent Madeira, but did we hear a word of thanks? Not a word! And here she has the colossal gall to imply that far from sending her the wine through a proper family concern for her welfare, I was trying to bribe her into leaving her fortune to me! I am glad she is not in this room, I can tell you, that miserable old maid, for I should give her a piece of my mind for such impudence!"

Mrs. Covington wisely said nothing. She knew only too well that George would do no such thing if his elderly aunt were standing before him. In fact, the reason he was probably so upset was that he had indeed sent the wine with the express intention of remaining in Aunt Cecily's good graces. She remembered now his airy statement about the gift. "It can do no harm to keep on her good side, m'dear. She must be about to totter off any day, and since I know she has not seen any of her relatives for years, why should we not remind her of our existence? It is not that I cannot support my family, but money is always welcome; the way Gregory runs through it, we can never have enough! And perhaps Caroline, with a larger portion, might still make an excellent match!"

Mrs. Covington had not needed to be reminded that her son Gregory was a spendthrift. She had always had a guilty suspicion that he had inherited

14

this trait from her side of the family, for although her lineage was impeccable, her father, the late Earl of Wye, had been an inveterate gamester, and his only son had dissipated whatever money that was left in such an expeditious manner that he had only just escaped to the continent before his pack of creditors could have sent him to Newgate. Janet Covington thought she had been very fortunate to attract her husband in her first and—as her father pointed out—her only season, for there was no more money to be spent on such frivolity. That she loved him as well was an unexpected bonus. As for Caroline, well, she was a Covington through and through. Sensible, steady, and serious. And although she seemed only amused that her mama was so upset that she had not contracted an eligible alliance by the great age of twenty-four, when taxed with her failure she only smiled a little and said, "But I have found no one I would like to spend the rest of my life with, Mama! The gentlemen of the *haut ton* are all so silly, so puffed up with conceit for their importance, their handsome good looks, and gorgeous attire. And their whole attention appears to be given to gaming and wenching and drinking! No, I thank you. I think on the whole, and even considering the alternative, I would prefer to remain an old maid!"

Mrs. Covington had thrown up her hands in horror, but not one of her warnings about the undesirability of the single state in the year 1814 could move Caroline to accept Lord Salford or even Mr. Tyson-Jones, both of whom had shown a distinct partiality for her daughter. It is not that she is unattractive, Mrs. Covington thought defensively. Of course she is not the blonde that is preferred in the current mode, for no one could call her soft wavy brown hair anything out of the ordinary, and it must be admitted that she was above average height, which eliminated many a gentleman from the possibility list, but her face was attractive and her figure excellent. Her best feature was her large blue eyes.

If only she would be more lively, Mrs. Covington had thought so many times. Instead of sitting mumchance beside me at a party, why could she not learn to flirt a little, to discover the benefits to be derived from a gay and lilting laugh, a demure blush, and lowered eyelashes? And it was not as if she had no conversation, either. Many a time her mother had had to take her to task for expressing her thoughts too vehemently. Gentlemen, as Mrs. Covington pointed out, did not wish a learned conversation with women, nor did they care to have their opinions questioned. She sighed and then was speedily recalled to the breakfast room. "For heaven's sakes, Janet!" her husband was saying in exasperation, "I have asked you the same question three times!"

"I am sorry, my dear!" she murmured, smiling lovingly at his stout figure and indignant face. "I was not attending. You asked . . .?"

"I asked if you thought we should comply with Aunt Cecily's wishes. Here she says that although she has no desire to see either you or me, and would turn us from her door if we should appear—such arrogance!—she is prepared to welcome Caroline and Gregory for a visit. Do you understand? They are to go alone! I cannot like it!"

"Cannot like what, Father?" his daughter asked, coming into the breakfast room and dropping a light kiss on her mother's frivolous morning cap before she took a seat.

For answer, her father handed her the letter. Caroline read it slowly while both her parents waited eagerly for her comments. When she had finished, she folded the letter and poured herself a cup of coffee.

"Well? What do you think of that, miss?"

Caroline looked at him over the rim of her cup, her blue eyes twinkling. "I imagine we are not required to go if we do not wish to, Father?" she asked. "I must admit this royal summons does not make me all anxiety to meet my great aunt! But I am confused

16

that she wishes to skip a generation in the disposal of her fortune. Whatever did you all do to give her such a dislike of you?"

Mr. Covington looked confused as he shook his head. "I haven't the foggiest notion!" he admitted. "I only met her once, when I was a green lad, but I know m' father said there was bad feelings between Aunt Cecily and the rest of her family, especially when my grandfather left her most of the estate. Everyone felt it was insane to leave so much wealth and power in the hands of a mere woman, and now we see the result—disastrous! Of course she was seven years younger than my father, a very late addition to the family. Perhaps that is why my grandfather doted on her . . ." He broke off these reminiscences and said, "Of course you are not required to go, Caro, but you can be sure all the others will be making plans to leave for the north immediately! I would not have you and Gregory left out of her will simply because you did not care to make the journey!"

"All what others?" Caroline asked calmly, buttering a piece of toast. "The only relative I know is Roger, Lord Danvers, and his wife, and, oh yes, Cecilia North, Aunt Mary's daughter. You remember, Mama, we met her in London two years ago when we went up for the season. To be sure, she is very young."

"She was not out then, that is true," her mother agreed, counting on her fingers, "but she must be nineteen now. Be sure she will be there! Your Aunt Mary will see to that!" Mrs. Covington sniffed; there was no love lost between the two sisters-in-law.

Mr. Covington took his seat again and looked thoughtful. "Yes, I imagine both Roger and Cecilia will be there. I have often thought it so very obvious that Mary practically named her daughter after my aunt; I am sure the old lady saw through the ploy! But there are some second cousins as well. Cecily

17

had two brothers and a sister. Her brother Anthony had only a single issue, a son, Hector, who died childless. Then there was my father, John, who had me and your Aunt Rose and Aunt Mary. But there was also Emily Covington, Lady Cecily's oldest sister. She married a man named Albert Russell and they had two children, Gloriana and Donald. Gloriana married Lord St. Williams; they had one son, who, if I remember correctly, came into a great fortune from his father's side. I am sure I don't know why *he* needs any of Aunt Cecily's! And of course Donald has one living son as well, by the name of Alistair Russell. I am surprised you never met them in London, Caro, but perhaps they were abroad at the time. They are both considerably older than you; I have no idea if they are married or single!"

"We do not appear to be a very close family, do we?" Caroline asked, stirring her coffee.

Mr. Covington did not reply, for he was reading through Aunt Cecily's letter again. "But surely that is only six; you and Gregory, Roger and Cecilia, and John and Alistair. Yet here the old lady mentions seven guests. Perhaps her mind has become addled with age, unless she is including Roger's wife, Sylvia."

"We can be assured that Sylvia Danvers will be among the first to arrive!" Mrs. Covington said tartly. "Do say you will go, Caro! If nothing else, it will be a change for you! It has been such a dreary winter, and there is still so much time before the season opens in London. Wouldn't you enjoy a change of scene from Falconfield? And if Gregory wishes to travel directly from town, why, then you might go with Cecilia. I am sure that with your maids to accompany you, it would be considered proper, and you will have a chance to get to know your cousin better as well!"

She beamed at this happy line of reasoning, and Caroline twinkled again. "But you remember, Mama, I thought Cecilia a most silly young miss, with more

18

hair than wit, when first we met? All airs and graces and affectations!"

When her mother would have interjected an indignant comment, she held up her hand. "I am teasing you, Mama! Very well, I will go to Great-Aunt Cecily's, since I see I shall have no peace until I agree to the scheme, and I will endure Miss Cecilia's company on the journey as well. Perhaps she has changed in the past two years; I can only sincerely hope so!"

She sighed again, but Mrs. Covington was already making lists in her mind of the clothing that Caro would need, and the particularities of the journey, so she did not rise to the bait. Mr. Covington kissed his daughter and said, "Good girl! I know you will do just as you ought, Caro!" which caused her to raise her brows as both her parents left the breakfast room to make their plans for her departure as soon as possible.

Mrs. Covington retired to her morning room to write to her son and to Lady North. Dear Gregory, she thought, what a wonderful opportunity! She was more than slightly partial to her son, as her husband was to his daughter, and she did not see how any woman, even one as elderly as Aunt Cecily, could fail to be attracted to his handsome looks and easy manner, and although he was only twenty-one and quite the youngest male relative to be invited, she was sure he would captivate his great-aunt at once! She made a note to point out to him how very important his attendance and courtesy to the old lady was, and was secretly relieved that this visit would remove him from his cronies in town. Mr. Covington might look understandingly at his escapades and tell her that it was only to be expected from a young man when he first began kicking up his heels, and that Gregory would soon settle down after he got these wild oats out of his system, but Mrs. Covington could not help worrying about her son as she never had about Caroline. Gregory was

19

a dear boy, but there was that odd kick to his gallop!

In London, Gregory Covington was sleeping very late, completely innocent of the changes about to occur in his future plans, for he had gone with several of his cronies of Totting Hill Fields, where they had spent a most adventurous evening drinking far too much Blue Ruin in one of the lowliest taverns. In wending their unsteady way home in the early morning hours, they had had the great good fortune to be set upon by footpads, who, unfortunately for them, had underestimated the young men's capacity for drink. Gregory thought the splendid mill that followed was the perfect ending to the evening, although he was sure to regret the Blue Ruin when he finally woke up.

Across the park, and in quite a more fashionable and elegant part of town from his bachelor rooms, two of his relatives were not so delinquent in their hours. Lord St. Williams had read his post during breakfast, and after he had spent several frowning moments over his Great-Aunt Cecily's unusual letter, was not at all surprised to hear his butler announcing the arrival of his cousin Alistair.

"I told Mr. Russell you were at breakfast, m'lord!" this worthy said, "*and* that you did not like to be disturbed, but he insisted!" Seavers sniffed, and Lord St. Williams smiled at his indignation.

"Never mind, Seavers! Show him in before he breaks down the door!" he said cheerfully.

His butler looked shocked. "Not while *hi'm* on duty, m'lord!"

Lord St. Williams waved him away and folded his newspaper. There was small chance he would be able to finish it until he had dealt with Alistair. The door to the dining room opened, but before Seavers could announce him, Alistair Russell pushed past him. Lord St. Williams raised his quizzing glass. This was most unlike his cousin, who generally affected a bored air of *ennui déjà vu* on each and

20

every occasion and was apt to move languidly when he moved at all. One of the *on dits* in town this year was that when Mr. Russell and some friends had been attacked by thugs while returning late from Lady Wallingford's ball, Alistair had managed to run one of them through with his sword stick within moments, causing the others to flee. Rumor had it that when Sir Thomas Graves had bent over the man and announced that Alistair had killed him, Mr. Russell had waved his handkerchief before his nose and murmured, "Then shall we be on our way, dear boy? These robbers, so fatiguing, and such a bore!" The story had been repeated and embellished for many days.

Now Lord St. Williams saw that his cousin, although he appeared to be as detached and indifferent as ever, was not dressed in quite his usual style. True, not even the highest stickler could have found fault with his coat of blue superfine tailored by London's finest, nor with his buff pantaloons or shining pumps, but John was quick to notice the absence of most of the fobs and jewelry he was accustomed to trick himself out with, as well as a slightly more tousled hairdo à la Brutus than was Alistair's normal custom. His cravat as well, although it was an impeccable pristine white, was hardly the symphony of pleats and creases he generally spent so much time in arranging.

"Do come in and sit down, Cuz, and tell me how I may serve you!" Lord St. Williams said. "Some coffee? Or perhaps a tankard of ale? Or are you one of those who cannot bear to drink anything so common, even in the morning? I shall be happy to order you some wine . . ."

Mr. Russell waved away all offers of refreshment impatiently. In his hand he clutched a letter, and Lord St. Williams indicated it with his knife.

"So, you received one too, eh?" he asked. "Most unusual letter I have seen in many a day! It quite surpasses the one I had from Dolly when I told her

21

our association was at an end. Who would have thought the old lady would have such cheek? It almost inspires me to travel to Scotland to make her acquaintance!"

Mr. Russell remembered to sink gracefully into a chair before he answered. He was a man of some thirty years, and considered himself the top of any tree you cared to mention. His clothing was always superb, and his manner such as to discourage any toad-eating mushroom who dared to impinge on him, and he had for so many years been unable to find a young lady worthy of his elegance that he had never married. Although they both resided in London for most of the year, he was not a particular friend of his cousin's, however, for their paths led them in opposite directions. Mr. Russell's set of exquisites were considered fops by John St. Williams and his friends. They did not ride or drive a team; they considered boxing disgusting and were never seen at Gentleman Jackson's rooms for instruction in the manly art and perhaps some sparring practice with the master himself. St. Williams had not questioned the veracity of the story of the thug and the sword stick, for he knew his cousin would never dirty his hands on such lowly scum, even if he had had the skill. Although there was a faint family resemblance between the two men, mainly in their height, which made them taller than most men, and in their strong-featured good looks, where Mr. Russell was blond and fair-complexioned, Lord St. Williams was dark and tanned, his powerful arms and muscular legs showing his athletic inclinations. Beside him, his cousin looked like a thinner pale shadow of his masculine virility even though he was always more gorgeously attired. Now he stared at St. Williams' plain dressing gown and carelessly tied ascot and tried not to shudder.

"Yes, I received one!" he said, in his curiously light baritone. "I have never been so offended in my entire life! If she were a man I would call her out, 'pon my word I would! How dare she insult my father and cast aspersions on my mother and our grandmother? Old hag!"

"But a very wealthy old hag, when all is said and done," Lord St. Williams reminded him, his dark eyes crinkling in amusement. "I take it then, Alistair, that you have no intention of obeying this command? I am delighted you are so well before with the world that the money is of no interest to you!"

His cousin shifted in his chair and looked away from his host's amused glance. "As to that, of course I have no need of her money," he said airily. "But I *am* undecided, for although Great-Aunt is unsufferably rude, we as gentlemen have standards of conduct to uphold. I came at once to seek your advice. You *are* older than I; I decided to ask if you are planning to attend her, since surely we owe some courtesy to such an elderly member of the family!"

"I hardly think two years' advantage makes me any great font of wisdom, dear cuz!" Lord St. Williams said, wiping his mouth with his napkin and rising to his full height of six feet four inches. "But come, since I cannot tempt you with refreshment, let us retire to the library, where I will be glad to prop up my gouty foot and wrap up in my shawl while I give you the benefit of my years of experience!"

He ushered a protesting Mr. Russell from the dining room and along the hall. There was a cheerful fire burning in the library, where the two cousins found Andrews, his lordship's secretary, at work, a great pile of papers on the mahogany desk before him. He rose at once and excused himself.

"I shall be with you presently, Andrews," Lord St. Williams said. "I do remember my promise to go over those papers with you this morning, never fear!"

As the secretary bowed himself out, Lord St. Williams remarked, "Business! There is always business to take care of! In this case, however, it can await your pleasure, Cuz. Here, take this chair. I think you will find it tolerably comfortable."

Since Lord St. Williams' library was exceedingly luxurious, as befitted a man of his wealth, and any one of the leather upholstered chairs would have been more than adequate, Mr. Russell did not reply, but took the seat indicated and waited for his cousin to speak.

"You asked my plans; I have hardly had time to formulate them. It would be awkward for me to leave town at this time; you yourself have seen the press of business that has descended on me, and frankly, after reading that letter, I am more than tempted to tell the old lady what she may do with her fortune—er, in a manner befitting my station as a gentleman with standards, of course!"

Mr. Russell allowed a small frown of irritation to pass over his usually expressionless features. It seemed that Lord St. Williams was determined to tease him, and he was not used to being so treated, but after a moment he composed himself and laughed gently.

"As you say, Cuz, my immediate reaction too. I even thought to consign the letter to the fire, unanswered, and think no more about it. And yet . . . perhaps it would be amusing!"

Lord St. Williams cocked an eyebrow at his cousin and waited.

"Have you considered how entertaining it would be, watching the others manuevering around, being pleasant and obsequious as they try to get on Great-Aunt Cecily's good side?"

"If she has one, which is an extremely doubtful assumption!" Lord St. Williams interjected.

"Town has become so tedious!" Alistair continued, changing his tack. "I swear I am worn down with

24

invitations to the most boring events! If I have to attend another card party or reception I think I shall go mad! Surely you have found it so too! And so many weeks before the season can properly begin!"

"It sounds as if you have made up your mind to travel north, then," John said, interrupting this monologue.

"Perhaps. And it would be infinitely more enjoyable if you would come with me. Come, John, are you not at all interested in the old family estate? Have you no desire to see your roots, the place where it all began so many years ago?"

"Situated as it is, by the sea and so far north, it is sure to be very uncomfortable at this time of year," Lord St. Williams said, not at all moved by this appeal to family feelings. "Probably leaks and is poorly appointed. The food is sure to be terrible as well, for I hardly imagine Great-Aunt the type to spend her blunt on a French chef, even if she could keep one so deep in the wilds, and I imagine the rooms are drafty and ill-lit as well. No, on the whole I think I shall be forced to decline. Do her a world of good to have one great-nephew who won't dance to her piping!"

Lord St. Williams was surprised to see the look of irritation that again appeared on his cousin's features. For some unfathomable reason, Alistair did indeed intend to travel north, and he wished his cousin to accompany him. It was a mystery, for he knew Alistair to be almost as wealthy as he was himself. He brought his mind back to the present situation as his cousin said, "But perhaps, John, your nonattendance might cause bad feelings among the others of the family? If you do not come and all the rest do, and then the old lady takes it into her head to leave her fortune to you since none of the rest of us measure up to whatever criterion she has set, there will be some who say your absence was a calculated move, and hardly fair!"

25

He paused as Lord St. Williams raised a haughty brow. "I must admit I had not thought of it in that light! And yet, Cuz, I have the distinct impression that what you really wish is for me to say I will go, so I can drive you north and you will not have to take the trouble. Forgive me when I say I cannot believe my company is so important to you; you have never sought it out before!"

His cousin flushed a little and admitted that there was that, for he knew how skilled St. Williams was with a team, and how much more quickly and in greater comfort they could travel if he held the reins. St. Williams waved away these compliments and rose. "Well, I shall send you word of my decision, Alistair. I promise to consider your proposal seriously. And now you must excuse me; I did indeed intend to apply myself to business this morning. In fact, if I do not get to it, there will be no question of my going anywhere in the foreseeable future!"

Lord Russell was forced to rise and take his leave, after appealing one more time to John's love of adventure, and had to be content with his cousin's promise to send word of his decision within the week.

Lord St. Williams did not summom Andrews immediately. Instead, he sat in a brown study before the fire, his eyes narrowed in thought as he stared into the flames. How very curiously Alistair was behaving! As for the rest of the family, he did not even know all of them and had no desire to make their closer acquaintance. In his opinion, relatives were seldom the type you wanted as bosom companions, and the more often they could be avoided, the better. The only one other than Lord Russell that he had met had been his second cousin, Roger, Lord Danvers, and his wife, and remembering the pair of them, he was almost tempted to send an immediate and firm denial to Alistair, and Great-Aunt Cecily as well. To be cooped up in an ancinet castle for several weeks with those two was an almost unbeatable incentive to remain in town, or almost anywhere else, if it came to that. He shrugged, determined to put the problem from his mind, and rang for his secretary.

At that exact moment, those two of whom he thought were deep in conversation in the salon of their town house in St. James Square. Or perhaps it would be more accurate to say that Lady Danvers was giving a monologue. She sat on the edge of a delicate brocade sofa, her salts and handkerchief in her hand, and occasionally she bounced excitedly as she instructed her husband in what she wished him to do. The sofa creaked in protest each time she did so, for although Lady Danvers was only twenty-three, she was an extremely fat young lady. At her marriage two years previous, she had been pleasingly plump, but since that time she had gained weight at an alarming rate. Some of her acquaintances thought that perhaps it was because she had accepted Lord Danvers, and one pert young miss had gone so far as to say that marriage to him would be enough to drive anyone to the comfits dish, if not worse! It was true that Lord Danvers was an unprepossessing young man. Exceedingly stout, with thinning mouse-colored hair and a double chin, his pale blue eyes tended to pop out of his head whenever he was surprised, making him look like an amazed and very fat baby. This condition occurred often, for Lord Danvers was not needlewitted by any means, and as he was very gullible as well, he tended to believe the most outrageous statements and take them as truth. He seldom had anything original to say for himself. When he did speak, it was generally in clichés, and most of the haut ton, although tolerating him for his title, made every effort to avoid being left in his company for more than a moment. Sir Roger was well known as a bore of the first water.

At the moment, he was standing before his wife,

his hands clasped behind him, looking for all the world like a small boy being chastised after he had been caught in the cookie jar.

"I say we shall go, Roger!" Lady Danvers announced, bouncing up and down in her vehemence, and causing the sofa to creak even more alarmingly. "After, of course, I have accepted your aunt's invitation!"

"But . . . but . . ." Lord Danvers began.

"I know what you are going to say, sir," his wife swept on, pointing a finger at his prominent middle and wishing for perhaps the hundredth time that her husband would consider wearing a corset. "But one can never have enough money, and even though *you* think we are well before with the world, I can assure you that that is not the case. You must look to the future! What if we were to have a large and costly family? You must remember that they would have to be provided for! And why should some other relative win this rich prize? I am sure we have as much right as anybody to inherit. After all, your mother was Grandfather Covington's *oldest* child!"

She paused for breath, while Lord Danvers wondered what that had to say to anything, but wisely he did not try to interrupt her again. With some alarm, he watched her toss her dark curls and bury her face in her handkerchief. He hoped dear Sylvia was not about to have one of her spells! He had not been married very long before he discovered the heights she could attain when she was upset. Such floods of tears, such impassioned screaming! Why, once she had even thrown a vase at him and it had only missed his head by inches before it smashed against the wall! He threw out his hands and would have tried to calm her, but she lowered the handkerchief, stared at him fiercely, and said, "I shall be most upset, Roger, *most upset*, if you do not agree to this visit! Do you understand?"

She stopped and waited for his reply, her little

dark eyes fixed accusingly on his face. Lord Danvers was forced to admit defeat. He had no desire to take a long and uncomfortable journey to Scotland, or to spend any amount of time with this great-aunt who was sure to be a terror and a bully, and he had several things planned to do in town this next month, but he mentioned none of these objections. There was no sense in trying to bring Sylvia around, not when there was money at stake. He had discovered even before she had her first spell that his wife was a squeeze-penny, nay, even worse, she was obsessed with money, and even his more-than-modest fortune was not enough for her. There was no need for them to dine on a neck of mutton or a boiled pig's face when they were alone, but Sylvia saw to it that they did, for both dishes were inexpensive and filling. He was not allowed to buy the best quality wine any-more, and she had forced him to sell one of his teams as an economy as well, and he was always replacing the servants, since no one would stay very long in a house where they were expected to do the work of at least two others. Sylvia paid very poorly and she would tolerate only a small staff to boot. In his more fanciful moments, Lord Danvers had thought it too bad his wife had not married someone who would derive more benefit from her tight, saving ways, but he knew she would never have considered anyone but as rich a man as she could find. It was amazing how different she had been when he was courting her, all smiles and tender looks and soft pats of her hands. Now he swallowed and nodded his head in agreement, and he was rewarded with one of the lady's warmest premarital smiles before she waddled away to write her acceptance to the invitation.

In due time Gregory was informed of the visit, and being a good-natured young man, was perfectly happy to obey his mama, especially since he was badly dipped at the moment and the summons came at an opportune time to rusticate and recoup his losses. He did not dare to ask his father for an advance on his allowance twice in one quarter. He planned to travel by stage, as an extra economy, and told his valet he might have a holiday until his return to town.

So all Great-Aunt Cecily's invited guests made preparations for the journey. Lord and Lady Danvers left London, predictably behind a single pair of horses. Even John St. Williams found himself unable to refuse to attend, not in any response to his cousin's pleadings, but from his own unholy desire to see the fun. Miss Cecilia North was delighted to accept Mrs. Covington's suggestion that she travel with her cousin Caroline. Her mother, Lady North, had been most effusive when she accepted the plan.

"A perfect solution, Janet, how kind of you to suggest it!" she wrote in her flowery script. "And since Caroline is *so* much older than Cecilia, she will be a *perfect* chaperone! Such a comfort for me to know that my dearest girl will be so well taken care of, by a *mature* woman well past any giddy, girlish ways!"

This letter so incensed Mrs. Covington that she went tight-lipped about the house for a week, and very uncharacteristically bullied the local dressmaker into finishing two very charming and attractive new gowns for her daughter; and lent Caroline her pearl set and a small diamond necklet, as well as a very pretty blue cape lined with fur that had a matching hood, to enhance her toilette. Caroline was more amused than insulted by her aunt's disparaging appraisal of her station of life, but she was delighted with these new acquisitions.

In quite another part of England, someone else was also preparing to travel to the ancestral estate of the Covingtons', but the intentions of this person to be a member of the party were as yet unknown to the rest of the family.

All young and healthy, perhaps it was not strange that not a one of them had the slightest premonition of the trouble that would come upon them as a result of this visit to Rockledge, Scotland, in February in the year 1814, and how this one simple alteration in their lives would forever change the course of their destinies.

CHAPTER 2

BY THE TIME Mr. Covington's carriage had reached the border between England and Scotland, his daughter Caroline had to admit that, far from improving in the two intervening years since they had met, her cousin Cecilia had become even more silly and affected. The two girls sat together facing forward, while across from them, with their backs to the horses, their maids clutched dressing cases, shawls, and extra rugs. Cecilia ignored both her own maid, Molly Deems, and Caroline's old servant, Miss Wentworth, while she chatted gaily about London, the season she was soon to enjoy, her clothes, her possessions, her beaux, and her family. Caroline made an effort to be attentive; it was, after all, a very long way they had to travel cooped up together, but after the third day she was fast becoming impatient, and wished the roads were not so rough that she could not read a book, thereby cutting off this monotonous monologue.

Besides the coachman, her father had sent a groom on horseback with them, to serve as equerry, and this servant did much to ease their journey. Every evening when they gratefully climbed down and stretched their aching bodies at the inn he chose for them, everything was in readiness, a hot meal waiting and their rooms prepared. Cecilia was inclined to turn up her pretty nose at some of these hostelries, but Grafton, the groom, told Caroline that as they got farther north, the inns were the best he could find.

To Caroline it was all an exciting adventure, and she watched the changing scene with interest, but as they got closer to Rockledge, she was surprised to find that Cecilia's artless chatter had stopped completely. She stole a sideways glance at her cousin, hoping the girl was not sickening, and saw her clutching the leather side strap as the carriage bounced over the rutted country roads, her face white and apprehensive.

Their way had become progressively more rugged, and the countryside more lonely and savage. This morning there was a cold rain falling which did not help cheer the dark February day. The widely scattered villages they passed through did not even seem to be inhabited; there were no children at play, no barking dogs or laden farm carts to be seen. If it had not been for an occasional plume of chimney smoke, they would never have known that anyone lived in those tightly shuttered gray stone houses, with their dreary empty garden patches. It was all very desolate, very wild, and very much unlike Middlesex County, where Miss Cecilia North generally resided.

"Are you all right, Cousin?" Caroline asked. Cecilia started, her face paling a little more, and then she whispered, "I do not like this place! Oh, it is so frightening—so lonely! Why did Mama make me come?"

Relieved that it was only fear of the unknown, and not that she had to arrive with a sick girl on her hands, Caroline patted her shoulder and sought to calm her. "It is just that we are not used to such scenery, Cuz! See there, through the mist! I believe that is what they call a tor; it is very mountainous, is it not? And just think, Cecy, all around us are the famous glens of Scotland, where the clans hid before they came out to fight, behind their lairds and swirling bagpipes! How very interesting it all is, for so much history has been made in this land!"

Cecilia peered through the rain, her face whiter now than before, as if she feared a band of kilted savages was even now stalking the carriage and getting set to ride down on them, swinging their cudgels and screaming their war cries. Caroline sighed. It appeared that her attempt to distract the girl had frightened her even more. After her earlier show of sophistication, she was turning out to be a very timid little country mouse, although Caroline had to admit she had seldom seen a prettier girl than Cecilia North. She had a slight, girlish figure, and her heart-shaped face, with its rose-tinged cheeks, gentle mouth, and melting brown eyes, was surrounded by clouds of chesnut hair. Until she spoke, she was captivating; when she did, it became obvious that no one, after all, is perfect.

Caroline drew her fur-lined cloak closer around her, for the morning was damp and chilly, even with the hot bricks at their feet. "Are you all right, Molly? Wentworth?" she asked. "Do use those extra carriage robes if you feel the chill!" Both maids smiled at her; such a kind lady, Miss Caroline! Cecilia looked amazed at her concern for such lowly people. The maids were only there to look after them, after all, not to comfort themselves!

When they stopped at noontime at a tiny inn so the ladies might refresh themselves, Grafton drew Caroline to one side.

"I have been asking the host, miss, and he says there is no decent place to stay between here and Rockledge. We must either remain here until morning or press on, even though that means we will arrive later than you had hoped. There is no chance that we can lose our way, however. He says the road is clearly marked."

Caroline looked at the gloomy hostelry with its

dark taproom that smelled so strongly of ale, and, remembering the one small bedroom she and her cousin and the maids would have to share, did not hesitate.

"By all means let us press on, Henry! I am sure we are all weary of this long journey and will be grateful to reach our destination even if we must do so after dark!"

She hurried her cousin through her tea and scones, and before very long, the carriage was again on its way. The owner of the inn looked after it regretfully, for he had hoped to convince the ladies to remain with him. Not many of the quality came this way; it was a lonely spot, and custom was poor.

As the afternoon wore on, Caroline tried to regale her cousin with a description of the comforts they would be treated to as soon as they arrived at their Great-Aunt's estate. "Just think, Cecy!" she said. "Warm beds with fresh dry sheets, hot fires, and I am sure a delicious dinner if our relative does not keep very early country hours!"

Cecilia did not reply. She was not looking forward to arriving at Rockledge, which she was sure must be a nasty place, or doing the pretty, as her mother had so carefully instructed her to do to a horrid old lady, and she had resented Caroline's insisting that they hurry along. Now she sat in silence, peering out at the scenery and pouting. Caroline shrugged and turned away to the window on her side. If Cecilia did not wish to converse, that was perfectly all right with her, and she even had the wicked thought that if the girl continued to sulk indefinitely, it would be much more restful.

The early winter dusk had fallen before they turned at last into a long, unkempt drive. As they passed the sagging iron gates, Caroline could just make out a deserted stone gatehouse. No cheerful lamps were lit to welcome the visitors, and as the carriage lumbered slowly up the drive, some leafless branches

35

scraped the sides. Cecilia, who had been dozing in her corner, woke up with a start.

"What . . . what was that?" she asked in fear.

"Nothing but a branch, Cuz! See, we are almost there!"

Both girls stared out the windows, but between the rainy darkness and the heavy, overgrown underbrush, they could see nothing. The carriage swept around a circular drive and halted at a set of steps. Caroline got down on Grafton's arm and squeezed it thankfully. "Bless you, Henry, you've done it!" she said, smiling at him, as her cousin stepped out beside her and clutched her sleeve.

"There are no lights!" Cecilia whispered. "Perhaps we are at the wrong place; see, no one is expecting us!"

Grafton tipped his hat. "Beg pardon, miss, this is Rockledge, all right! There was a sign at the gates."

"Do help Miss North, Grafton," Caroline ordered, gathering her skirts and starting up the steps. "Come, Molly, Wentworth! We will soon be warm and comfortable. And Henry, you and John Coachman go round to the kitchens after you have seen to the horses and the baggage; tell them you have not eaten and that you require a room for the night. I will make the arrangements."

All the time she was speaking, she was herding her small party up the shallow stone steps. Rockledge loomed above them, dark and cold and, she had to admit, extremely unwelcoming, but not a trace of her own apprehension showed in either her expression or in the cheerful tone of her voice. Beside the moaning of the wind, she could hear the dull booming sound of the surf; it had a very sad and ominous effect.

The groom gave the door knocker a mighty crash, and they all waited, but not a sound could be heard of any approaching footsteps. "Oh dear," Cecilia whispered again, "I am so afraid!"

Any impatience that Caroline might have felt,

vanished as she felt her cousin shivering, and heard the chattering of her teeth, and she put her arm around her to steady her. Just as Grafton was raising his hand to signal their arrival again, the heavy door swung open. Thankfully, Caroline went forward, drawing Cecilia with her. An elderly butler stood there bowing, and she gave him her warmest smile.

"Good evening! I am Miss Covington, this is Miss North. I believe we are expected?"

The butler bowed again and, holding the door wider, admitted the party. He did not speak, and Caroline looked about her with curiosity. It was a massive hall they had entered, the ceiling of which could not even be seen in the gloom, for outside of the branch of candles the butler was holding, there were no other lights. At one end of the hall a small fire burned in the huge fireplace, and Caroline could make out some dark chairs and tables, and at one side a wide staircase with a heavily carved railing that stretched upward in a spiral to the next floor. She turned to the butler. "Perhaps Lady Cecily was not expecting us to arrive so late . . . er?"

"My name is Crowell, miss," the butler announced in a quavering voice.

"Very well, Crowell! If it is not convenient for us to see our Great-Aunt this evening, we shall pay our respects in the morning."

"Not very likely!" the butler muttered to himself, and Caroline's eyebrows rose as a feminine voice came from the dark at the back of the hall. "Who is there, Crowell?"

Everyone turned to see a middle-aged woman, dressed in black, with her graying hair scraped back into a tight bun, who was coming towards them, holding a single candle up to peer at them.

"This here be Miss Spenser," the butler said in some relief. "Lady Cecily's companion."

Caroline held out her hand. "We are delighted to make your acquaintance, Miss Spenser. We have

37

been on the road for a very long time today, and we are tired and hungry. Since it appears that our Great-Aunt cannot receive us tonight, perhaps it would be best if we went immediately to our rooms. A light supper will be all that is required, and of course, accommodations for our servants."

"Oh dear!" Miss Spenser said, one thin white hand going to her face. Caroline thought she looked like a frightened rabbit, with her plain face and her startled gray eyes magnified behind a pair of thick glasses. "Lady Cecily will most certainly not receive you, oh no, it is not to be thought of!"

For a moment Caroline was dumbstruck at their uncivil reception, but before she could insist that they be shown to their rooms at once, another door opened at the side of the hall and light streamed out, illuminating the stone flags of the floor on which they stood and the little party of travelers.

"Can it be that another contingent of relatives has arrived?" a haughty, lazy voice inquired as a tall handsome gentleman appeared at the door. "Ah, I see I was correct! Do come into the library, 'cousins'; it is the only fairly warm room in this whole enormous and decrepid castle!"

Miss Spenser threw up her hands, and as Caroline moved past her, she heard her whisper to herself, "So many candles! So much coal!" As she entered the library, a nervous Cecilia right on her heels, she said over her shoulder, "Perhaps you could summon the housekeeper, Miss Spenser, and see that our maids are taken care of before you order us something to eat. I assume dinner is over, since we are so late?"

"You would be most untruthful to call what we had this evening 'dinner,'" the tall gentleman said as he led them towards the fire.

"John! I am desolated to have to ask you, but you must give up your chair; these ladies are in need of warmth!"

Even as he spoke, the other gentleman in the

room was rising to bow to them. "Since my cousin has not seen fit to introduce us, allow me to do the honors," he said, his deep voice at odds with his cousin's light baritone, and his keen dark eyes inspecting the two girls carefully. "I am John St. Williams; this is my cousin Alistair Russell."

Caroline suddenly felt somewhat better. At least they were not alone anymore! As she curtsied, she studied the two men before her. Alistair Russell was handing a smiling and blushing Cecilia to a seat close to the fire. He was everything that Caroline disliked most in a man, a complete London fop, she thought, elegant, affected, carefully groomed, and, she was sure, extremely conceited. His evening dress might not have been out of place in a London drawing room, but here in the north of Scotland it was absurd, and the number of rings and fobs he wore, excessive in any place. She would have agreed he was handsome, with his straight features and glistening blond hair, but if she had had to choose, she would certainly have picked Lord St. Williams as the better of the two. He stood looking down at her, his eyes intent but with a twinkle lurking in their depths. Unlike his cousin, he had not changed for dinner, and wore buckskin breeches and a dark riding coat. She could see a faint family resemblance between the two men, but when Lord St. Williams smiled at her, his white teeth brilliant against the tan of his face, she decided that on the whole she had always preferred dark men.

"I am Caroline Covington, m'lord, and this is our cousin Miss Cecilia North," she said, turning to see from the pleased expression on the girl's face that she had completely recovered her spirits. Gratefully, Caroline held out her hands to the blaze. "How good that feels!" she said. "Now, if only Miss Spenser does not forget to feed us! We are ravenous!"

Lord St. Williams chuckled. "Unfortunately, you will find that in this house, Miss Caroline, you will always be ravenous! But you may leave the matter safely in my hands."

He strode to the door and called out, "Here, Crowell! Bustle about, man! Some food for the ladies, some wine and a pot of tea as well!"

Caroline could hear the old butler mumbling as he shuffled away, and then Mr. Russell claimed her attention. "I am sure you found the journey as tiresome as we did. So tedious, traveling!" He sighed and yawned before he continued, "We had no idea it would take so long to reach Rockledge, but then, we underestimated the condition of the roads in this backward part of the world, the state of the weather, and the fact the estate is, after all, located on the Moray Firth. I cannot imagine why any civilized person would choose to live here, especially in the winter!"

"But Alistair," Lord St. Williams said as he rejoined the group by the fire, "you have so often said that about an estate located only twenty miles from London!"

His cousin agreed calmly. "It is true that I find the country an abomination. May I tell you how delighted I am to have your company, cousins? We have seen no one but servants since our arrival yesterday. So boring!"

"Is Great-Aunt Cecily ill, sir?" Cecilia asked, her eyes widening.

"We have been informed that Her Royal Highness will see none of us until the entire party is assembled," Alistair said. His words were light and bantering, but his expression was somewhat grim. "I hope the others are not far behind us, for I intend to make this as short a visit as possible. There is nothing to do here, absolutely nothing!"

"But now we have such *charming* company, Alistair, we can get up a game of cards, or perhaps explore the estate if it ever stops raining!" St. Williams added. "Do you ride, cousins?"

As they conversed together, Caroline wondered

why she felt so uneasy in this room. There were undercurrents here she could not understand, but perhaps that was just because she was so tired, she was imagining things. Just then the butler brought in a large tray and set up a table so they might eat their supper by the fire, as directed by Lord St. Williams. It was not much of a meal, some bread and cheese and a bowl of apples, but the wine was excellent and the hot tea refreshing. Cecilia became very chatty after Mr. Russell pressed another glass of wine on her, and in a few moments, when Caroline saw her trying to hide a yawn behind her napkin, she rose and excused them both. Cecilia pouted again, but she was forced to rise and curtsy to her new cousins and to follow Caroline from the library. After they had made sure the butler was there to take them upstairs, the two men sat down again over their port.

"Pretty things, ain't they?" Alistair asked idly.

"Exceedingly so, especially the younger one, but she's a widgeon for all that, Alistair!"

"Lord, I know that!" his cousin agreed. "Besides being so very young and naive as well, but any company is better than none, and although Miss Caroline has all the brains and *some* conversation, neither you nor I would spend a minute with either of 'em in town. Here, I am afraid, we must be grateful for even *their* meager charms! I find myself alarmed by the prospect that if we have to spend more than two weeks here, I will probably propose to one of 'em out of sheer boredom!"

John St. Williams opened his mouth to reply, and then shut it as he eyed his cousin lounging so gracefully before the fire, his handsome face petulant.

Upstairs, Caroline inspected the room the butler had designated was to be hers. She found Wentworth unpacking her portmanteau and sniffing in disdain as she did so, and she could not blame the maid. The room was large and at one time must have been a handsome apartment, but it had evi-

41

dently not been used for years. The furniture was dingy, the hangings of the bed and the draperies faded, and the rug worn. As she ran one slender finger over a tabletop, the maid said, "It's a disgrace, Miss Caro, that's what it is! But don't you worry, *I'll* take care of it tomorrow! There's no use asking the servants here—they are all elderly, from what I have seen, and under no supervision, for there isn't even a housekeeper! That Miss Spenser seems to be in charge. Ha! I have never seen such dust and neglect; your mother would be horrified. It's an insult to you, that's what I say!"

Caroline laughed as she got ready for bed. "I am so tired, Wentworth, I don't care what it looks like. At least the sheets are fresh! And perhaps tomorrow we can persuade someone that four coals doth not a fire make! Brrr!"

"Just so, miss!" Miss Wentworth agreed, promising to take care of it and helping her between the covers at last. "You sleep well, Miss Caro, and I will be here to wake you in the morning!" But Caroline did not even hear her reassuring words, for she was immediately asleep.

When she woke the next morning, she lay very still for a moment, wondering where on earth she was, but then she heard the sound of the sea and remembered. Rockledge, her absent and unwelcoming great-aunt, this old, neglected stone pile, and her two new cousins. When Wentworth came in with her morning chocolate, she was still pondering the situation, and she continued to do so as she dressed in a warm gown of sky blue woolsey. She and Lord St. Williams ate breakfast alone since Cecilia was still asleep and he told her that Alistair never rose before eleven, his face carefully expressionless. After they had devoured the porridge and cold toast which was all that was on the sideboard, Lord St. Williams suggested he show her around the ground floor, which, he said, seemed to be one dark, neglected room after the other. As they stood talking in the hall, the knocker sounded, and he went at once to answer it.

"My staff would be amazed to see me playing butler, cousin, but if we wait for Crowell, whoever is at the door may go away in disgust!"

Caroline gave a glad cry as he threw the heavy door open, for her brother Gregory stood on the steps, a bewildered expression on his face. Lord St. Williams watched the two indulgently as Caroline brushed past him to throw her arms around her brother and kiss him.

"Cut line, Caro!" he growled in embarrassment as he caught sight of Lord St. Williams, whom, he congratulated himself, he would never be such a flat as to take for the butler. After she had introduced him, Gregory grinned and said, "I am delighted to find someone else here, sir, at the end of the world! I have been traveling forever, and after I left the stage and hired a horse for the final miles, I was sure I was about to ride and ride, never reaching my destination!" Caroline laughed at him as he added, "And coming up that long, overgrown drive—whew! I can see we are to have a real adventure here!"

He looked and sounded so pleased at the prospect that John St. Williams had to laugh with Caroline, and then Crowell finally arrived, mumbling about this new visitor, but taking him away to show him his room and to arrange to accept his baggage when it came later by carter.

By the time Gregory came downstairs again, Cecilia had arrived, and she positively bloomed as she made the acquaintance of yet another handsome young man. They all sat chatting in the library until Alistair Russell made an appearance, the very picture of London gentility. Gregory's mouth fell open slightly as he tried not to stare too hard at this vision of perfection before him; boots by Hobey, coat by Stulz, breeches by Goren, and cravat by Mr. Russell's own accomplished hand.

There was some time before luncheon, so the five

of them went out to stroll briefly in the grounds, although Alistair announced that even if the sun was *almost* shining, the wind was an abomination! A strong breeze was blowing from the north, and even though there was a refreshing salty tang to it, it was the kind of wind that went right through the thickest clothing. Caroline, in her warm gown and fur cloak, did not mind it, but Cecilia said she must go back in within moments, and Alistair was quick to say that he would be glad to escort her, leaving Lord St. Williams and the Covingtons to continue to investigate.

"I wonder why Great-Aunt put us all on the side of the house facing the firth," Caroline mused. "Surely a room overlooking the drive and the park would be more comfortable this time of year!"

"But it is so healthful, Cousin Caroline," m'lord assured her. "You may always have the benefit of fresh air without the danger of opening your window, for the drafts stir the curtains almost continually, and help to fan the very inadequate fire as well!"

The three strolled around to the back of the house, and as they came from behind a windbreak of firs, Caroline was forced to grasp her unruly skirts. Her brother took her arm and eagerly led her down a sloping lawn that led to a low stone wall.

"My word!" Caroline said faintly as she stared over the edge.

Far, far below her, the waves rolled in towards the huge ledges that gave the estate its name, and were tossed upward on impact into a cascade of foam and turbulent water; all the while they were accompanied by the tremendous booming sound she had heard all last evening. Lord St. Williams stared down for a moment, frowning, and then he looked out to sea, and Gregory clasped his sister's arm tightly as he leaned over for a better look.

"I say! This is something like, isn't it!" he yelled, for it was difficult to speak normally over the sound of the surf. Caroline shivered as she stared down at those black rocks, now covered with slate-gray water, now glistening and darkly wet as the waves receded until yet another breaker came rolling in to do battle with the earth. It was as if all that ferocious, restless energy was determined to undermine the very ground on which they stood. Caroline brushed back an errant curl with one shaking hand, and Lord St. Williams noticed and took her arm, saying to Gregory, "Very exciting, I'm sure, but your sister is cold. Shall we go in?"

He led them away from the precipice, and Caroline felt grateful and relieved. It had been an awesome sight, but somehow it frightened her to be so far above such majestic, relentless power. She was glad to leave the back of the house and return through the unkempt gardens to the front door. They found Alistair and Cecilia in the library, their heads together over an old book, and Caroline went away to tidy her windswept hair.

When the gong sounded for lunch and they all went towards the dining room, they passed a pair of closed doors in the middle of the hall, and Gregory asked, "Is that the drawing room? Why do we not use that room instead of all being crowded together in that dark library?"

"That is Great-Aunt Cecily's lair," Alistair replied. "Miss Spenser says she uses it as a bedroom, sitting room, and receiving room—when, that is, she ever condescends to receive, of course! Let us hope the Danvers are not far behind us! I am all impatience to meet our most unusual hostess!"

Again his tone was light and casual, but Caroline noticed Lord St. Williams' intent, speculative look.

They had barely begun their luncheon, when a commotion could be heard in the hall, and Lady Danvers' sharp voice raised in command.

"Your wish appears to be granted, Cuz," Lord St. Williams remarked. "Perhaps you will be sorry you voiced it, before long."

Gregory Covington raised an inquisitive eyebrow, but he did not ask to be enlightened. He knew both these gentlemen by reputation, and he was aware he was far beneath their august notice, even if he was related to them. Who was he, after all, but a callow twenty-one-year-old of no distinction, when set beside m'lord and that leader of fashion, Alistair Russell?

It was not very many more minutes before Lord and Lady Danvers joined them. Lord St. Williams introduced everyone at the table, and while Lord Danvers smiled and bobbed and said he was very pleased, his wife glared at each of the other guests with a suspicious, beady eye and a truculent frown. Gregory kicked his sister under the table, but Caroline was careful not to catch his eye.

"Well!" Lady Danvers said as she took her seat and stared now at the small portion of baked eggs that Crowell was presenting to her. "We are quite a *large* group, are we not? I did not expect so many, and I find it strange that Roger and I have never met some of you before!"

Her tone seemed to imply that there was something havey-cavey about relatives one had never met, as if they had been up to something disreputable all these years that she would most definitely not approve. She glared at each one again in turn as she ate her lunch, causing Cecilia to drop her fork, and Gregory to hate himself for blushing. Only Caroline returned her scrutiny with an indifferent nod, while Lord St. Williams and Alistair studiously ignored her.

"I suppose you have all been very busy, worming your way into Great-Aunt Cecily's good graces?" the lady asked next, waving away a sorry-looking platter of vegetables, but taking three scones and a large dollop of butter.

"Oh, I say, Sylvia!" her husband said weakly, as Alistair Russell raised his quizzing glass in hauteur to inspect the lady, and the others sat dumbstruck at her temerity.

46

The lady had the grace to flush a little. "Well, why beat about the bush?" she asked. "Why not come right out with it?"

"Perhaps because it might be considered—oh, only by the *highest* sticklers of the haut ton, of course—to be in rather bad taste, m'lady?" Russell asked gently.

"I do not believe in subterfuge and play-acting! That is why we are all here, is it not, to try to gain sole possession of a very large inheritance?" she replied. "But I do find that for all of you to come before us a most suspicious occurrence!"

"You may be calm, Lady Danvers," John St. Williams remarked in his deep voice. "Our great-aunt has decreed that she will receive no one until the entire party of guests is assembled. So you see," he added as the lady's expression brightened at this intelligence, "no one has stolen a march on you, and you and your husband shall have the same opportunity as the rest of us!"

"I am aware that you disapprove of my honesty, m'lord," Lady Danvers acknowledged, nodding at the custard that was put before her, "and I am also aware that you, the least of all of us, have no earthly need for money! I wonder why you came?"

She looked straight at him belligerently, and Caroline felt forced to intervene, since Lord St. Williams' face looked dangerously rigid, and the lady's husband had become afflicted with a coughing spell behind his handkerchief.

"Allow me to tell you, Lady Danvers, that no one here has so much as spoken of the inheritance. After all, as far as we know, Lady Cecily is not about to die! She may live for many more years; indeed, I hope she does!"

"Do you, Caroline?" Lady Danvers asked in a stunned voice. "I find that hard to believe! Unless, of course, at your age, and in your circumstances, you have given up such worldly matters!"

Since Caroline was only a year older, she did not take offense at this bald reference to her spinsterhood, but instead tried to turn the conversation to another topic.

"We had a most interesting walk this morning, Cecy, after you and Cousin Alistair returned to the house. You both must go and see the firth, as we did. The house is built so high up, you stare down at the breakers from a great height; it is most impressive!"

Cecilia shuddered, but she did not speak for fear Lady Danvers would turn her guns her way. Mr. Russell raised his wine glass to Caroline in a silent toast for her efforts. "It sounds frightening, Miss Caroline!" he said. "I have always dreaded heights; I am not sure my health is up to such excitement!"

Lord St. Williams put down his fork and wiped his lips, his composure regained as he said, "Do try to forget your consequence as London's finest exquisite, Alistair! The view is probably the most interesting thing here! You must allow me to escort you to the precipice so that I can support you if you feel overcome by weakness!"

For a moment, a dangerous light flamed in Alistair's eyes, but it was gone so quickly, Caroline felt she must have imagined it. Lady Danvers, who had discovered the comfits dish, was now blessedly silent as she selected all the best sweets and neglected to pass the dish to the others. Lord Danvers looked relieved, but Caroline could not help feeling disgust at the woman as she chewed and gobbled, her fat cheeks bobbling with her effort. What a horrible, unattractive woman, she thought! If she does not have us all at dagger-drawing in a day, I shall be surprised! Cecilia rose and excused herself in a faint voice as soon as she possibly could, and Caroline could see she was being asked to go with her, from the pleading expression in her eyes. She rose, and after bidding everyone a good afternoon, left the room with her cousin.

As soon as they gained the hall and the doors were safely shut behind them, Cecilia whispered, "How are we to bear that horrible woman? She frightens me, Caro, truly she does!"

She grasped Caroline's arm as she spoke, her eyes wide. "I feel she is very dangerous! Certainly she will let nothing stand in the way of gaining control of Great-Aunt's fortune! I wish my mama had not insisted I come here! I do not want the money that badly!"

Caroline led her along to the library, and when both girls were seated with their needlework, she remarked, "Then if you do not want the money, all you must do is tell Lady Danvers so, and be as rude to our Great-Aunt as you can contrive!"

"But . . . but Mama will kill me if I do not make a push to be the favorite!" Cecilia wailed, dropping her tapestry to wring her hands. "For Lady Danvers is right, of course! We are all here for one reason, and one reason only. It is so lowering!"

She sniffed, and Caroline pushed down the feeling of impatience she was always beginning to feel when she had to reason with her cousin.

"I think, Cecy, that the only possible way to go on is to pretend at least that that is not so, and that we are merely here to pay our respects. Otherwise the situation *will* become impossible! Do try and help me to draw Lady Danvers' bow; I am so afraid that Lord St. Williams or possibly even Alistair Russell will kill her. Did you see the way they looked at her at the table?"

"Oh, I couldn't! You are so very brave, Caroline, I do envy you, but I intend to stay as far away from the lady as possible, and never open my mouth at all if I can help it!"

"In that case, you will starve to death in short order!" Caroline said tartly, taking up her dark-green thread and measuring out a length of it. "There is little enough to eat here, and if you do not nip in and get your share before Lady Danvers, there will be nothing at all!"

She laughed a little, remembering the gluttony

she had seen at the table, but Cecilia only shivered and said that starvation would be preferable to having the lady's attention focused on her.

That afternoon, Lord St. Williams took Gregory off for a long ride, Alistair Russell retired to his room and was not seen again until dinnertime, and Lady Danvers insisted her husband take her around every room of the house so she might inspect them carefully, noting any items of value that she could find. Although she was royally ignored, Miss Spenser followed them around, her gaze behind the thick glasses worried and upset. Caroline and Cecilia remained in the library until it was time to dress for dinner.

When all were in their rooms changing, another knock came on the front door, but only Crowell, who for once was there to open it, knew that the last member of the party had arrived, and he quickly ushered the gentleman upstairs to his room, as he had been instructed to do, and acquainted him with the plans for the evening. The stranger nodded and disappeared into his room, followed by his manservant with his baggage, while Crowell went downstairs to report to Lady Cecily that her house party was now complete.

CHAPTER 3

CAROLINE COVINGTON WONDERED why she had chosen to wear her most becoming new gown, the one of dark-brown velvet edged with creamy lace at the sleeves and neckline. Surely she was not as anxious as Cousin Cecilia was to appear at her best before the gentlemen! Of course not! It was just that the gown was new and flattering, and fit her so well. She sat at the old dressing table that Wentworth had somehow managed to steady by propping up one shaky leg with a piece of board, and allowed the maid to brush her hair into smooth waves and fasten on the necklace, eardrops, and bracelets of her mother's pearl set. There was no way she could see the whole effect in the small dingy mirror, but Wentworth assured her she had never looked so well. Caroline smiled at her and remembered to thank her for the clean, orderly room and the comfortable fire, and Wentworth was not slow to relate the trials she had undergone to wrest another hod of coal from Miss Spenser. When the gong sounded, Caroline went downstairs, wondering why such stringent methods of economy were being practiced in a home where the owner was so exceedingly wealthy!

She was the last to arrive in the dining room, and John St. Williams, this evening attired in formal dress, led her to a seat beside him, smiling down at her and openly admiring the creamy expanse of white shoulder that her gown exposed. He was surprised that his scrutiny did not cause her to flush or look at all conscious. A point for Cousin Caroline, he thought as she ignored his admiration to smile across the table to her brother.

Since he was without the services of his valet, Gregory had tried as best he could to turn himself out in a style that would not disgrace his sister nor disgust his male relatives, but he had succeeded only in looking very young. His brown hair was brushed casually, but since he, rather than Caroline, had inherited his mother's curls, it was attractive, and his fresh, open face helped to distract attention from his poorly tied cravat and unbrushed, wrinkled coat. He seated Cecilia North with a flourish, and she blushed. Tonight she was wearing a gossamer gown of palest blue, with sapphire combs set in her chestnut hair, and it would have been a much younger and more unimpressionable young man than Gregory who could have ignored her beauty.

Alistair Russell was of course as impeccable and polished as ever. As he took his seat, he wondered idly if he had enough family feeling to send his valet to young Covington to assist him in his toilette, and decided that after all was said and done, he did not, even though some slight inconvenience to himself might be preferable to looking across the table at such disarray!

Lady Danvers was resplendent in a gown of maroon peau de soie and a beautiful set of rubies her husband had given her on their betrothal. She took her seat eagerly, and tapped one impatient finger on the table while her husband went around to greet everyone. This evening he had decked himself out in a pale-gray coat and tight satin pantaloons, and he wore a waistcoat of scarlet silk, embroidered with peacocks, vines, and flowers, which unfortunately focused attention on the vast expanse of his stomach. As he bowed and beamed at Caroline, she thought one did not have the slightest desire to smile at his dandyism, for he was so eager to be liked, like a puppy that gambols around you, begging to be petted.

At last Crowell shuffled in with the soup tureen, followed by the oldest footman Caroline had ever seen, and dinner commenced. Conversation was general and innocuous, for which everyone felt a vast relief, and when Lady Danvers had not insulted anyone for two entire courses, even Cecilia was bold enough to speak up and add her mite. Gregory and John St. Williams told about their ride and the surrounding countryside, Alistair Russell discoursed on the London theatre, and Lord Danvers told several long and extremely boring stories about his journey north. Caroline wondered if he had had a talk with his wife which had resulted in her good behavior, not knowing that in reality he would never have dared such a thing. His wife was quiet only because she was busy eating and because she was wondering whether she could possibly take away with her when she left, concealed in her trunk, that very old and very valuable antique gold salver she had seen in one of the back salons.

When the table had been cleared and Caroline was wondering if she, as the eldest lady present, should give the signal for the ladies to retire, the doors to the dining room opened to disclose Miss Spenser, swallowing rapidly and hesitating at the entrance.

"Er . . . I beg your pardon, ladies and gentlemen!" she said in a strained high voice, which cracked a little with nervousness. Or was it excitement? Caroline wondered as she turned to the lady. The room stilled, and Miss Spenser coughed and said, "Now that everyone has arrived at Rockledge, Lady Cecily has instructed me to tell you that she will receive you after dinner, for brandy or any refreshment that you might wish!"

Before anyone could question her, she scuttled

away like a frightened mouse and Crowell closed the doors behind her.

"How very unusual!" Alistair remarked to no one in particular. "I wonder why she did not join us at the dinner table?"

Lady Danvers stirred the fallen soggy soufflé before her and asked, "Why would she want to? She has probably dined very well in her own room, leaving us to eat the most unappetizing, poorly cooked, and sparse meal I have ever seen! Imagine, only two removes for each course!" She reached down into her lap and drew out a small enameled box, which she opened with a flourish to select a sweetmeat. "I, at least, will not starve!"

John St. Williams raised one dark brow and murmured to Caroline, "Now, why did we not have the forethought to provide ourselves with additional sustenance, Cousin Caroline? You, for example, will be a skeleton long before *that* lady wastes away!" Caroline tried to look disapproving at this levity, but her eyes twinkled in response in spite of her good intentions.

Gregory and Cecilia had their heads together and were speaking in rapid whispers, and from the excited look on her brother's face, and his sparkling eyes, Caroline knew he was anticipating the coming confrontation. Cecilia, on the other hand, looked scared and apprehensive, and Caroline saw her brother pat her hand in reassurance, while Cousin Alistair looked around the table and sneered. Lord Danvers rose from his chair and said in his ponderous way, "Perhaps this evening, cousins, we should all retire to the drawing room together, instead of lingering over our port?"

"What port?" m'lord inquired. "I do not see any offered to linger over! But come, of course Roger is right! Let us not delay, but all go together like deferent children to obey Lady Cecily's command! Come!"

He rose to draw out Caroline's chair, and in a

moment they were all moving from the dining room and down the massive hall to Great-Aunt Cecily's room, preceded by the elderly butler. No one spoke; the only sound was that of their feet on the flagstones.

Crowell knocked and opened the door and bowed them in. Caroline was not the only one who could not restrain a gasp when she saw the fantastic, crowded room, dominated by the huge bed at one end, and so very warm it was like stepping into a conservatory. Her eyes were drawn immediately, as were the eyes of all the others, to the thin old lady sitting in the large wing chair before the fire, with Miss Spenser hovering behind her. She had never seen anyone so old, or so very unusual, she thought as she moved into the room, as Great-Aunt Cecily. From her powdered wig to her overornate gown of stiff white brocade, worn over the hoops of the last century, she looked like a caricature of a young girl at her presentation to society, except that she wore more rubies and diamonds and opals and pearls than Caroline had ever seen on one person. The bracelets alone covered almost her entire forearm. Now she crooked an imperious finger and beckoned them to the chairs that were set near her. Cecilia had deserted Gregory to stand as close to Caroline as possible, and she could hear her frightened breathing.

Lord St. Williams spoke first, since all the rest appeared to be dumb with shock. Bowing, he said in his deep, commanding tones, "Good evening, Lady Cecily! I am John St. Williams, at your service!"

Aunt Cecily peered up at him, her dark, hooded eyes snapping. "Yes, yes, of course! Emily's descendant! She always did have a bossy way with her. I might have known you would take over the party!"

St. Williams' eyebrows came together in a quick frown before he replied, "I am unable to defend my grandmother, ma'am, for I never knew her!" But Great-Aunt Cecily had turned away.

"Let me see if I can guess your identities! You, sir," she said, pointing her cane at Alistair Russell's

55

elegant figure as he made her a deep bow, "you are also of Emily's stock, are you not? Neither of you seems to have inherited any Covington features at all. Well, she might have been opinionated, but she was nothing out of the ordinary way, I can assure you, for all her airs. No wonder she didn't have the strength to pass on her own family traits. Weak, spineless, and simple!"

Alistair would have spoken, but she said abruptly, "Sit down!" and both of Emily Covington's hapless descendants subsided without demur.

"You two, yes, you! Tweedledum and Tweedledee! Or Lord and Lady Danvers, I'll be bound! Roger, is it not? Your mother was Rose Covington before her marriage?" Lord Danvers nodded his head, his little eyes popping in amazement and his fat cheeks reddened, while his wife curtsied, her most winning smile creasing her round face. "We are so pleased to meet you, Lady Cecily," she said in a warm, soothing tone as the others stared at her in wonder.

"BAH!" her hostess returned, and then she said, "Miss Cecilia North; you're a pretty thing! At least your hair has the tint of the Covingtons'! Mine was a more brilliant red, you know, like my father's!" She sighed and stared at the portrait over the mantel for a moment, and then she turned back to Cecilia. "Your mother is a fool, girl; I hope you are not one too." She paused, but Cecilia seemed incapable of speech, and Caroline could feel her trembling as the old lady continued, "Why she thought to turn me up sweet by naming you for me—well, almost for me—I shall never understand. Does she think I am as silly as she is?" Still Cecilia did not reply, and Lady Cecily waved her hand in dismissal. "Pooh! Silly, and dumb as well, I see!"

"And you last two; yes, I see the family resemblance between you. You are Caroline and Gregory Covington!"

Gregory bowed and Caroline said "Good evening,"

in a quiet, composed voice, standing erect and looking at her great-aunt with calm interest.

"I do not frighten you, girl?"

"No, m'lady."

"Excellent! How very strange that of all you here, only these two still bear the Covington name." She pointed her cane at Gregory and said, "You must marry at once, my boy, and produce a great many children as fast as you can, else the name will die out! Do not tarry, man! Marry a good, strong breeder of a woman and get her with child!"

Gregory blushed a deep, painful red, but she continued as if she did not notice. "Mr. Russell, if you will be so kind as to pour me a glass of port!" There was a small sound from Miss Spenser, which she ignored. "The rest of you gentlemen, help yourselves. The ladies may drink what they like, probably muddle their insides with negus or cordials, or even tea! I myself drink like a man, as my father taught me, and I can vouch for the port! I keep a good cellar!"

"I have already noticed, m'lady," Alistair remarked as he moved to do her bidding. There was a large tray of bottles and glasses on a table to the side of the group, and he poured her a glass of port as ordered. His movements seemed to break the spell, and the ladies settled themselves as the men moved to the table. "A glass of wine, Gregory, if you please," Caroline said at his inquiring expression. "Cecy, some wine?" The girl nodded but still seemed unable to speak a word.

As Alistair stepped up to hand the port to his hostess, he stepped on the dog that lay asleep at her feet, which no one had noticed before, since it was half hidden by her hoops. The dog yelped in pain, and he drew back in surprise as an old English bulldog staggered to his feet and moved away.

"I beg your pardon, m'lady!" he said, startled out of his usual indolence.

"You did not step on me! Better apologize to Excalibur!"

57

"What a dear doggie!" Lady Danvers purred, although she had not taken her eyes from Lady Cecily's jewelry since she entered the room.

"Excalibur is old and blind and of no earthly use to anyone! The sooner he dies, the better!" Lady Cecily replied to this blatant lie. "You are all thinking the same of me, of course! Well, my dear relatives, I would be the first to agree with you! But come, if you have all been served, sit down. I have a surprise for you!"

She chuckled as she grasped the embroidered bell-pull by her side. Alistair moved back to the table to pour himself a snifter of brandy, his elegant face once again expressionless, although somewhat paler than usual. John St. Williams obviously did not care to sit, for he lounged against a large table, somewhat removed from the others, his glass in his hand and his expression stern and unsmiling. Lady Danvers popped a sweetmeat into her mouth as she accepted a glass of liqueur from her husband, whose fat face was damp with perspiration in the heat of the room, as Crowell appeared at the door. Lady Cecily nodded to him without speaking, and he bowed and turned away. Caroline took a grateful sip of her wine and watched her great-aunt. Now, why does she look so pleased and excited? she thought. She had not seemed to like any of them, with the exception of Gregory, and he only as the future sire of many little Covingtons! And perhaps she liked me a little, she mused, because I refused to kowtow to her! But everyone else has earned only her insults and sarcasm, even Lord St. Williams!

Her thoughts were interrupted by the quavering voice of the butler, and all eyes turned to the door.

"Mr. Covington-More, m'lady!" he announced, and a man stepped into the room and came towards them. He was not of any great height, but he was strongly built, with powerful hands and muscular legs that could be seen plainly under his tight pantaloons. He had a broad, pale face, with a large nose and bushy brows over a pair of light hazel eyes, but his most arresting feature was his brilliant red hair. No one spoke as he came up to them and bowed, his thin mouth sneering unpleasantly.

"Covington-More?" Alistair Russell asked in wonder, his snifter halting halfway to his lips.

"The very same, sir!" the man said in an uncultured voice. "M'lady!" He bowed again to Lady Cecily, who sipped her port, her eyes over the rim of the glass darting from one to the other of the guests to gauge their reactions to her surprise. She smiled in delight when she saw their stunned faces, and nodded her head.

"Get yourself a drink, sir!" she said, and then added, "You are all amazed, are you not? Mr. Covington-More is the grandson of my brother Anthony. His father was Hector Covington!"

"But ... but Hector Covington never married!" Lord Danvers burst out. "How is this possible?"

"More easily than you think, my dear *legitimate* relative!" Lady Cecily said. "He is a bastard!"

Over by the drinks table, the back of the gentleman's neck turned a dark red, but he did not speak. "There are many Covington by-blows around, you know; why, my father himself had several besides his legal issue. Now, there was a man for you! Spenser, here, is a descendant of one of 'em! But her mother was lucky enough to marry before she had her, thereby sparing her her own shame!"

Everyone looked at Miss Spenser, who was wringing her hands and looking miserable to be singled out and stared at, and Caroline felt very angry at her great-aunt for holding her up to ridicule this way. It was obvious the lady was deeply uncomfortable and hurt.

"Mr. Covington-More is the son of Marjorie More, a barmaid in Edinburgh. He has such a look of my father, don't you agree?" She waved her glass at the portrait before she added, "I see no reason why I should not consider him as one of my heirs, if so I wish!"

Lady Danvers choked and raised her handkerchief to her lips, so stunned by this information that the comfit she had been about to bite into fell to the rug.

The newest member of the party came back to the group and took the only vacant seat, near Cecilia North, who paled and tried to turn away from him. Lady Cecily chuckled. "It's not contagious, goose! But come, another glass of port? Spenser, fill my glass, and none of those meager rations you generally try to give me, mind! We are having a celebration this evening!"

Spenser obeyed without a word as John St. Williams spoke. "You live in Edinburgh, sir?"

The man nodded, his lips still twisted in a sneer. Caroline thought the late Lord Covington must have been a very ugly man, if this by-blow of his was anything to go by, and then Lady Cecily, who seemed determined to hold center stage, broke in.

"I should tell you all that I have already made a will, *dear* relatives, but my solicitor has been summoned for two weeks' time. By then, I am sure I will be able to decide which one of you should inherit my fortune. Of course, if I die before then, not a one of you will see a penny, for I have left it elsewhere! I shall ask each one of you to attend me here alone so that I might get to know you better in the meantime."

She paused and then added, "Of course, I may decide that none of you is worthy of the fortune, which I can assure you is considerable!" Lady Danvers nodded eagerly, squirming a little in her chair, her face all smiles. Caroline stole a look at Cecy; the girl was still very pale, but she had better control over herself now that the conversation had turned away from her. "I am so looking forward to your visits!" the old lady chortled. "I have not had so much fun in years!"

John St. Williams went to pour himself another drink. "We are delighted, of course, to be such a source of amusement to you, m'lady!" he said in a carefully expressionless voice. Lady Cecily did not take offense. "Come, John, it will do you good! You are thirty-two, I believe?" He nodded, and she continued, "Had your own way for years, and were left enough money that you are probably thoroughly spoiled! Do you good to dance to someone else's tune, for a change!"

M'lord returned to his perch by the table, stepping around the old bulldog, who was wandering among the guests, sniffing at their feet, as if bewildered by all these strangers in a room generally only populated by his mistress and himself.

"How disappointing if I refuse to dance! Or any of the others, m'lady!" John said.

"You would not be so cruel! And as for the others, I know you are all here for one reason only. I do not mislead myself as to think it was only family concern that brought you all so far north in the winter! Of course, I do know of one other who has not the slightest interest in my money, but I will not tell you who that is. That will remain *my* secret!"

Everyone looked around at all the others, including Covington-More, who had not spoken again, all wondering which one of them was so rich and independent that they did not want the old lady's fortune.

Suddenly Caroline exclaimed, "Look at the dog! Whatever can be wrong with him?"

Indeed, Excalibur was behaving very strangely. He moved backwards and forward in some agitation, pausing now and then to shake and tremble, and then he began to whine and toss his old blind head about in distress. "Oh dear," Cecilia said, pulling her blue skirts away from him as he staggered near her. Suddenly, he halted, gave a loud bark, and fell to the carpet, where he lay, his sides heaving for a moment, before he was abruptly, ominously still.

"Excalibur!" Lady Cecily cried, struggling to her feet, her glass falling unheeded to the floor. Miss Spenser was immediately at her side, holding her arm as she tried to reach her dog. John St. Williams knelt down and felt the old bulldog's side.

"He is dead, m'lady," he said quietly, a faint frown creasing his forehead.

"Dead? Excalibur? No, no!" she cried.

"Sit down, m'lady, do!" Miss Spenser urged. "There is nothing you can do to help him, and it will distress you!"

"Of course I am distressed!" Lady Cecily snapped, tears running down her wrinkled cheeks. "Excalibur and I have been together for so many years; you remember, Spenser, when he came here as a puppy, years ago? I did not mean for him to die, when I spoke earlier about his uselessness! Oh, how I shall miss him!"

She sank back in the wing chair and took the handkerchief that Miss Spenser produced, and buried her face in it. Alistair Russell was also holding his handkerchief to his nose, an expression of profound distaste on his face for the scene he had just witnessed, and Caroline glanced quickly around at the others. Cecilia was looking horrified; Mr. Covington-More, bored; Gregory, perplexed; and Lord Danvers was patting his wife's hand and saying, "There, there!" for he was very much afraid that dear Sylvia would have one of her spells, since the dog had expired practically at her feet. His wife did not seem to be that concerned, as she lifted her glass to gulp the last of her liqueur. Lord St. Williams rose, giving the others a hard stare.

"But I say!" Gregory exclaimed in bewilderment. "The dog acted as if he had been poisoned!"

John St. Williams whirled around and glared at him, and Caroline wondered why. She had never seen anyone look so dangerous as he did at that moment, and Gregory seemed to feel something was wrong as well, for he hastened to add, "But he did! He behaved just like a dog of mine who got into some poison put down for the rats in the barn! I remember it well, for he was a favorite bird dog of mine!"

"Poisoned? Nonsense!" Alistair said, startled out of his usual nonchalant pose.

"Not nonsense at all; the boy is right!" Mr. Covington-More said. "I've seen rats act just like that!" He smiled a little, as if he had enjoyed the spectacle, and Caroline tried not to shudder.

Lady Cecily sat up straighter in her chair. "But who would want to poison him? The thing is absurd!"

Gregory seemed about to speak again, but one glance at Lord St. Williams' glowering face silenced him. Instead, Alistair spoke again.

"I do think we might have the ... the unfortunate animal removed. So distressing to be talking of him this way while he lies at our feet!"

John St. Williams beckoned to Gregory. "Come, help me carry him outside, Gregory! Alistair is right. There is no need to discuss this now."

No one said anything as the two men carefully lifted the old dog and carried him out the door of the drawing room, although Lady Cecily wiped her eyes again and sighed. Miss Spenser patted her shoulder until the old lady twitched impatiently away from her concerned hand.

It was a few minutes before the men returned, and Caroline's eyes went immediately to her brother's face. He seemed pale and subdued and miserable, as if John St. Williams had spoken to him sharply while they were out of the room, and this angered her. What right had he to reprimand Gregory, and besides, what if her brother were right? So she sat up straighter in her chair and, setting her glass down on the table by her side, said, "But if the dog was poisoned, as both Gregory and Mr. Covington-More suspect, who could have done it, and to what purpose?"

St. Williams frowned at her, but she stared right back at him, her chin lifted in defiance. He was not going to ride roughshod over *her*, arrogant man that he was!

"Yes, that is what I cannot understand!" Lady Cecily added. "None of you knew I had a dog until this evening, but I do not think Excalibur could have gotten into any poison by himself. He never leaves—oh dear, left—this room except to be taken out for short walks by Spenser. Spenser!"

The lady spoken to jerked, one hand going to her throat.

"Yes, m'lady?" she asked in a shaky voice.

"Did Excalibur get into anything this afternoon when you took him out?"

"Oh no, m'lady! We only went a short way down the drive, and I watched him carefully! As soon as he had . . . er, finished, I brought him right back to you!"

Lady Cecily nodded as if that was what she had expected to hear.

John St. Williams moved to the center of the group and, giving Caroline another dark look, began to speak.

"Since you are all so determined to speak of the incident, let me say that I do not think the dog was the intended victim!"

"Not the victim? Surely you are mistaken, John!" Alistair interrupted. "He hardly went about sipping from our glasses, and that is all that has been served in this room. Besides, we are all in excellent health—so far!"

Cecilia gave a little cry and stared down at her glass in horrified suspicion.

"That will do, Alistair!" St. Williams said in a harsh, deep voice. "There is no need to upset the ladies any further, and bouts of hysteria can do no good at all! The poison was not in the drinks, of course! Think—what else was consumed in this room this evening?"

Caroline's mind was working quickly, and without thinking she blurted out, "Lady Danvers! Her comfits box!"

John St. Williams gave her an ironical bow. "An excellent deduction, Cousin! And if you recall, Lady Danvers dropped one of her sweetmeats on the floor.

I suspect that the dog, in wandering around after Alistair stepped on him, found it, and ate it."

"But . . . but . . ." Lord Danvers sputtered, while his wife sat frozen, with her eyes wide with shock, "that means, m'lord, that you believe someone was trying to kill Sylvia!"

"I have to believe it, Lord Danvers, but for what reason, I have no idea!"

All were staring at the lady and thinking their own thoughts, and so it was a complete surprise when Lord Danvers gave a little moan and fell heavily to the floor. Quickly, Lord St. Williams was at his side. Lady Danvers stared down at her husband as he lay at her feet, her fat hands going to her mouth in horror.

Cecilia North began to cry hysterically. "He has been poisoned as well! Dear God!"

"Nonsense! The man has only fainted!" Lord St. Williams said in an ordinary voice, trying to calm her as he loosened Lord Danvers' cravat and tight scarlet waistcoat. "Has no one any salts? An vinaigrette?"

Miss Spenser hurried to fetch these articles from Lady Cecily's bedside table, while Caroline tried to comfort Cecilia, who did not appear to have heard St. Williams' diagnosis of the situation. She was forced to give her several hard shakes before she could quiet her, but soon had her feeling better, with only an occasional sob or hiccup to show her agitation. In the meantime, Lady Danvers, who had not spoken, continued to stare at her husband in disbelief. Eventually, he commenced to moan, and in a few minutes was able to sit up. "Do rise, Roger!" his wife hissed at him. "Whatever will Lady Cecily think of such unmanliness?"

Caroline stared at the lady. Such concern for her beloved husband! she thought. All she was interested in was that he not give Lady Cecily a disgust of him so that she might leave her fortune elsewhere! No wonder someone wanted to do away with her!

65

Lord Danvers took John St. Williams' arm and struggled to his feet and then was assisted to a chair, apologizing profusely for his momentary weakness. Alistair brought him a glass of brandy. "Here, drink this, m'lord! It will revive you!"

"Do not drink it; it might be poisoned!" Cecilia said in a high, nervous voice.

The irony of Alistair's bow was not lost on the girl, as she blushed bright red. Mr. Covington-More turned to her and said, "Try not to be so silly, girl! Of course the gentleman is not trying to poison the fat man!"

"Thank you!" Alistair said, bowing again distastefully in his direction. "One is of course gratified to have such a vote of confidence, even from you!"

Mr. Covington-More glared back at him, and suddenly Lady Cecily said, "GO AWAY!"

"I beg your pardon, ma'am?" Alistair asked, much shocked.

"I want you all to go away! I am tired and upset, and I do not think I can take any more of these dramatics! Oh, do go away!"

This last was said in a querulous, elderly whine, and everyone rose immediately as Lord St. Williams gestured to them.

"Of course, m'lady," he said to her. "We will leave you now to rest. Perhaps tomorrow we can discuss . . ."

But Lady Cecily did not hear him. She was struggling to her feet, grasping her cane, and allowing Miss Spenser to support her as she made her way to the bed. She looked very old and very confused.

None of the guests attempted to bid her good night as they filed from the room. As one, they moved down the hall towards the fire burning on the hearth.

"Allow me to congratulate you, Lady Danvers," Alistair Russell said. "I am sure I could never behave so phlegmatically if I knew someone was trying to kill *me!* I am all admiration for your self-control and fortitude! But then, they do say the woman is the stronger of the species, do they not?"

Lady Danvers stared at him as he bowed to her.

"How else should I possibly behave?" she asked in her sharp voice. "Of course I do not believe Lord St. Williams' explanation, for I have never heard anything so absurd in my entire life! Why on earth would someone want to kill *me?*"

There was a pause while everyone assembled, with the exception of her husband, began to count the reasons, and then John St. Williams said, "We must hope you are right, Lady Danvers! But just to be on the safe side, I would not eat any more of those sweetmeats if I were you!"

"No, no, she shall not!" Lord Danvers assured him in a hurry.

His wife stood and pouted, but finally she nodded and said, "Very well, if you insist, but you will see it was all a mistake. That Spenser woman undoubtedly let the dog eat something he should not when she had him out this afternoon, and now, of course, does not dare to admit it! I think that this suspicion that you all have of an attempted murder shows a lamentable lack of stability in the family. *I* intend to rise above such speculation and sensationalism!"

Thus chastised, the guests remained uneasily around the fire, no one making any move to adjourn to the library to discuss the events of the evening further. Lady Danvers took her husband a little apart from the others and began to lecture him in quick, querulous whispers; Cecilia North seemed to have decided that remaining glued to her cousin Caroline's side was the only possible safe place to be, Mr. Covington-More lounged at his ease in a chair near the fire and watched them all, and Alistair Russell was intent on removing an imaginary speck from the sleeve of his evening coat. John St. Williams watched Gregory as he paced up and down the hall, his quick footsteps and excited expression showing that he was pondering the problem. John was sure he considered the whole thing a terrific lark, and the best thing that had happened to him in years, and that he was all ready planning how he would confound his friends with the adventure when he returned to town. M'lord could not help smiling a little at such boyish enthusiasm, and Caroline, looking up just then, wondered what on earth he had to smile about! If what he suspected was true, and there was a murderer in the house, then surely they were, all of them, in a great deal of danger.

CHAPTER 4

THE NEXT MORNING, Caroline was surprised to receive a visit from Molly Deems, Cecilia's maid. Watched by a disapproving Wentworth, the girl stood near the foot of the bed, wringing her hands under her apron and begging Miss Caroline to be sure and let her mistress know when she was about to go down to breakfast, so Miss North could accompany her.

"Didn't sleep a wink, miss, not a wink, she didn't!" Molly elaborated. "Miss Cecilia 'as a very sensitive nature, wot *feels* things, if you take my meaning, miss! Poor lady, that frightened, she is, and so am I! Murder! 'Oo would o' thought it!"

Caroline thought the maid did not sound at all frightened. After all, no one was interested in disposing of *her,* and this was all as good as a play to her. So Caroline looked into her eager eyes and coldly told her to control herself, that there was nothing to worry about, and the best thing she could do for her mistress was to remain calm and not encourage the girl to dramatize the situation. She was so pragmatic and so completely unmoved by Molly's histrionics that the maid went away completely subdued.

Caroline sighed as Wentworth helped her to dress,

but she was distracted this morning and did not chat with her maid, as was her wont. It was plain to see that she was to be treated to her cousin's company throughout the waking hours, and she knew she would be bored with Cecilia's endless discussions of the situation and conjectures about the culprit in a very short time. She had hoped to have a few minutes to herself to think about this puzzle; now, of course, that would be impossible.

The two girls went down the stairs together, Cecilia hanging onto Caroline's arm until she was told sharply to stop behaving like a such a ninny! Crowell bowed to them as they entered the dining room, and informed them in a gloomy voice as how Miss Spenser had had to send for the doctor, first thing! Cecilia gave a little cry and sank into a chair, which was just the reaction the old butler had hoped for.

From one end of the table, Mr. Covington-More said thickly through a mouthful of ham, "No need to take a pet, missy! The old lady's not feeling up to snuff after last evening, but there's naught that much amiss with her but the usual; old age, and too much port!" He sniffed, and Cecilia, who was sure that someone had been taken ill or died during the night, managed to recover her spirits after a cup of strong tea, while Caroline and the gentleman conversed about the weather. She wondered that Caroline cared to talk to him; he was, after all, not the type of person young ladies of their quality were supposed to have anything to do with, so she kept her eyes averted as she ate her breakfast. In spite of her show of timidity and fear, Miss Cecilia North was enjoying herself very much, although she would have hotly denied it if it were pointed out to her. Her favorite kind of reading was the more terrible gothic tales, and this castle in Scotland, gloomy and run-down, with its ominous scenery and howling wind, was a setting she knew perfectly well. There was of course a beautiful heroine in residence (herself), and several handsome heroes to choose from, as well as any number of villians. To think she would be living just such a tale as she had finished reading in her room the previous afternoon! The fair Rosalinda of that story would have nothing on her!

After breakfast, she begged Caroline to walk up and down the hall with her before they went into the library, for she had something of great importance to discuss with her privately. Taking Caroline's arm again, she asked her if she thought it would do any good to write to her mother and beg that she might be allowed to return home. Since she knew as well as Caroline did that her mama would firmly order her to remain where she was until Great-Aunt Cecily's will had been signed, with, it was hoped, her as the sole beneficiary, this was only a ploy to talk about the events of the previous evening. Caroline checked a tiny sigh and said that although she was sure Lady North would be delighted to hear from her daughter, by the time the letter reached Middlesex and an answer was returned, they themselves in all probability would already be on their way home, and she advised her cousin not to alarm her mother unduly. Cecilia nodded at this prosaic wisdom and felt sorry for her cousin. She did not seem to have a romantic bone in her body. Did she not feel the excitement? Was she not at all afraid? How terrible it must be to be so calm and sensible all the time!

Just as Caroline was about to bear her off to the library and a morning of needlework, there was a knock on the front door, and both girls waited curiously to see who might be there. When Crowell opened the door, he admitted a middle-aged man carrying a black bag, who was obviously Lady Cecily's physician. He bowed slightly in the girls' direction, but before he could speak, Miss Spenser came out of Lady Cecily's room to greet him. She rudely brushed by the young ladies without a word, in her haste to reach the doctor's side. Caroline thought she looked very excited this morning; there was an unhealthy flush on her face as she took the doctor's hat, and her gray eyes were large and distended behind the thick glasses. The doctor did not seem to notice that anything was amiss as he courteously asked after Miss Spenser's health, and was finally introduced to Caroline and Cecilia, as Dr. Matthew Ward.

Although he had a pleasant face under his graying hair, you would not have called him a handsome or dignified man. He looked as if he rarely got enough sleep, and his black suit was poorly pressed and his cravat darned. Caroline thought Mrs. Ward must be a poor wife to send her husband out dressed so carelessly, even as she shook his hand and said she was pleased to meet him. They had only a minute to talk before Miss Spenser took his arm and led him away, promising to come and tell the girls his report on Lady Cecily's health as soon as he had examined her.

The girls entered the library to find Gregory standing by the window, dressed in riding clothes, and John St. Williams reading an old newspaper before the fire. He rose and bowed, and when Cecilia importantly announced that the doctor was even now with Lady Cecily, he did not return to his seat but folded the paper and excused himself. "I want a word with that doctor!" he said as he left them. Caroline smiled at her brother.

"Why are you still indoors, Gregory?" she asked, sitting down and opening her workbasket. "I see the sun is shining; I was sure you had gone for a gallop long ago!"

"Go out, Caro?" he asked, his eyes wide. "Why, I might *miss* something exciting if I do!"

"I hardly think we are going to be continually assaulted by dying dogs, fainting husbands, or suspected murders, Gregory!" she said.

"But how can we be sure?" Cecilia added. "Do remain with us, Cousin Gregory! I feel so much safer with a man to protect us!"

The two youngest members of the house party soon had their heads together in the window seat, and Caroline bent to her tapestry, wondering why she felt about a hundred years older than either of them!

Lord and Lady Danvers were the next to make an appearance. Lady Danvers very kindly took it upon herself to give Caroline a critique of her tapestry and told her several ways she might have improved it, if only she had had the benefit of the lady's good advice before she was so far along, and Lord Danvers went to stand near the window seat and ask Miss North how she did, effectively putting an end to the confidences the young cousins had been sharing. Cecilia blushed prettily, but it was not because of his attentions, as Lord Danvers suspected, but the fact that she had just whispered to Gregory that perhaps Cousin Roger was using this occasion to do away with his wife, and what did Gregory think of him as a possible murderer?

Since Gregory knew he would have killed the lady several times over if he had had the misfortune to be married to her, this suggestion met with his hearty approval, and until Lord Danvers had arrived, they had been talking over every possible way he might have done the deed.

"For, of course, it was easier for him to put the poison in her candy than anyone else!" Cecilia pointed out.

"Very true!" Gregory agreed. "But remember, cousin, how he fainted? Surely he could not have faked that?"

"Well, perhaps that was just because he was so disappointed that his foul deed miscarried!" Cecilia reasoned, loath to abandon this promising culprit.

Since Lord Danvers remained beside them, the two cousins were unable to continue, although they exchanged several knowing glances the rest of the morning, especially when Cousin Roger kept calling his wife "my love."

"Coming it much too thick, to throw off suspicion!" Gregory muttered once when the gentleman turned aside for a moment.

73

Mr. Covington-More did not join them that morning, nor did Alistair Russell, but Miss Spenser came in after a while and said that the doctor had insisted that Lady Cecily remain quietly in bed for at least a day and had forbidden her to receive any of the company. She did not add that Dr. Ward had given the old lady a severe lecture for indulging in not one, but two, glasses of port, which she knew very well she should not drink, and that Lady Cecily must be feeling especially low, for she had not replied to this typical admonition in her usual way, by telling the doctor to stop being an old woman, for she would, as she always did, do exactly as she pleased!

Miss Spenser went away without thinking to tell them another item: how Lord St. Williams had been waiting in the hall for the physician and had carried him away for a private conversation, and how the two men had then left the hall together.

This gentleman was late to the luncheon table, although Alistair Russell was there, studiously ignoring Mr. Covington-More, who did not seem to be at all downcast to be treated in such a way, when the others came in. Alistair did not look well this morning; his face was unusually pale, and although he was beautifully dressed with his customary complement of fobs and chains and rings, he seldom spoke to the others but appeared to be lost in thought. Caroline herself had a headache. She told herself that even if it were insufferably rude, she was not going to spend the afternoon with her female cousins, not after she had endured a morning of Cecilia's artless chatter and Sylvia's superior lectures.

John St. Williams, who had taken the chair at the foot of the table, thereby enabling him to watch all his relatives carefully, noted Alistair's pallor and preoccupation, and the way Caroline rubbed her temples with a little frown and was so unusually quiet. He could not fail to see the supressed excitement of both Gregory and Cecilia, nor the occasional looks they exchanged, for they were so very obvious.

He thought Lord Danvers exceptionally chatty, as if he were determined to behave as if nothing had happened, and saw Mr. Covington-More's almost habitual sneer as he stared at the others while chewing large mouthfuls of his lunch. Of all the guests, only the intended victim seemed at all at ease. Lady Danvers sat erectly at the table, steadily working her way through several large plates of food, and every now and then interrupting her husband to tell the story he was trying to relate to them all, in her own, more accurate, version.

When Mr. Covington-More put a large hand over his wineglass when Crowell would have filled it, St. Williams could not resist asking why.

"I do not touch spirits, sir!" the man said, staring with disapproval at Lord St. Williams' brimming glass.

"But last night, surely you had a glass of port, did you not?"

"I drink only Adam's ale, the only drink man should permit himself! I certainly do not approve of all this swilling of spirits that the rest of you indulge in! Disgusting!"

His face had turned very red, and Alistair looked up and asked, "Can it be that *you*, you of all people, are one of those Methodists?"

"And what if I am?" Covington-More asked belligerently. "I know the ways of the devil, the evil that waits to engulf the unwary, the snare that . . ."

"Oh, spare us! It needed only that," Alistair muttered, lifting his wine glass to sip defiantly, "that the bastard among us should be a religious fanatic!"

Covington-More made as if to rise from his seat, but one look at John St. Williams' face caused him to sink back again into his seat. "That will do, Alistair!" his cousin said harshly. "Let us all endeavor to keep our opinions to ourselves. There is enough trouble in this house without stirring the caldron to a boil!"

"I see that you still hold to your ridiculous suspicions, m'lord!" Lady Danvers said, taking another biscuit. "However, I believe you are right about self-control and the need to maintain harmony, so I will say no more about it! We will see, however, who has the right of it in the end!"

Caroline thought John St. Williams was about to speak, but then he closed his lips firmly and only nodded.

It seemed a very long time before she was able to excuse herself, and, ignoring Cecilia's pleading eyes, left the room alone. She went up to her bedchamber to fetch her fur cloak and hood and a warm pair of mitts, and when Cecilia came to find her, had already left the house.

There were a great many clouds massing in a sky that looked as if a storm was brewing, but at the moment, the sun was shining and there was only a little wind. Caroline walked slowly through the gardens, careful to keep well out of sight of the hall, taking deep breaths and enjoying the fresh tangy air and the solitude after a morning of being cooped up in the library.

She could hear the breakers, strangely muted today, and thought of going around to the front of the hall to admire the firth. Somehow she could not make herself move in that direction, and even though she scolded herself for her timidity, she knew she would remain here on the sheltered side of the hall. She was walking down a brick path between two overgrown hedges, and thinking the garden might really be very pretty if anyone were to take the trouble to care for it, when she came to a crossing and ran into John St. Williams.

For a moment, she was so startled to find she was not alone that she gasped in fright, her face going white. Instantly, he put out two strong hands to steady her. "I am sorry I startled you, Cousin Caroline!" he said as she tried to recover her poise. "I did not realize that anyone else was out here!"

She tried to smile, even as she noticed that the

path he had been walking led only to an old gardener's shed. What had he been doing there? she wondered even as her calm voice assured him she was quite recovered from her fright and could now stand alone.

John St. Williams let her go, though he continued to stare down into her face, his own face stern and thoughtful. Caroline felt her color rising and would have turned away,when he said abruptly, "Do me the honor of walking a way with me, Cousin. I have something I would like to discuss with you."

Such was her curiosity that she agreed at once, and they began to retrace her steps up the brick path. "Shall we walk down the drive?" he asked. "It will be more private."

At that, her eyebrows rose, but she allowed him to lead her to the front and down the drive. He did not seem to be in any hurry to tell her what he had in his mind, for they had covered almost half the drive in silence before she was forced to put her hand on his arm to halt him. He looked down at her again and was surprised to see her panting. "I must ask you to moderate your steps, m'lord!" she managed to get out. "I cannot keep up with such long strides, and whereas you are having a nice stroll in the country, I am having a nice run!"

He smiled and apologized, saying he continually forgot his height, and as if this reminded him of the purpose of their walk, he began to speak. "I had not meant to mention it, but I find I must, if only to warn you. One must trust someone, after all," he said, tucking her hand in his arm and commencing their walk again, at a much slower pace. "Tell me what you thought of last evening, Cousin. Do you believe, as Lady Danvers does, that it was all an accident?"

"I am not sure, m'lord," Caroline replied. "Of course, it could have happened as she said, that the dog ate something when he was taken outside, but somehow it is hard to believe that Miss Spenser would not have noticed! And yet, it is impossible to believe that anyone would be trying to kill Sylvia Danvers, although I am sure we would all *like* to, several times a day! But who among us would murder her just because she was annoying? It is impossible!"

"Yes, you can argue the case both ways," he agreed. "The dog *was* poisoned, by the way. Dr. Ward looked at the body this morning. He said there was little doubt of it, but he put it down to a dismissed servant who might have had a grudge against Lady Cecily, or a small-boy's prank. She is not much liked in the neighborhood, I understand."

"But you do not believe that, do you?" Caroline asked, hearing the doubt in his voice as she stared up at his dark, frowning face.

"No, I think the candy was meant for Lady Danvers, but for the life of me I cannot imagine why. She only arrived yesterday at noon, and I did not see her after luncheon. Do you have any idea what she and her husband did until they joined us all for dinner?"

Caroline admitted she had no idea although she could try to find out, as he continued, "Abrasive and maddening as she is, I find it hard to believe that the lady could so enrage someone on a few hours' acquaintance that they would immediately try to poison her!"

Unconsciously echoing her brother and Cecilia's theory, Caroline said, "Of course, her husband is very well acquainted with the lady . . ."

John St. Williams nodded. "And has the best of all possible reasons! But why would he do it here—to throw discredit on the rest of us? There are other ways of disposing of an unattractive wife; ways that would seem completely innocent as well."

"There are?" Caroline could not help asking, wondering what her mother would have had to say about this extraordinary conversation.

"Oh yes, you can arrange a carriage accident, or perhaps the lady's saddle is not properly secured before she goes for a gallop, or you can have her set upon by thieves while returning from a ball . . ." He stopped. "What am I thinking about, to be telling you these things?"

"I have no idea, m'lord," Caroline said demurely as they reached the end of the drive, with its sagging gates and empty gatehouse, and turned and prepared to retrace their steps.

"What I most wanted to tell you was that I think you should be very much on your guard; that we, all of us, should be on our guard!" Suddenly he stopped still in the middle of the drive and turned her to face him, his strong hands bruising her upper arms where he grasped them so tightly. "And what the devil, my girl, were you doing wandering around that garden all by yourself? Suppose there *is* a murderer, and suppose he came across you there, completely alone in a deserted spot, unable to call for help? I thought you had more sense!"

For a moment, when he had pulled her to him so harshly, Caroline had felt terrified, suddenly remembering that she did not know very much about this man who was her second cousin, and that they were far from the house, where no one could come to her rescue. Now, at his words, she felt anger that he had frightened her so, and she pulled away from him, her breath coming fast.

"You are right, m'lord! For all I know, *you* might be the murderer!"

For a moment she was sure he was going to strike her, and she wished she might recall those hasty words, he looked so dangerous, but then he lowered his hand and nodded bleakly.

"Of course I might be—or anyone else at Rockledge, from the lowliest servant on up!" He sounded angry, but before she could interrupt, he continued, "And you yourself, *dear* Cousin Caroline, might be the murderess! After all, poison is so often a woman's choice of weapon! But I do not fear you, for I am better able to defend myself than you are against a man!"

Caroline agreed, still trying to control her breathing and obscurely wishing she had a loaded pistol in the pocket of her cloak just to frighten him as he had frightened her.

"Do not go out again by yourself, and lock your door when you are alone in your room. Although I have no proof, I feel the situation is very dangerous. You must promise me that you will take more care!"

Caroline would have liked to ask what business it was of his, but she saw the wisdom of his words and agreed meekly, not wanting his anger to flare up again.

"You know, of course, that you have doomed me to the endless chitchat of my cousin Cecilia, m'lord?" she asked, and then said, "But stay! Perhaps I should remain in a group at all times. She did say that she thought Lady Danvers was dangerous and that she was afraid of her! I cannot imagine Cecilia as the guilty one, but I suppose anything is possible!"

John St. Williams had resumed walking, and he suggested that if she wanted fresh air, she recruit her brother as her escort. "I would offer my services, Cousin, but now that you suspect me, I am sure I would be denied with a royal snub!"

Caroline thought it wisest to ignore this provocative statement and, changing the subject, remarked on the poverty of the household.

"If Great-Aunt has such an enormous fortune, why does she allow things to be run so economically? What a farce it would be if she turns out to be one step from the workhouse!"

"Have no fear of that; there is a fortune," he said, "a very considerable fortune besides what she wears as jewelry!" He paused, and Caroline stole a glance at his profile and wondered how he came to have that information. Then he continued, as if he were not much interested in the topic, "I think it is only the way of some elderly persons to be parsimonious, no matter what their circumstances."

For a moment they continued up the drive in

silence. He had not taken her arm again, and Caroline wondered why she regretted this. She had liked striding along beside him with her hand tucked in his arm, for he was so very tall that even with her own considerable height, she had felt tiny and feminine and fragile. Somehow, being next to a man well over six feet was very pleasant; she wondered what it would be like to dance in his arms? And she liked his eyes, too, so dark and intent, and that strong mobile mouth, and ... giving herself a mental shake, she was relieved when he began to talk again.

"Shall I tell you who I think it is, Cousin?" he asked, and at her eager nod he said, "Surely the prime suspect is Mr. Covington-More!"

"A Methodist, Cousin?" she asked, pretending horror.

He grinned down at her, and she was glad his wrath had disappeared.

"Never mind the man's religion; after all, we only have his word for his piety. But here he is, thrown into a bevy of legitimate heirs, while he alone is a by-blow! He must hate us! And suppose he thought that in doing away with us, he might gain control of Lady Cecily's fortune?"

"But to plan in cold blood to kill so many people!" she said, her hand creeping up to her throat in horror. "That would be an act of madness, sir!"

"Murderers *are* madmen!" he replied.

"Or madwomen!" she murmured, her brows knit in a frown. "Yes, I can see where he might be a suspect, and only by reason of his birth. How very unfair the world is; it is not his fault, poor man!"

"The only thing that bothers me!" her cousin continued, "is, when could he have done it? He was not present at dinner, and he did not even meet the woman until we were all assembled in Lady Cecily's room, and then he never went near her!"

"That is true!" Caroline thought for a moment and then said, "There is another possibility, John. Sup-

81

pose there is one among us legitimate heirs who thinks that in killing off some of the others he or she will have a better chance to inherit the whole? But I have to ask myself, why Lady Danvers at all? She inherits only through her husband; why not kill him, instead of her?"

"That is an excellent point, Cousin!" St. Williams congratulated her. "You have an intelligent mind; how refreshing in a woman!"

They had reached the last bend in the drive and could see Rockledge looming before them through the trees, and once again he stopped. Putting one hand on her sleeve, he said, "I most sincerely hope you will keep all such observations to yourself, however! I would ask you to trust me, for I do trust *you*, you see, but that would be unfair. You must guard against giving the murderer—if there is one—any clue that you might be on his trail. Promise me to be careful!"

Caroline looked up at his intent face, bent over hers, and could only whisper, "Yes, I promise to be careful!" For a moment they stood there staring at each other, and for the first time since she had come to Rockledge, Caroline did not hear the sound of the sea. She wished she might look away, but somehow she could not, and she wondered about it; the moment was too long, there were too many currents here, too much that had not been spoken!

He seemed aware of it too, for presently he shook his head a little and then said in his harsh, deep voice, "I shall leave you here, Cousin! It will be better if we arrive back at the hall separately, and I want to see to the care of my horses in any case." He stepped back, and she drew a shaky breath as he tipped his hat to her and moved off behind the screen of bushes towards the stables.

She put one mittened hand up to her mouth and stared after him. Whatever is the matter with me? she thought, and then she became aware that the early dusk of February was falling and the storm clouds had thickened. She hurried from behind the shelter of the trees up the circular drive. It seemed to be much colder and windier; perhaps they would have snow before morning, she thought as she knocked for admittance.

To her surprise, the door was opened immediately, and when she went into the hall, it was to find everyone assembled, including all the servants, everyone staring at her and all talking at once. She saw that the men were dressed for the outdoors, while the ladies huddled around the fire, looking frightened. Cecilia was crying, as well.

"Caroline!" Gregory shouted. "Where the devil have you been?"

"Why . . . why, I have been out for a walk, Gregory! I had no idea it was so late!"

"Do you realize how worried we have been? Missing most of the afternoon, and no one could find Cousin John, and what were we to think? You should be whipped!"

Alistair Russell strolled up to her as he removed his hat and gloves and handed them to Crowell. She thought his eyes very cold and bleak as he took her chin in his hand. "How very inconsiderate of you, Cuz!" he said in his light baritone. "It is hardly my idea of a pleasant afternoon to have to worry about you and even contemplate a search of the grounds. Have you, by any chance, been with John?"

For some obscure reason, Caroline lied to him. "No, I have not seen him. I went first to the gardens, and then I decided to walk to the end of the drive. It is longer than I remembered. I am so very sorry to have caused this trouble; please say you will forgive me."

She looked around at the others, smiling her most pleasant smile, and the servants reluctantly began to make their way to the back of the house, now that Miss was safe and the excitement over. Alistair flicked her chin with a careless finger and nodded. "As long as I did not have to scramble through the underbrush, scratching my boots and tearing my coat after all, I suppose I shall forgive you, Cousin Caroline!"

"Well!" said Lady Danvers, rising from her chair. "I am sure it was most unwise of you, Caroline, and very thoughtless as well. One certainly expects more good sense from a woman of your years!"

"She is not so very old!" Gregory put in when he saw his sister's anger rising.

Lady Danvers glared at him. "As you say, but she is certainly of an age when such mad starts are most inappropriate. I have always in the past considered you to be a mature woman of good understanding, Caroline," she continued, "but after this afternoon I have changed my opinion drastically! Come Roger! Let us retire to rest before dinner!"

No one spoke until the Danvers had disappeared above stairs, and then Mr. Covington-More said, "No need to fret, girlie! No one cares what SHE thinks, anyway!"

Caroline smiled at him for his support even as she remembered Cousin John's naming him as the chief suspect.

Alistair turned to the butler. "Fetch Miss Covington some tea, Crowell, and bring it to the library. You must be chilled, Cuz!"

Caroline took her brother's arm and moved in that direction, as the others, with the exception of Covington-More, followed. "Yes, it is growing colder and there are heavy clouds overhead. I expect we will have snow before morning."

Gregory squeezed her hand as he took her cloak and hood, all anger gone now he knew she was safe, and she went to hold out her hands to the fire.

"That is all we need!" Alistair said, lounging against the bookcase and raising his eyes to heaven. "To think we may be snowed in here!"

He spoke in such a gloomy tone that the others laughed. "Yes, you laugh now, but consider the food, the fires, and our charming rooms, to say nothing of the alarums and upsets we have already suffered in this barbaric location! Bah!"

Caroline drank her tea and listened as the others talked. Cousin John had given her a lot to think about, and she wished she might go to her room, but she felt she owed it to the others to remain and chat. She noticed that St. Williams did not come in and join them, and he had still not made an appearance when the first dressing-bell sounded and they all went up to change for dinner.

He joined them at the table, however, but not by a flicker of an eye did he give any indication that he was aware of her presence. She had put on another new gown this evening, a deep blue silk that matched her eyes, and Alistair had complimented her on it when he escorted her in to dinner by saying it was much too fine for such a savage setting!

Conversation that evening centered mostly on the state of Great-Aunt Cecily's health. Miss Spenser had told Gregory that she was resting comfortably and planned to remain in bed for the evening. She had no plans to join them after dinner but hoped she might see them tomorrow.

Accordingly, the ladies withdrew to the library after dinner, leaving the men to enjoy Lady Cecily's port, and in the case of Mr. Covington-More, water from the Rockledge well. Caroline wondered what on earth they would talk about; surely it would not be a very convivial conversation with the usual witticisms and jokes that the ladies might not hear.

Lady Danvers claimed the most comfortable chair, closest to the fire, and Cecilia and Caroline sat across from her on the sofa. Cecilia had not been especially pleased that afternoon when all the attention was focused on her cousin's disappearance, but she was sure she could redirect it to herself when the gentlemen arrived. She was wearing a gown of palest yellow muslin, and after Lady Danvers told her how very unsuitable, immodest, and unbecoming to one of her years it was, she was sure it was stunning.

The men did not linger long over their port. Alistair was the first to come to the library, his handsome face set in petulance. "I do not know how I am to endure the boredom!" he said, sinking into an armchair and gracefully crossing his legs while one slim white hand went to his forehead to shade his eyes. "Surely even a fortune cannot be worth it! I am almost convinced I should retire to town at once!"

Lady Danvers leaned forward and eyed him eagerly. "Perhaps that would be best, sir!" she said, and he dropped his hand to send her a look of complete loathing. She flushed, for once embarrassed to be caught so obviously in her greed, and then the others came in.

Lord St. Williams had found a chessboard, and he challenged Gregory to a match, and they were soon settled by the window, deep in play. Lord Danvers stood before the fire, his hands behind his back under his coattails as he rocked back and forth on his heels, and even Covington-More took a seat near a branched candelabra so he might read one of the week-old newspapers, the light turning his red hair to flame.

After a few moments, when Lord and Lady Danvers monopolized the conversation, as usual, Caroline was deep in thought, Alistair had retired behind his hand again, and the others were ignoring her, Cecilia rose from the sofa and went to inspect the bookcase, a pout on her pretty face. This was not at all what she was used to, to be ignored in a room full of gentlemen, and although she was sure she would not find anything to read, she was aware of the attractive picture she made in the pale-yellow gown that floated around her, fragile and ethereal against all the old leather bindings.

The Danvers' had stopped speaking, and for a moment there was only the sound of the fire snapping in the grate and the muted roar of the sea. Then

Cecilia gave a sudden piercing scream and, putting her hands to her throat, fell to the floor.

"Dear God!" Alistair exclaimed, jumping to his feet and looking around wildly, his careful pose of *ennui* forgotten. Lord Danvers had paled and his wife was gasping in shock as Caroline rose and quickly went to her cousin, now lying still and quiet on the library floor. Gregory and John were right behind her as she knelt and took up one of the girl's hands to chafe. She could see Cecilia'a breath stirring the yellow gown, so her first fear, that death had occurred, was assuaged, but her heart was pounding and she was still frightened. No sign of this showed in her demeanor, however.

"Gregory! Get me a napkin and some water!" she ordered. "Sylvia, have you your salts with you?"

St. Williams went to get the bottle the lady held out, as Gregory brought back the jug and a napkin from the tray near the door.

"Is she . . . is she dead?" he asked in a hoarse whisper.

"No, my dear, she has only fainted!" Caroline told him.

"Now, I wonder why?" John asked, handing her the salts and staring down at Cecilia North, so pale and still.

"This is THE END!" Alistair said in a trembling voice. "My health is not such that it can support these almost constant jolts to the system! I have never been so unmanned, and I hope I shall not have to remain in bed for a week with a nervous attack! Dear God, why ever did she give that ghoulish shriek?"

"I am afraid we will have to wait until she regains consciousness to find out, sir," Mr. Covington-More said from behind him, folding his newspaper calmly.

Alistair gave a little squeak of alarm; he had forgotten the man was there, and then he looked very angry, to be caught out so.

All the while, Caroline was bathing Cecilia's temples with the damp napkin and waving the salts under her nose, and it was not much longer before the girl groaned and opened her eyes. Caroline could see the fright in them as John St. Williams commanded, "Cecilia! Come, wake up! It is all right!"

Gregory knelt beside his sister and helped his cousin to sit up. She put one hand to her head and began to moan and weep.

"What happened, Cecy?" Caroline asked, patting her hand.

"Oh, I am so frightened!" she whispered, her eyes going wildly from one to the other. "It was so dreadful, so awful!" Her voice rose again, and she began to wail in earnest.

"What was?" Mr. Covington-More asked in a normal tone of voice, which cut through all the drama effectively.

Cecilia started and shuddered, and cried helplessly. "No, no! I cannot say!"

"Here, let me carry her to the sofa, Gregory," St. Williams said, taking command. "We must let her regain her composure before we question her any further." Gregory helped her to stand and John picked her up and carried her to the sofa, where she was gently deposited, a pillow behind her head, as an anxious audience watched her carefully.

"Here, give her this!" Covington-More said, holding out a glass of brandy.

"From you, sir?" Alistair asked in astonishment. "A Methodist advocating hard drink? The angels are weeping, sir, at your downfall!"

Mr. Covington-More reddened, and he sent Alistair a look of complete hatred. "This here's medicinal!" he said, handing the glass to John.

Cecilia would have pushed it away, but St. Williams was having none of that, and she soon had taken a sip or two, which caused the color to come back into her face.

"Now, Cecilia!" Lady Danvers began in her piercing voice, having recovered from her initial shock.

"Be quiet!" John said, glaring at her. "Give the girl a chance to recover!" Lady Danvers bridled, but she was forced to settle back and wait.

"Caro! Where is Caro?" Cecilia moaned next, from the depths of John's arms as he sat beside her, holding her close.

"I am right here, my dear!" Caroline assured her, wishing she did not look so comfortable in his arms.

"Oh Caro, how horrible it was, staring at me!" She shuddered and then whispered, "I . . . I saw an eye?"

"An EYE?" Caroline asked, perplexed. "What do you mean? Where?"

"While I was looking for a book! I had just put one back in the case when—oh dear, shall I ever forget it?—there was an eye, right there in the wall behind the books, and it was glaring at me!"

She shook and began to sob again, and St. Williams gestured to Caroline to take his place. When she was holding Cecilia, he went to join Gregory, who was already searching the bookshelves where the girl had been standing.

"There is nothing here!" he said in disappointment. "Do you suppose she only thought she saw an eye?"

Lady Danvers sniffed. "Of course! Trying to dramatize herself, most likely!" she said. "I do not consider Cecilia, although of course it pains me to say so, to be of more than moderate understanding!"

Caroline watched John take down one book after another and almost cried out, for he was searching in much the wrong place. Both he and Gregory had forgotten that Cecilia was only a slip of a girl, only a few inches above five feet, and they were busy searching at their own eye levels, several shelves above.

Why she did not call this to their attention she did not know, but she was glad when at last Cecilia was calm and she was able to leave the library and take her upstairs to bed. It was very late when she and the maid had soothed and comforted her and put her between the covers, and since Molly volunteered to spend the night with her mistress in case she should wake and cry out, Caroline felt it safe to go to her own room. She had heard the others when they came up to bed, and for a moment she paused at the top of the stairs with her candle, thinking she might go down and conduct her own search of the library bookcases.

But then she remembered her promise to John St. Williams to be careful and, shrugging, decided the morning would be time enough. She did not consider herself a coward, but the thought of going down those dark stairs and across that massive, echoing hall with its stone floors to the library, and searching all by herself to find—and *what* might she discover?—was unnerving. Besides, she told herself stoutly, I am really very tired!

But for the first time, that night, after Wentworth left her, Miss Caroline Covington locked her bedroom door.

CHAPTER 5

CAROLINE WOKE EARLY the next morning, even though the day was dark and gloomy. When she went to the window and pulled back the drapes she discovered that the snowstorm she had predicted had begun in earnest, the thick white flakes swirling past the glass and the wind moaning. She shivered, and then, remembering the mysterious eye, dressed quickly in her blue woolsey dress and went downstairs to the library, hoping to be the first one down.

The library was empty and had the disheveled look of a room that has not been tended by a maid. There was no fire in the grate, and Mr. Covington-More's paper lay where he had dropped it. The chessboard still lay open and Cecilia's glass of brandy had not been moved, nor had the room been dusted or swept.

Caroline went at once to the bookcase where Cecilia had been standing. The old books were grimy and looked completely innocent, but she took several of them off the shelf and peered closely at the back of the case. Yes, there *was* something! She reached out and touched the wood. Although invisible to the naked eye, her fingers felt the circle that had been cut there, and looking down at the shelf, she saw a few grains of sawdust. She had returned the books to their places and was dusting her hands on a handkerchief when the door opened and John St. Williams came in.

"So, you found it, did you?" he asked. "Somehow I knew I would meet you here, diligently searching!"

"Yes, there is a circle cut out here, well below where you and my brother were looking last night. You forgot how much shorter Cecilia is than you, m'lord!" she replied, proud of her detecting.

He laughed. "I did forget it at the time, but I did not need to get my hands dirty to solve this mystery; I merely went and asked Crowell!"

At her questioning look, he held out his arm. "Come, let us retire to the dining room. There is nothing more to learn here, and I want my breakfast."

Caroline allowed herself to be settled at the table and served before she spoke again.

"What did you ask Crowell? And why him?" she asked when she could stand the suspense no longer.

"Well, from his age, it is obvious that he has been here forever, and since so many of these old houses have hideaways and priest holes, I was sure if Rockledge boasted one, he would be the one to know of it. You remember the religious persecutions, Cousin, when a man was hunted and slain if he admitted his devotion to Rome, and the priests who came secretly to say Mass at the homes of the faithful?"

She nodded, impatient with his history lesson, and he grinned as he poured another cup of coffee. "Of course there is a priest hole here, very cleverly hidden between the drawing room and the library. It can be reached from Lady Cecily's room or from a closet in the hall. Crowell knew nothing of the spy hole, though; that is a new development, for, according to him, the secret room has not been opened for years!"

"How very excited Gregory will be when he learns

of it!" Caroline said, her eyes twinkling as she spread some honey on her toast. "And how very lowering for Cecilia to find out that far from the supernatural, it had to be a very human eye she saw!"

John St. Williams put down his cup and frowned a little as Caroline asked, much perplexed, "But who could it have been? We were all of us in the library, even Mr. Covington-More."

He nodded. "Yes, it had to be a servant, but I cannot imagine why they would want to spy on us. In my experience, they always know all about everything, but where they get their information I have never understood. My valet, for example, can often be found packing my portmanteau only minutes after I have decided to travel!"

"It might not have been a servant; it might have been Great-Aunt!" Caroline said. "If there is an entrance to the secret room in her own room, perhaps she is not as ill as we thought and was not resting in bed last evening."

"I certainly wouldn't put it past her to have had the hole cut deliberately so she might listen to our conversations," he agreed. "After all, she was the one who decreed that we should all use the library as a sitting room. And what we have had to say to each other, and about her, might very well help her to choose her heir!"

Just then Alistair came into the dining room, and it was so unusual for him to be up at this early hour that both his cousins stared at him in amazement.

"I know, I know!" he said in a weary voice. "The country is ruining me! Such an uncivilized hour to be dressed! But I was barely able to sleep last night, so I decided I might as well rise. I have always been told how peaceful the country is after the racket in town, but after two days here I am sure I would be able to sleep better in the middle of a noisy London street. Just some tea, Cousin Caroline. I may be up and dressed, but I shall certainly not eat at such an ungodly hour!"

He sat down with them, and without hesitation John told him what they had discovered about the priest hole. Caroline was at first surprised at his openness, but then she realized that he did not think the incident had any connection with the poison in Lady Danvers' sweetmeat, nor did she think so herself.

"Of course it was our *dear* Great-Aunt!" Alistair said dryly. "I can only hope she was as startled by that piercing shriek as we were!" Then he began to chuckle, and Caroline looked at him, a question in her eyes.

"But how funny! Only think, Cuz, of all the comments she has heard these last two days. They say eavesdroppers never hear any good of themselves, and from what I can remember, there was nary a compliment to the lady that she might treasure! Instead we have discussed her parsimonious ways, her eccentricity, and her crumbling old castle! I can hardly wait to acquaint Lady Danvers with this information. *She* has been so very rude, she bears the palm! How she will gnash her teeth, all her hopes of garnering the Covington fortune quite cut up!"

John St. Williams excused himself, his eyes on his still grinning cousin as he rose from the table. Caroline prepared to follow him, but Alistair put out a lazy hand and stopped her.

"Do stay and bear me company, Cuz! Do you think we will be summoned to the queen's chamber today, or has what she heard given her such a disgust of us that we will be asked to leave instead?"

"Even if she did ask us, Cousin Alistair, there is no way we could comply. There is a blizzard raging; how could we travel?"

He looked to the window. "I had not noticed. So, you were right. Let us hope it is not a storm of very long duration!"

He changed the subject and began to discuss London with her. She decided he could be a fascinating man when he forgot his affected manners, for he had a quick wit and turn of phrase, and his comments on the latest fashions, as well as some of the more fabled of the haut ton, were completely amusing. She sat beside him willingly for an hour, but when the Danvers came in together, she excused herself so she might go and see if Cecilia had recovered from her indisposition. He rose and bowed and then he took one of her hands and kissed it lightly, and whispered with a wicked gleam in his eye, "Too bad you do not stay to see for yourself the lady's reactions to the news! But I will report to you all the amusing details!"

As Caroline was closing the dining room doors behind her, she heard Lady Danvers exclaim, "You cannot be serious, sir! How . . . how very unethical!"

Smiling to herself, she went to the stairs, not noticing Lord St. Williams watching her from the door of the library, a frown on his dark face.

Caroline found Cecilia languishing in bed, her face pale and her eyes heavy. She gave a little start when Caroline slipped in, after only the most perfunctory of knocks.

"Do not do that, Caro! How you frightened me! And after I told Molly to lock the door behind her, bad girl!"

"There is nothing to be frightened of, Cecy!" Caroline said briskly, coming up to the bed and smiling at her. She told her what she and St. Williams had discovered, and as she had suspected, Cecilia was very disappointed that the eye had not belonged to a ghostly apparition.

"Of course, it could have been the ghost of a long-dead priest!" she insisted. "Suppose one had been shut up there centuries ago and forgotten, and now his spirit cannot rest!"

She shuddered in delight, and Caroline, seeing the books on her nightstand, understood completely. Besides *The Secret Ordeal of Rosalinda or, The Castle of Rundello,* there was also a copy of Mrs. Witherington's latest opus, which she had heard contained a villian who went about killing young ladies at every opportunity in his run-down castle, which was complete with bats, creaking doors, and moaning ghosts.

"I hardly think it likely," she said in a damping way. "How difficult to sit reading in your library while someone was banging on the wall, trying to get your attention. How could you concentrate?"

Cecilia pouted and said she supposed it was lucky that Caroline did not have any imagination, but as for herself, she had always been very sensitive to nuances and auras. Before she could develop this theme, Caroline went away.

She found her brother in the library and told him the story, and he was as delighted as she had known he would be, and went away at once to the hall to see if he could locate the entrance in the closet. Mr. Covington-More came in shortly thereafter as she stood at the window watching the storm, and he told her that Lord St. Williams had just been summoned to his great-aunt's room.

"So, it begins!" she said, coming back and sitting down.

"Aye, that it does!" he agreed. Caroline looked at him. There was something in his tone, something she could not place, that disturbed her, but before she could think about it further, both the Danvers arrived and effectively put an end to any thinking she might have done. The lady was furious, her face red and her eyes dangerously angry, and Lord Danvers hovered around her, all but wringing his hands in his distress.

"But, my love, we cannot be sure that it was Great-Aunt!" he said. "It might have been a servant!"

"Will you be silent, Roger!" his wife hissed in a breathy whisper, pointing to the bookcase while making grimaces at him and shaking her head. Mr. Covington-More put down his book and stared at her in amazement, sure the lady had gone mad. Caroline remembered that no one had thought to tell him of

96

the morning's discoveries. After she had finished, he broke into laughter, long husky brays of laughter, while Lady Danvers waved her hands and frowned.

"No need to fear the old girl's at her post, m'lady!" he said when he was able to speak. He wiped his streaming eyes on his handkerchief and added, "She's called in Lord St. Williams, so you are safe for a while!"

"Well," Lady Danvers said, casting a still nervous eye in the direction of the spy hole. "I am glad to hear it! Not, of course, that anyone would say anything derogatory about such a sweet old lady, I am sure! I myself am quite taken with her; she is such an original!"

Caroline quirked an eyebrow at her. Was Sylvia practicing or just covering all her bets? she wondered.

It seemed a very long morning. Caroline had always felt imprisoned in bad weather when she knew she could not get out, and after a while she went to walk up and down the hall for some exercise. She was soon joined by her brother, who, by the dust he was brushing off his coat, had had success in his search, although he told her that any child could have discovered the secret. You only had to press one of the pegs at the back of the closet and turn it slightly to the left, and a panel slid open. He said he could hardly wait to show Cousin Cecy, after Caroline declined to get her gown dirty by joining him in the priest hole.

"Can you hear what is said in the library, Gregory?" she asked.

"Oh yes, clear as anything! I heard every word even though the spy hole has been shut. There must be air vents somewhere else, for I could feel a definite draft. But there were no clues as to who has used it; there is nothing in there but spider webs and an old stool. I say, Caro! Sylvia Danvers is a flat, isn't she? I almost called out that it was only me in there, but I was afraid I would startle you!"

John St. Williams joined the others for lunch, but

he would answer no questions about his conversation with Lady Cecily that morning, and he seemed preoccupied throughout the meal.

Crowell came with measured steps during dessert to inform Mr. Russell that her ladyship would do herself the honor of receiving him after lunch, and Alistair's eyebrows rose as he caught Caroline's eye. Lady Danvers sniffed.

Caroline went up to her room with a book after lunch, and it was some time later when a knock came on the door and Cecilia slipped in. Caroline was glad the girl had left her bed and dressed, even as she shut her book and prepared herself for the inevitable chatter and gossip. Cecilia knew all about the visits to Lady Cecily. "I am glad she has not summoned me; if she never does so I will not repine!" she said, tossing her chestnut curls. "I was passing in the hall when Miss Spenser took in a tray of medicine, and I heard Lady Cecily laughing with Alistair in such a hearty way! I wonder what he said to make her laugh. I am sure I would never be able to do so!"

She stayed with Caroline until it was time to dress for dinner. The storm had worsened during the afternoon, and now the wind was howling around the windows, and the snow seemed to have turned to sleet, for Caroline could hear it striking the glass with sharp little taps. She was glad to put on the warm cashmere shawl that her maid insisted she take before she went downstairs to join the others.

After Crowell and the elderly footman had served the last meager course and had left the dining room, Alistair Russell began to tease Lady Danvers by telling her what a pleasant visit he had had with Lady Cecily that afternoon. She had questioned him, much as she had tried to question John St. Williams, all through dinner, but Alistair had turned away all her queries with light answers and had changed the subject again and again. Caroline could not help smiling a little at his tactics. The lady did not seem to realize how obvious she was, or how amusing to the others. Now, as if he had tired of teasing her, he gave a detailed account, and she leaned forward in her seat, her little black eyes intent with interest.

"You say she was pleasant? That she actually laughed with you?" she demanded to know. "How very extraordinary! She did not seem the type for levity!"

She fell silent for a moment, as if she were thinking of several jokes that Roger might tell his Great-Aunt when they were summoned, or some pleasantry that she herself might relate.

"Yes, she was very amused with my poor tales of London life and the haut ton," Alistair assured them all, one eye on Lady Danvers.

"I wish you would tell me what to say!" Cecilia interrupted. "I am so afraid of her, I know I will look a perfect fool! How very strange it is; I am never at a loss for words with gentlemen!"

Everyone laughed, and the conversation became more general after Alistair commiserated with her on her bad luck in finding an Aunt Cecily instead of an Uncle Cecil, "for," he said, "then of course you would have had no trouble at all bamboozling the old gentleman, and wrapping him around your pretty little thumb, Cuz!"

Lady Cecily was seen no more that day. Crowell told them that she was in her room, attended by the faithful Spenser, for the visits had tired her, and she was planning to retire early. Her relatives adjourned to the library, even after Lady Danvers suggested that perhaps they might have the fire in the hall built up and spend the evening there. "I cannot be comfortable, Roger!" she said, "Knowing that she— that someone might be listening to us!"

"I do not think you will find the priest hole used again, m'lady," John said. "Not now that we know about it!"

Gregory, who had been about to offer to sit there with a candle to see if he might catch the eavesdropper, was delighted with this analysis, since such a course promised a long, lonesome evening, and happily agreed to make a fourth for whist, with Lord St. Williams, Mr. Russell, and Lord Danvers.

Caroline had found an old journal that some long-dead Covington had long kept and was deep in its pages, every so often relating an incident to the others as she read. Cecilia had brought her embroidery, and Lady Danvers knotted a fringe, and if you had looked in on the group that stormy night, you would have thought it a pleasant family gathering, for Mr. Covington-More had excused himself immediately after dinner and gone to his room.

The group retired early. Somehow, the howling of the wind made everyone restless, and they were all taking up their candles by ten o'clock. Caroline found herself next to John St. Williams for a moment and could not resist asking him, in an aside, what he thought of Alistair's account of his visit. He looked down at her intently, and had the irrelevant thought that she was a very attractive woman, with her candle lighting up her expressive face and those beautiful blue eyes, but he did not smile in return.

"Alistair may regret his moment of fun!" he said finally. "I wish he had not made so much of it, how much Lady Cecily liked him!"

He paused, as if he had said too much, and, bowing, wished her a restful night. But Caroline could not sleep for a long time, for she was going over in her mind what he might have meant by his statement.

The snow stopped falling sometime during the night, and a weak sun was trying to break through the clouds when they woke the following morning. After breakfast, Caroline was trying to decide if it would be possible to go for a short walk with Gregory or if the wind was still too strong when the Danvers joined her in the hall.

"Good morning, Cousin Caroline!" Lord Danvers beamed at her. "I see the sun is shining, what? So

100

much more pleasant for us! And what are you planning to do this morning?"

Lady Danvers nodded to her and sat down before the fire, for once content to let her husband do the talking. Caroline mentioned a walk; Lord Danvers could not recommend such an undertaking.

"Drifts, you know, drifts!" he said, waving one hand vaguely towards the ceiling. "Dangerous things, drifts! Why, I recall a time when . . ."

"Roger!" his wife interrupted. "Summon that butler and have this fire attended to at once. It is smoking, and there are not nearly enough coals to warm even this end of the hall!" She shivered and wrapped her shawl around her shoulders more closely as her husband went back towards the servants' quarters to give the old butler a shout. "And bring a hod of coal, man! The ladies are cold!"

Crowell came at last, grumbling and complaining, and after he had grudgingly put a few more pieces of coal on the fire and poked it up a bit, he stood and announced that Lady Cecily wished to see Lord Danvers that morning, at his convenience.

At once Sylvia rose to her feet, smoothing her curls and straightening her gown. "Why did you not tell us immediately? Come, Roger! We will go at once so as not to keep the dear old lady waiting!" she said, taking his arm.

"Beggin' your pardon, m'lady," Crowell said, his voice quavering, and somehow triumphant, Caroline thought, "Her Ladyship only asked for Lord Danvers!"

Sylvia stared at him. "You must be mistaken, Crowell!" she said in her positive way. "Of course Lady Cecily wishes to see me as well as Roger! Come, my dear!"

"Well, you can go in, m'lady," Crowell announced, "but you'll come right out again! Lady Cecily said to me, she said, 'And tell that wife of his there is no need for her to push her way in here. I don't want to see 'er!' Them was her exact words, m'lady!"

Lady Danvers sank back into her chair, her face

101

now ominously red, and her mouth working as if she were suddenly speechless. Roger patted her hand, his eyes popping as he looked around desperately for help. Spotting Caroline, who was trying not to laugh, he beckoned to her.

"Do me the kindness to stay here with Sylvia, Cousin," he said. "You can see she is upset! Perhaps it is all a misunderstanding. There, my love"—turning back to his wife—"I will attend to this. I am sure Lady Cecily did not mean it—er, in quite that way!"

He bowed to them both and followed Crowell to the doors of the drawing room. Sylvia Danvers watched him go, still without a word. Caroline thought she looked as if she might have a fit of apoplexy, she was so very angry. After a few pregnant moments, she spoke.

"*I*," she said slowly, "have never been so insulted in my entire life! One would like to make allowances for the elderly and their little whims and caprices, but this . . . this rudeness, this complete disregard for what is proper behavior, makes me seriously doubt that Lady Cecily has all her wits! She must be deranged!" This thought seemed to afford her a great deal of pleasure, for her expression brightened and she seemed to be thinking. "Yes," she went on finally, "that must be the explanation! And if that is the reason, then of course any will that she makes in her present state will not be valid!"

Caroline was sure that the lady did not trust her husband to make a good enough impression to influence his great-aunt in his favor without her assistance, and she felt only disgust for Sylvia's greed and devious mind.

"I cannot agree at all," she said, not caring a whit when the lady's expression darkened, for of course she had never been treated to one of Sylvia's "spells." "She seemed to be completely in touch with reality when we all saw her the other evening. Perhaps, Sylvia, she only wishes to deal directly with the immediate members of the family."

"Immediate? Immediate?" Sylvia sputtered. "As the wife of Roger's bosom and the future mother of his children, who is more 'immediate' than *I*? And I meant to point that out to her, for of all of you, Roger is the only one who has seen his duty plain and entered into holy wedlock!"

And at such a cost, Caroline thought wickedly, but she did not reply, but bent her head meekly so her cousin could not see the laughter in her eyes.

Somehow, she lost all desire for a walk that morning, for she found she could not bear to miss Lady Danvers' account of her humiliation to the other members of the party as they straggled down to breakfast. Alistair Russell was among the last, and by this time, Sylvia had perfected her performance. He heard her out without speaking, both he and Caroline avoiding each other's eyes, and then he said, "How very mortifying for you, m'lady! I am sure you feel it deeply! But Roger has not come out; perhaps he is making an excellent presentation of his case? And even amusing Lady Cecily with a few *bon mots* and well chosen on dits in his own inimitable way?"

Lady Danvers' face flushed dark red; even she knew that she was being ridiculed, and Caroline rose hastily and excused herself in a quivering voice, to go to the library before she burst into laughter.

She found John St. Williams there, dressed to go out, and deep in conversation with Mr. Covington-More. Both men stared at her as she shut the door and then leaned back against it, her hands over her mouth and her eyes sparkling as she tried to contain her laughter. One helpless giggle escaped, and John smiled in sympathy as Covington-More said, "Well, I'm glad someone finds something funny in this house!" before he went out, shaking his head at the ways of the quality, as she moved away from the door.

Caroline explained to her cousin what had caused her amusement, and he gave a great shout of laugh-

103

ter before she hushed him. "Do be still, Cousin! What if she hears you?"

St. Williams looked down into her flushed face and smiled lazily. "Do you know, Caroline, I find myself completely uninterested in the lady's feelings, even as I most sincerely pity Roger!"

"I almost forgot to tell you," Caroline added, "Sylvia is very anxious to point out to Lady Cecily that Roger is the only one of the heirs to have married; she seems to feel this shows a steadiness of character and observance of duty that the rest of us, alas, lack!"

John's eyebrows rose, and she wondered why she had thought to mention that. "Perhaps," he said softly, not taking his dark eyes from her face, "that might be rectified. Who knows?"

Caroline moved away from him and took up her book, feeling breathless and confused. What did he mean by that? Did he intend to marry? And who was the lady? These were things she could not ask him outright, of course, so she pretended a great interest in the journal until he gave a little chuckle and begged to be excused.

"The grooms in Lady Cecily's stable seem as reluctant to feed the horses as her cook is to feed us. I must make sure they have been given enough oats," he said as he left.

Caroline sat down near the fire, all thoughts of reading gone from her mind. She was glad no one came in, for she wished to be alone and think.

Half an hour later she was still alone and deep in contemplation when the quiet of the morning was shattered by a loud explosion. Jumping to her feet, one hand to her rapidly beating heart, she hurried to the door of the library. The scene that met her eyes caused her to gasp in shock, for in the center of the hall, lying very still on the flagstones, was her cousin Alistair. Even as she watched, a dark-red stain crept from under his body to darken the flags, and for a moment, everything was still except for that slow trickle. As she was telling herself to go to him and see if she could help and to stop being a coward, the confusion began.

Lady Danvers stood at the door to the dining room and gave a piercing shriek, Gregory and Cecilia came hurrying down the stairs, both exclaiming, and Lord Danvers appeared from the back of the hall and hurried to his wife's side. Part of Caroline's mind registered all these things as she made herself move forward. Then the front door opened, and Mr. Covington-More stood there, a cigar in his hand, which he threw away as he stepped inside. Caroline was delighted to see him hurry up to Alistair and begin to examine him.

"You, Danvers! Call Crowell and tell him to bring bandages at once! The man's been shot!"

"Is he . . . is he dead?" Caroline could not help asking.

Mr. Covington-More did not look up as he turned Alistair over onto his back. He thrust his handkerchief beneath the bloodstained coat, and Caroline, staring at the hole in that beautiful garment, swallowed hard, her hands tightly clenched. Gregory reached her side and put his arm around her, and she was glad for his support. Cecilia, she noticed, had sunk down on a lower step as if she dared come no closer, and all the while Lady Danvers kept up her keening.

"Shut that woman up, m'lord, if you have to throttle her!" Covington-More commanded. "No, he is not dead, but it may be serious for all that. I wish that doctor chappie was here; we could use him!"

Crowell tottered into the hall, bearing bandages and followed by one of the footmen and Miss Spenser, wringing her hands and looking very distraught. Covington-More looked at them and shook his head.

"Come here, boy!" he said to Gregory. "It looks like it is up to us to get the gentleman to his room. You take his feet and I'll take his shoulders." Gregory moved quickly to help as Caroline stared down

105

at Alistair's still, white face. She knew Covington-More had no reason to lie, but how deadly pale her cousin was, how ominously still! She twisted her hands, wishing there were something she could do, when she heard the front door open again, and Lord St. Williams was there. Immediately, she felt better, as he joined the group around his cousin to hear Covington-More's terse explanation. John would take care of Alistair, she thought, John would take care of everything! St. Williams turned to the butler and took the bandages from his hands and said, "Send someone for the doctor—now!"

The old butler opened his mouth to protest—the state of the roads, their isolation—but one look at m'lord's dark, furious face and he bowed without a word.

Caroline wondered why Great-Aunt Cecily did not come out of her room with all the noise and confusion, for even though Sylvia had subsided into a few occasional moans, the servants were chattering, and Cecilia was still crying softly at the bottom of the stairs. Miss Spenser moved to the drawing room doors. "Oh dear," she said, to no one in particular, "how very upsetting for her ladyship! I must go to her!" As she went into the drawing room, the little procession started up the stairs, Gregory and Covington-More carefully supporting Alistair's body, followed closely by Lord St. Williams. He turned after he reached the fourth step and stared back down at everyone, his dark eyes intense and angry as they swept over the assembly. When his gaze reached Caroline, he spoke. "Bring the doctor up the minute he arrives, Caro. I will come down and tell you everything as soon as I can! No one is to leave the hall except for the servant who is fetching the doctor. Is that clear?"

She nodded, unable to speak, as the men moved around the bend in the stairs and went along the gallery at the top. Everyone stood frozen until they heard the door of Alistair's room close, and then

106

Caroline went to her cousin Cecilia, hanging on to the newel post and white with shock.

"Come, my dear! You need a cup of tea, or perhaps a glass of wine. I know I do!" She put her arm around the girl and helped her into the dining room, saying to Lord Danvers, "Bring Sylvia, Cousin! She could use a restorative too, and there is nothing any of us can do until the doctor comes!"

Lord Danvers supported his very shaken and frightened wife to a chair. She continued to moan and cry, which seemed very much out of character since Caroline knew that the lady heartily disliked Alistair Russell. Why should his being shot upset her so? It was not many more minutes before she learned the answer. Faced with this mysterious shooting, it had suddenly dawned on Lady Danvers that perhaps the comfit *had* been poisoned, and most definitely meant for her! This so unnerved her that she began to make preparations for a swift departure.

"You must tell Lady Cecily that my nerves cannot support a longer stay and that she must make up her mind about her heir as soon as possible!" she commanded her husband. "It is not at all what I am used to—poisoned candy, someone spying on me in the library, and now this!"

Her husband looked unhappy. He had not had a pleasant interview with his great-aunt, and did not look forward to approaching her again; furthermore, he was just as upset as Sylvia at the turn of events. His eyes protruded in his agitation, and his hand shook, and it was not until he had downed two very large glasses of wine that his complexion resumed its normal hue.

Caroline sat holding Cecilia's hand. The girl still had not spoken a word. It appeared that although this kind of thing figured prominently in her novels, it was not nearly as exciting when it happened in real life. Her first words to Caroline were, "Please let us go home, Caro! Please!"

Crowell served luncheon eventually, but no one

did more than toy with the food, and when Gregory came into the dining room, even the pretense of eating ceased in their eagerness to question him.

Gregory Covington was very white and nervous, and he was glad to drink the wine Lord Danvers poured for him, before he began to speak. He told them that Covington-More had managed to stop the bleeding and that Alistair had regained consciousness briefly, but that Lord St. Williams said the bullet was still lodged in his side and must be removed. They thought Alistair would be all right as long as they were able to keep him from moving restlessly and opening the wound again, until the doctor arrived, and that he had been sent down to tell the others since there was nothing he could do to help the older men.

This news cheered everyone considerably, for at least Alistair was still alive! They all began to discuss who might have been responsible, and Caroline excused herself to go and await the doctor in the library. She was glad that Cecilia seemed perfectly content to remain at the table with Gregory and the Danvers, for she wished to have a few minutes alone.

Sitting down at the writing desk, she took up paper and quill and began to list the guests, and where they had been right after Alistair was shot. Gregory and Cecilia were easy, for they had both come down the stairs together, and Mr. Covington-More had been on the front steps and John St. Williams in the stable. But Lady Danvers had appeared at the door to the dining room, and her husband had surely come from the direction of the back hall. Alistair had been lying facing in that direction, so it had to be an inmate of the house, guest or servant, for no one could have come in from outside and shot him, not with Covington-More on the steps, smoking a cigar!

She studied her list and sighed. With the exception of herself, she could not be sure of any of the others; they all could have managed. Even Cecilia or Gregory, for they had not been together upstairs, she knew, and there were two sets of back stairs from the servants' quarters that could have been used. And although she could not picture either one as the murderer, it was entirely possible to fire the shot and then run up the back stairs, appearing moments later in the upper hall, exclaiming in horrified tones over the incident.

Even Mr. Covington-More or John St. Williams could have done it, she supposed. Getting up from the writing desk, she went quickly into the hall. She was glad someone had wiped up the bloodstains, but she still could not help shuddering as she passed the spot where Alistair had lain. Methodically, she went into every room on the ground floor and inspected every window. Her heart sank when she reached the back salon, near the door to the servants' quarters, and found that the snow had been heavily trampled outside the French doors leading to the terrace. So she had been right. Either John or Covington-More could have shot Alistair, run out of these doors and down to the stables or around to the front door, with no one the wiser. As she stared at the confused footprints, she saw that it was beginning to snow hard again; in a short while this evidence would be gone.

Slowly she went back to the hall and, suddenly weak, leaned against a large table on which reposed several candles, the butler's tray, a large vase, and some odds and ends. Putting her hands to her face, she thought how horrible this was, to be suspecting any of the others! Then she remembered that Lord Danvers had come from this direction, and over there across the hall were the dining-room doors, where Sylvia had been standing. She began to tap her fingers on the table as she thought. Surely either of them was in the ideal position to shoot Alistair, or at least to see who had done it!

She was still standing there, deep in thought,

when Miss Spenser came out of Lady Cecily's room, carrying a tray, and gave a startled exclamation.

"How you frightened me, Miss Covington, standing there so still!" she exclaimed, one hand fluttering to the throat of her black dress.

Caroline apologized and asked for Lady Cecily.

"It is surprising she is so well," Miss Spenser said. "She heard the shot but she is taking it calmly, asking only that someone report to her as soon as Dr. Ward has seen Mr. Russell. I should be glad to wait for the doctor, Miss Covington, for you!"

Caroline thought her gray eyes were distraught behind the thick glasses and said she would not dream of imposing on Miss Spenser when she already had so much to do, before she went back to the library. Carefully she put the lists she had been making away, and then went to stand at the library windows, watching the snow and waiting for the doctor's gig to come up the drive, and praying that Cousin Alistair would be all right.

CHAPTER 6

EVENTUALLY, TOWARDS THREE in the afternoon, Dr. Ward arrived. The others had joined her in the library, and Caroline began to think she would scream if she had to hear one more conjecture, one more comment, or one more word from any of them, her nerves were so on edge with waiting. Even her brother Gregory annoyed her with his constant referring to the situation, and finally she told him to hold his tongue and let the matter rest! Gregory was much offended by this high-handed treatment, and studiously ignored her to whisper to Cecilia North. The Danvers too were whispering together, and Caroline turned back to her vigil by the window. She was beginning to wonder if the doctor would be able to make it through the deepening snow, when his gig struggled up to the front door and he leapt down with his black bag and hurried up the steps. As Caroline was taking him upstairs, relieved that at last help was at hand, she saw Miss Spenser at the back of the hall and called to her to tell Lady Cecily that the doctor had arrived.

She was dismissed at the door to Alistair's room by Lord St. Williams. He looked tired and distraught, and had only a small welcoming smile for the doctor, and none at all for Caroline. She went to her room for a moment to compose herself. In a little while they would know whether Alistair was going to recover, or if they would have to face the fact that Rockledge harbored a murderer.

"How silly you are, Caro!" she told herself. "Even if he is all right, and pray God that he is, there is still a murderer on hand!"

She closed her eyes and prayed for her cousin, for although she had not liked him at first, with his foppish manners and exquisite clothes, she had come to see that he was not as foolish a man as he pretended to be, and she had even felt stirrings of liking for his quick wit and intelligent mind.

Sitting by her fireside in the comfortable old wing chair, she fell asleep, and it was not until Wentworth came in to see to her clothes for the evening that she awoke.

"Oh dear, Wentworth, how could I sleep?" she exclaimed, rubbing her eyes. "Have you heard how Mr. Russell is?"

Miss Wentworth was able to tell her that the doctor had removed the bullet and was sure that with good nursing the young man had a fine chance of recovery, for the bullet had not struck any vital spot, and Caroline breathed a prayer of thanks. But when she would have hurried downstairs to hear the news firsthand, Wentworth announced that the first dressing-bell had gone, and she would be obliged if Miss Covington would change for dinner first, for she looked a perfect fright in her creased and crumpled gown, with her hair every which way!

Caroline laughed at her, but she submitted to her ministrations, not really caring this evening what gown or jewels she wore, or how her hair was dressed. At last the maid declared she was satisfied, and Caroline ran down the stairs to join the others, all standing before the huge fireplace in the hall, waiting for Crowell to announce dinner.

She saw Cecilia and Gregory with their heads still

together and the Danvers standing somewhat apart, looking identically nervous, and there before the fire, Lord St. Williams and Mr. Covington-More. Shyly, she went up to them to ask how Alistair did. John St. Williams frowned at her, and the tentative smile on her face faded, and it was Covington-More who assured her that the young man was better, that his valet was sitting with him, and that Dr. Ward had retired to Lady Cecily's room to have dinner with her there, and that the doctor intended to remain at Rockledge until the storm had abated and he was sure Mr. Russell was out of danger.

Caroline thanked him for the information, always aware of Lord St. Williams standing so tall and straight beside her, with that dark, thunderous look on his face, and wondered what she could have done to incur his wrath.

Crowell announced dinner and the seven remaining guests filed into the dining room. Conversation was very limited this evening, and often only the tinkling of silver or crystal could be heard, or the elderly footman's nasal breathing as he cleared away the plates, for there were long pauses in the talk.

After dessert, when Crowell brought in the decanter of port and the glasses and had bowed himself and the footman from the room and the ladies rose to leave the men as was customary, John St. Williams said in a harsh, deep voice, "I think it would be best if you remain here this evening, ladies, instead of adjourning to the library. There is no point in putting this off; we must discuss what has happened and try if we can to find out who fired the shot at Alistair so we might prevent it happening again. Next time he might not miss!"

Lady Danvers gave a squeal and sat down again, and Cecilia went very white at his words, while Caroline took her seat and folded her hands before her on the table. The decanter went around, and then St. Williams said, "If anyone has any suspicions, it would be wise to air them now when we are all together!"

There was silence, so he sighed as he looked around the table.

"I see. Can it be possible that there in the main hall, surrounded by all the other guests and servants, Alistair could be shot and no one saw a thing? Come, who was first on the scene?"

Caroline spoke up. "I believe I was, m'lord. I was in the library when I heard the shot, and I ran immediately to the door. There was no one in the hall but Alistair, lying where we found him."

"No one else? Not even the glimpse of someone disappearing? No skirt whisking around a corner, or a coattail?"

"Nothing!" Caroline said, and then added honestly, "But of course, I was so horrified and so startled, I did not really look, for my attention was all on Alistair, bleeding there on the flagstones!"

Cecilia whimpered and then was quiet as all eyes turned towards her.

"Come! We must press on!" St. Williams declared, running his hand through his dark hair in an impatient way. "Who came next, Caroline?"

"I cannot be sure of the exact order, but Cecilia and Gregory came down the main stairs together, and then . . . then Sylvia appeared at the dining room doors and began to scream, and Lord Danvers came from the back of the hall. And then the front door opened and Mr. Covington-More came inside and went at once to Alistair." She paused, and then, looking directly at John St. Williams, she said, "And of course, you arrived a few minutes later."

He nodded. "Yes, I had been to the stables, as I told you. But there was no one else? No servant, or perhaps someone whose face was not familiar?"

"No one," Caroline said firmly. "Later, of course, Crowell and a footman arrived with bandages, and after them Miss Spenser, who went in to Lady Cecily almost immediately, and there were some other

114

servants. I did not attend to them particularly, but I am sure there was no stranger among them."

"Of course you would not notice anything unusual, for there was nothing to see!" Gregory said, coming to her rescue, for John was staring at her in an accusing way. Almost as if, she thought, if only I had paid more attention, I might know the name of the murderer. Or does he think I am keeping something back?

"Very well," St. Williams said. "Let us go around the table and see what we can add to Miss Covington's statements. Gregory, where were you when you heard the shot?"

"Why, in my room! I had gone back up to fetch my greatcoat, thinking I might interest Caro or Cousin Cecilia in a walk! When I came out of my door, I ran right into Cecy; isn't that right, Cuz?"

Cecilia nodded. "And what had you been doing, Miss North?" John asked gently, for he could see the girl was still on the edge of hysteria.

"I . . . I had gone to fetch my needlework after breakfast. I intended to join Caro in the library," she whispered.

"And you and Gregory came down the stairs together?"

"Yes. I thought to run ahead," Gregory said, "but I could see Cecy needed support, so I stayed by her side."

"Did either of you notice anything out of the ordinary?"

Cecilia shook her head, and Gregory admitted reluctantly that he had not.

"Now, then," John St. Williams said, turning towards the Danvers. "Let us find out what you two were doing, there at the back of the hall."

Lady Danvers bridled. "How dare you question *us*, m'lord? I should like to know who put you in charge of this . . . this investigation! And I must say that I resent your tone and inferences. Neither Roger nor I have anything to say to you. Why, one might suppose that you suspect that it was one of *us* who shot Mr. Russell!"

"I not only suspect it, Lady Danvers," John said softly, "I am almost positive that it had to be someone in residence in the hall!"

The lady drew in her breath. "Roger! How can you sit there mumchance when this man has insulted your wife? How dare you, sir!"

"Very easily, m'lady!" St. Williams replied, pointing a finger at her. "Do you not understand how dangerous a situation this is? Here we all are, cooped up in this remote castle, with a blizzard raging outside, and somewhere here with us also is a murderer! Who can tell where he or she will strike next? Or do you feel safe, m'lady, because an attempt has already been made on your life? If, indeed, it was!"

Lady Danvers was now as white as her shawl, but it was Cecilia who drew everyone's eyes as she gave a little cry and fainted, sliding off her chair to the floor beneath the dining-room table. Lord St. Williams rose, as Caroline hurried around the table to help her.

"Seems to make a habit of it, don't she?" Covington-More asked no one in particular, and not seemingly very worried about the young lady's health.

Caroline shook Cecilia and gently slapped her face while the rest sat in silence. "She has not really fainted this time; it is only a momentary weakness, I believe!" she said as Cecilia stirred.

And so it proved to be, for in a minute the girl was back in her seat, sipping the glass Gregory handed her, and in control of herself after a few whispered words from Caroline. All that it had taken for her to return to normal was Caroline's suggestion that she would be so much safer here with the rest, instead of having to retire to her room, where she would be alone.

"Shall we continue?" Lord St. Williams asked, looking around the table. "Come, Roger! You can see we must try to get to the bottom of this! Of course we are all suspect, every one of us! Now, I ask you again. What were you doing at the back of the hall?"

"Why . . . why I had gone to fetch Crowell to bring some more coal for the dining-room fire," the gentleman gasped. "Sylvia and I went in there for a private conversation after my visit to Lady Cecily, and the fire was almost out! This house is run disgracefully! I seem to be constantly running back to the servants' hall and the butler's pantry, for no one answers the bells promptly. It is most unsettling to a man of my position!"

"Truly disgusting!" Lord St. Williams murmured. "But forget that, Roger! Surely *you* must have seen something! The would-be murderer had to have been standing there, from the way Alistair was lying!"

Lord Danvers gasped, his eyes bulging with shock, but before he could reply, Covington-More said, "Beggin' your pardon, m'lord, but that is not necessarily so. If the bullet struck him with enough force, he could easily have spun around as he fell. You cannot be sure he was shot by someone standing back there in the shadows!"

John nodded, but he stared for a moment at the man. "But such a theory is to place you more firmly on the list of suspects, sir!"

Covington-More nodded. "That is so. I could have fired the shot and then gone out the front door. You have only my word I did not."

"And of course, that means Caroline could have done it as well," Lord St. Williams mused. Gregory sprang to his feet, his face flushed. "How dare you insult my sister, m'lord? As if Caro would shoot anyone! I've a mind to call you out for such an insult!"

Caroline had never been so shocked, but her voice, although bitter, was firm. "Sit down, my dear! I thank you for your support, but if what Mr. Covington-More says is true, of course I could have done it! We are none of us exempt!" She felt her head was reeling. Why, during their walk, Lord St. Williams had said he trusted her! She felt a pang as she realized that he had lost that trust somewhere between now and then.

"But why *was* he?" Cecilia asked in a plaintive little voice, and everyone turned towards her, for she had been so quiet that they had almost forgotten her.

"What I mean is," she went on as she saw their confused faces, "why was Cousin Alistair shot at all? I do not understand! Can it be that there is a madman here?"

Caroline could see that she was already imagining a dungeon deep beneath the castle, and a deranged monster who had escaped his chains to prowl the hall at odd times of the day and night to seek his victims. Fortunately, Lord St. Williams spoke before she could enlarge on this theme. "It seems to me that Alistair was shot because he was on such good terms with Lady Cecily after his visit with her yesterday. I think we are all aware of how he amused her and had her laughing with him. He bragged openly to us about how taken she was with him, remember? Someone might have thought he stood too good a chance of being named sole heir!"

"But . . . but that is to accuse one of us of all these things which have been happening!" Lord Danvers protested. "It might not have been for that reason at all!"

"Well, it is true that Alistair delighted in insulting people; there is hardly a one of us present that he has not annoyed, but I hardly think anyone would murder him for that!" Lord St. Williams replied. "Does anyone have a better motive to suggest?"

They all shook their heads, and then Lady Danvers, who had remained quiet for some time, remarked, "It appears to me, m'lord, that *you* are the only one among us who cannot be considered a suspect, for you were not even in the house! How very convenient for you!"

John St. Williams looked very dangerous, and as

if it were someone else who spoke, Caroline heard herself say, "But he is most definitely a suspect, Sylvia! I must tell you all that while I was waiting for the doctor, I went around the ground floor and inspected the snow beneath all the windows. In the back salon, near the servants' hall, someone had used the French doors that lead to the terrace. The snow there was disturbed by many footprints, coming and going, so it is entirely possible that Lord St. Williams came back into the house that way, shot his cousin, and then made his way around the house and entered by the front door, as we all observed."

Dear Lord, she thought, looking down the table at him, what have I done? There was a hushed moment of silence while Caroline and Lord St. Williams stared at each other, and then he raised his glass to her.

"How very observant of you, Cousin! If the footsteps were there, and I, for one, do not doubt that you saw them, then someone indeed could have used that exit, and of course you are correct when you say it might have been I. I hope it makes you feel more serene, Lady Danvers, to have me join the rest of you as a suspect?" He spoke sarcastically, and Caroline felt a lump in her throat, for she had seen his look of distaste before he turned away from her.

"Unfortunately, I cannot prove it," she added, determined even now to be truthful, "for even as I found the prints, they were being obliterated by the fresh snowfall." She looked down at her hands and wished she might burst into tears, or faint, or leave the room. She could not remember when she had been so unhappy!

"Well, well!" Mr. Covington-More observed. "So we are all in this together, eh? Since I do not see how this problem is to be resolved, ladies and gentlemen, I suggest we remain as close together as possible, and when alone in our rooms, make use of the locks. If this snow continues to fall, there is small chance the local justice can reach us!"

119

"I don't know what he could do if he did!" John remarked. "This is very serious, for until the culprit has been found, none of us is safe."

"I did hear something from Crowell today!" Lord Danvers said in the silence that followed these remarks, as he tried to change the subject. "That is one good thing, I suppose, about all this running back and forth to the servants' quarters—you do hear things! It seems that one of the footmen reported that he had found an open can of rat poison in the gardener's shed. Seems he was meeting one of the maids there—frightful morals, the lower classes, what?—and he said it had not been there last week."

Lady Danvers glared at him. "Why did you not mention this before, Roger? How very upsetting!"

"Went right out of my mind, my love," he hastened to say, "what with all the excitement we have been having!"

Caroline stared down at her tightly clenched hands, noticing how her knuckles had whitened with the tension. In her mind's eye came a picture of John St. Williams hurrying along the path from the shed the day she had met him in the garden. She also remembered how angry he had been when Gregory mentioned he was sure the dog had been poisoned, but none of this made any sense to her, for the very reasons she had explained to him earlier. Why kill Sylvia Danvers? And who had been spying on them all in the library? And who had shot Alistair? And was it possible that all these incidents were not at all related, as they all believed?

"Caro! I have spoken to you twice!" Gregory said, and she looked up and flushed as the others stared at her. "Come, we are all going to adjourn to the library!"

But when they had reached the library, Lord St. Williams excused himself, saying he was going to sit with Alistair for a few hours, so his cousin's valet, Mr. King, might have a few hours' sleep before he again took over the task of watching over his master.

"Perhaps tomorrow we had better take turns sitting with Alistair," Lord Danvers volunteered. His wife frowned, and he added, "Perhaps we should do so in pairs? . . . I mean . . ."

He turned bright red and subsided as Lord St. Williams bowed to them all, his stormy gaze going right through Caroline as if she were not even there.

It was a very long evening. Dr. Ward did not come in, and there was no summons from Lady Cecily's room for anyone to join her there. Caroline tried to read, but John's stormy face kept appearing between her and the page. Cecilia and Gregory played cards in a halfhearted way, and after thoroughly cowing her husband with a severe lecture for neglecting to tell her immediately about the rat poison, Lady Danvers subsided and stared into the fire in an injured silence. Only Mr. Covington-More appeared at his ease. His eyes darted from one to the other of the guests, a little half-smile on his lips as if he found them all—indeed, the entire situation—vastly amusing. Everyone was glad when the clock on the mantel struck eleven and they were able to go to their rooms.

Caroline did not call Wentworth, but undressed and put on a warm dressing gown of navy velvet and sat down to brush her hair. As she brushed she reviewed what she had heard that evening. There was something that bothered her, something more than the identity of the person who had tried to kill her cousin. It was something that none of them had thought about. Now, what could it be? Suddenly, she put down the brush and stared at her reflection. Of course! No one had mentioned the gun! And where was it? The murderer must have had to get rid of it very quickly, for Caroline could see that keeping it in a pocket would be very dangerous. No, as soon as the shot had been fired, the gun must have been hidden in a safe place.

She rose and began to pace the bedroom. She did not believe Mr. Covington-More's theory that the

121

shot could have been fired from the front of the hall, for surely either he or she would have seen the person making an escape. And, she thought, nodding her head, I would have heard the door! There was a distinct creak when the front door was opened or closed; she had noticed it the evening they arrived. Surely she would remember if she had heard that distinctive sound!

So the shot had to have been fired from the back of the hall, and by someone who had stepped into the back salon or escaped through the servants' quarters. She closed her eyes and tried to remember that particular room. It had been dark and cluttered, the furniture covered by dust cloths. What could be easier than to push the gun under a cushion and cover it with a cloth, until such time as it was safe to retrieve it? She knew she should go down at once and search for it before that happened, but she could not summon the courage.

Finally, she removed her gown and slippers and climbed into bed. It would be foolhardy to go down there alone, in the dark, she told herself as she drew up the covers. And then, as she closed her eyes, a picture of the hall table where she had stood that afternoon appeared in her mind, as clear as if an artist had painted it just for her to see. There were the candles, and over there, Crowell's tray, and right in the center, the large vase!

Without stopping to think, she threw on her robe and slippers and, taking up her candle, softly unlocked and opened her door. There was not a sound from the hall; all the other bedroom doors were shut tight, and locked as well, she was sure. She had no idea of the time, but it must be very late, and everyone else asleep. Before she could lose her nerve, she crept down the dark stairs, obscurely pleased that the hand holding the candle did not shake. She went at once to the back of the deserted hall and, putting down her candle on the table, reached out and lifted the vase. Her excitement grew as she heard something metallic knock against the china, and she reached inside and drew out a gun.

And then, as she was holding it gingerly and trying to replace the vase, the dining-room doors were flung open and light streamed out from a high-held candelabra.

She whirled, her heart beating wildly with fright, to see Lord St. Williams standing there, pointing a very dangerous-looking pistol at her head. The gun she was holding clattered to the floor.

"YOU!" he said, "I do not believe it!"

"No, m'lord!" Caroline exclaimed. "No! You are mistaken!"

St. Williams came out of the dining room and strode towards her. As he reached the gun on the floor, he kicked it away, never taking his eyes from her face or relaxing his aim.

"Pick up your candle, Miss Covington, and walk slowly into the dining room, if you please!" he said in a commanding voice.

Caroline swallowed and did as she was bid, her candle now shaking dreadfully as she carried it before her.

She turned to find him shutting the doors and motioning her to a seat. She saw he had been sitting there at the table alone, perhaps trying to resolve the puzzle, and he must have heard some small noise that caused her discovery. She looked up into his dark face, and then quickly lowered her eyes. There was anger there, and disgust, but there was something else as well; something very like regret.

"Before we begin, a glass of wine?" he asked. "You must be distraught to be discovered!" Without waiting for her answer, he poured her a glass and pushed it towards her as he took his seat, carefully putting his pistol within easy reach of his right hand.

"I am sure you have a perfectly good explanation! Come, what have you decided to tell me?" he asked, his eyes never leaving her face.

"I will tell you the truth, m'lord!" Caroline said. "I

suddenly remembered the weapon, and in thinking it over was sure that the person who shot Alistair must have disposed of it as soon as possible. But where had he put it?"

"He?" Lord St. Williams inquired in a deceptively soft voice, one eyebrow quirked.

Caroline flushed. "I am aware how this must look, but you must allow me to tell you what happened! If you keep interrupting me, I shall not be able to do so!" Her blue eyes flashed for a moment with anger, and he nodded his head.

"I remembered the footsteps in the snow," she continued, "and it seemed to me that the murderer might have hidden the gun in that room before he—or she—went out the French doors. But then something else occurred to me. I recalled the large vase on the hall table. Surely that was the easiest hiding place. I did not want to come downstairs, but I was afraid that if I waited until morning, the gun would be gone! And I could not sleep knowing that, for then the murderer would have had the weapon back, perhaps to use more successfully next time!"

She stopped and glanced at him, and saw his frown. "A very plausible and pat explanation, Cousin. My congratulations! But how foolhardy—although brave—of you! Were you not the least bit afraid that you might meet the murderer on the same errand?" There was a pause, and he added, "But of course, if you are indeed the one, you would know there was no danger of that!"

Caroline drew a shaky breath and said with as much dignity as she could muster, "I can only give you my word, m'lord, that what I have related to you is the truth."

"And yet, by your own admission, *you* were the first on the scene, and had plenty of time to drop the gun in the vase and then hurry back to the library door as if you had just come out of that room!" he said, and she bowed her head in defeat. He did not believe her; there was nothing more she could say to convince him! Suddenly she heard him groan and looked up in astonishment to find him staring at her and then rising and coming towards her to pull her to her feet, his strong hands tight on her arms as he looked down at her pale face.

"I want so much to believe you, Caro! So very much!" He groaned again, and then pushed her away, so she staggered a little and had to grasp the back of a chair to keep her balance, while she watched him pace up and down the room. She noticed that he had picked up the gun again, but at least he was not pointing it in her direction. She felt confused at his words, and for a moment felt she might break down and cry, so she put up her chin and said, "I know how this looks, John! And of course I have no proof, no proof at all, that what I have been telling you is the truth. But it *is!* On my word as a Covington, it *is!*"

He stopped and went to lean against the mantel as if he were very tired, not looking at her now, but staring down at the dying coals instead.

"How dangerous women are!" he mused, as if speaking to himself. "I have known it for a long time, but until now was not aware of the extent of their perfidy. What a mistake it is for men to think they can understand women, that it is safe to care for them, even to love them!"

He looked at her, his eyes bleak, and Caroline stood very still, in her navy dressing gown with her hair streaming down her back. There was nothing more she could say. The silence continued, and finally he sighed and came towards her again.

"Come, I will escort you upstairs. You must forgive me if I take the precaution of locking you in your room tonight, dear cousin. I think we will all sleep more soundly for it! I know I shall!" His voice sounded sad and resigned, and strongly determined as well.

Caroline picked up her candle and went past him to the door, trying to keep her head up and her tears in check. There would be plenty of time to cry later;

all night, in fact. As she stepped into the hall, John St. Williams close behind her, she stopped suddenly, her hand at her throat, and he jumped back as if she had been planning a trick.

"M'lord!" she whispered, staring at the flagstones, "Where . . . where is the gun?"

With a startled oath, he held the candelabra high, but the gun that he had kicked to one side was nowhere in sight. He turned to look at her again, despair on his face for the accusations he had made, and in the deathly silence that followed, they both heard, very clearly, the sound of a door closing somewhere above them.

CHAPTER 7

"CAROLINE! DEAR CARO, forgive me!" came his agonized whisper in the silence that followed the shutting of that door.

"I would be glad of your escort upstairs, m'lord," she replied in a tight little voice, "especially now that the gun has been reclaimed by the person who made use of it in the first place. I trust you will not find it necessary to lock me in now, although of course I intend to do so from the other side of the door!" All the time she had been speaking, she had been moving towards the stairs, and John St. Williams was forced to follow her.

"Caro, you must listen to me! . . ." he began, reaching out for her, but she stopped him by raising her free hand before she picked up the skirt of her dressing gown to climb the stairs.

"Do me the favor of not speaking to me further, m'lord!" she said, her voice icy. "We have nothing more to say to each other; not tonight, and not ever!"

St. Williams, catching sight of her set jaw and the angry eyes that sparkled with tears, desisted, and it was not much longer before he was bowing to the lady's back as she swept into her room. He stood there, his shoulders slumping, until he heard the key turn in the lock, and then he went to his room although he knew he would be unable to sleep.

Mr. King was amazed when Lord St. Williams came to relieve him well before daybreak. He had not expected such consideration from one of the quality, but he was glad to take himself off to bed for what remained of the night. He told m'lord that his cousin had been restless, often calling for water or needing his position changed, but that he did not feel this warranted waking the doctor.

After King had bowed himself from the room and John had locked the door after him, he went up to the bed. Alistair was sleeping now, and looking a very young man as he did so. John adjusted the covers and then went to stand by the window. He was still there when the sky lightened slowly in the east over the firth, and he could see that it had stopped snowing. In his ears were the muffled sounds of the breakers beneath the window, and as the dawn came, he could have seen them if he had only looked down. But he stared out across the water to the far horizon. In truth he was not seeing anything at all but Caro's angry face, and he was not hearing anything but her voice saying, "On my word as a Covington, I am telling you the truth!"

And he had not believed her! Even though he had known he was more than half in love with her, still he had not believed her! What kind of man could he be to doubt her? He tried to tell himself that anyone would have reacted just as he had after catching her in the act of retrieving the gun from its hiding place, no matter how she had pleaded her innocence. But somehow this did not make him feel any better, and he put his hands on the sill and bowed his head, a groan for his folly escaping his lips. Alistair, in the act of waking, turned his head to see his cousin leaning there, the very picture of despair.

"Never say that I am worse, John!" he exclaimed in a weak voice. "The doctor assured me I would recover, but to see you in such a pose unsettles my mind!"

John straightened up and ran one hand over his unshaven face as he tried to smile. "No, no, Cuz! 'Twas not on your account I looked so ill. I am afraid I am tired from a sleepless night, that is all. What can I do for you? Some water, or perhaps a cup of tea?"

Alistair waved these offers away and tried to shift his position. In an instant John was there beside him, lifting him gently, and turning and fluffing up his pillows. Alistair sighed as he was laid back down again.

"Thank you, John! You are much more adept than King is! I am afraid he will be turning in his notice, for he sniffed most disapprovingly all last night, this situation not being at all what he is used to! Scotland in February is bad enough, without adding to it this horrible house, and now someone run amok with a gun! I will be lucky if he remains another day!"

"No one is going anywhere, Cuz, not in this weather," John replied, pulling up a chair to the bed. Alistair's remarks reminded him that he had wanted to question his cousin as soon as he regained consciousness.

"Did you see who shot you, Alistair?" he asked.

Russell frowned, as if trying to remember. "I am afraid I did not. I was crossing the hall, going towards the fire, when suddenly, without warning, the shot was fired from the back of the hall. It was dark there; I certainly did not *see* anyone! And yet . . . I have the strangest feeling that at the time I *did* know who it was, but now I cannot remember!"

"You had better keep that to yourself!" John told him, explaining a little of what had happened last night, although he neglected to mention how he had accused Caroline of attempted murder.

"You mean she went down there alone, in the dark, to find the weapon?" Alistair asked, his voice incredulous, as if such bravery was not to be believed. "What a gallant, plucky girl she is; women constantly amaze me! But now you say the gun has disappeared again, I shall most certainly forget to mention any suspicions! You don't think the mur-. derer will come back anyway and try again, do you, Cuz?"

John was not at all sure that this might not happen, but he told his cousin that the door was always locked now, and that he would never be left alone. Alistair dropped off to sleep again shortly thereafter, and John was beginning to wish he might go and shave and change his clothes, when Dr. Ward knocked, and on identifying himself, was let into the room, Miss Spenser behind him, bearing a tray of medicines and bandages.

They both insisted John leave the patient to them, Dr. Ward claiming Miss Spenser an excellent assistant, which caused her to lower her eyes and brought two red patches to her thin cheeks as if she were flustered by his compliment.

John was not hard to persuade. He asked his valet to bring him up a tray of breakfast, for he did not feel ready to face the company yet. After he had shaved and had put on fresh linen and fortified himself with some toast and coffee, he sat down at the writing desk and began to make a list. Even if last night had lost him Caroline Covington, it had provided some progress. He wrote down her name, his own, and Alistair Russell's, for these three could not be guilty. In another column he listed both the Danvers, Cecilia North, Gregory, and Mr. Covington-More. He stared at that list for a long time, and then he drew a line under it and added "Lady Cecily" with a question mark, and finally the word "servants." Drawing another sheet of paper towards him, he listed all the incidents that had occurred and, as best as he could remember, the location of everyone in the hall when they had taken place.

In the meantime Caroline had gone downstairs with Cecilia North. She wished she might stay in bed, for she was very weary and depressed this morning. She had not slept any more than John St. Williams had, for after her initial anger at him had died down, she had felt a sense of loss and regret. She had liked her cousin John, liked him very well indeed, and it upset her to know that he had not trusted her. And that is all it is, this malaise I feel, she told herself as she turned over yet again and tried to go to sleep.

When Cecilia had come and knocked on her door, accompanied by a wide-eyed Molly Deems, she had been dozing, but after Cecy was in the room, chattering away, she got up to wash and dress. Even after Wentworth brought the morning chocolate, she was still chattering, but Caroline knew it was nervousness. She did not tell her cousin what had happened in the night, for she saw that to announce that the gun had been recovered by the murderer would only upset her further. Besides, she did not want to speak of Lord St. Williams.

At last they went downstairs to the dining room, where Crowell was waiting to give Miss North the message that Lady Cecily would be pleased to see her that morning. He tottered away as Cecy sat down very quickly and stared at Caroline in horror. "No, no!" she exclaimed. "I will not go!"

"Come, now, Cecy!" Caroline said, helping herself to bacon at the sideboard. "She is not a dragon or a witch, you know! And you must make some push to make her closer acquaintance after your long journey here."

"I will not see her alone!" Cecilia said, her voice rising, and her pretty face set in mulish lines. "Not if she were as rich as Golden Ball! But stay! We are all supposed to remain together, are we not, Caro? I am sure that was the plan that was made last night, that we stay in groups, or at least pairs? Well, then! Of course you must come with me, in that case."

She brightened up and poured herself a cup of coffee, while Caroline studied her from the sideboard. "But Cecy, she did not ask to see me! I hardly think it the thing to . . ."

"We go together or I do not go at all!" Cecilia said, and Caroline wondered why she had never noticed what a determined little jaw she had. "Please, Caro! What difference will it make? I certainly don't care if you hear what she asks me, or my replies!"

She continued to plead and beg, and finally Caroline agreed, more because she could feel a headache coming on than from any desire to help her cousin. When Roger and Sylvia came into the dining room, Cecilia was happy to announce her scheme. Lady Danvers shook her head and sniffed at Caroline. How could she be so foolish as to assist another aspirant to the fortune? She was beginning to think that Caroline Covington's intelligence had been vastly overrated!

The two girls left the Danvers at the table, Lord Danvers busy drawing up a roster of people who should sit with Alistair that day, and arguing with his wife about who should draw the duty with Mr. Covington-More. Lady Danvers declined, even though as a married woman it should probably have fallen to her lot, and assigned Caroline to him; Lord Danvers demurred and suggested Gregory.

Caroline knocked on the drawing-room door, and her great-aunt's voice bade her enter. She pushed Cecilia ahead of her, and the two of them went to where the old lady was sitting by the fire, her bushy eyebrows rising as she saw them together.

"And what is this, miss?" she asked Caroline in a haughty tone. "I did not ask to see you!"

Caroline explained that the guests had decided to go everywhere in pairs, in the interest of safety, and Lady Cecily snorted and shook a bony finger at Cecilia.

"This is all your doing, I'll be bound, miss! Scared to death to face me alone! Well, never mind, never mind! Come in and sit down, both of you!"

Caroline took the armchair across from her, and

Cecilia settled nervously between the two, smoothing her gown with a shaking hand.

"Tell me what is happening!" Lady Cecily demanded. "I never leave this room, you know, and so I have to depend on Spenser to give me the news. I know that Mr. Russell was shot at yesterday, but since Dr. Ward has arrived, Spenser is not nearly so attentive to me as she ought to be!"

She chuckled to herself, as if she were secretly amused, and Caroline said, "I believe she is assisting Dr. Ward, m'lady, when he attends to Alistair. I heard from my maid this morning that although he spent a restless night, he has no fever and, now that the bullet has been extracted, is expected to recover completely."

"I am glad to hear it, very glad indeed! I like him, you know!"

Caroline nodded. "So do I; I did not at first, but after I came to know him better, I discovered his many good points."

Lady Cecily stared at her. "Put off by those foppish clothes and mannerisms, eh? Take a lesson from me, Miss Caroline, and never judge a book by its cover! Now, I'll be bound that Lord St. Williams is much more to your taste!"

Caroline turned even paler and shook her head. "Not in the least, m'lady! He is arrogant, opinionated, and untrusting!"

"I would love to know why you say so, but of course you would not tell me. But come, Miss North, have you nothing to say for yourself? How is your mother, girl? Tell me something about your home, your life, the things you like . . . ."

Cecilia said in a little voice that Mama was very well, thank you, and had sent her love. Caroline was glad that Lady Cecily refrained from one of her acid comments, for probably that would have brought Cecilia's conversation to a complete standstill before it was even begun. When the old lady did not interrupt her, she was bold enough to go on and describe her home and her friends, and to tell Lady Cecily how much she was looking forward to her first season.

"Yes, you'll be fired off with no trouble at all, I can see," Lady Cecily said, "for you're so pretty. How fortunate that there are still some gentlemen who do not care particularly if the wife they choose has a brain in her head or not! Just as long as her face is beautiful and her figure attractive, they are satisfied."

Caroline smiled a little, and Lady Cecily turned to her. "And you, miss, not married yet? And you all of twenty and four! Take care or you will end up an elderly spinster like me!"

Caroline looked at her closely, but there was no disappointment or bitterness in her face, so she remarked, "I would prefer it so, m'lady, rather than marry a man I cannot love and respect! So far, at least, I have not found anyone to suit me."

Lady Cecily cackled with amusement. "Neither could I! You may not believe it, looking at me now, but I was a great beauty in my day; had any number of men dangling after me. But not a one could compare with my father, and I vowed I would never settle for second best. I have not been unhappy, but it takes a special sort of woman to live alone without regrets. I wonder if you are such a one?" She stared keenly at Caroline for a moment. "You have honest, clear eyes, gel, and a determined look. It might work, but of course you are much too young to put yourself on the shelf as yet!"

The conversation moved on to other things. Cecilia asked about Miss Spenser and some of the other servants when she felt a lull. Her mother had told her to be especially attentive to what interested her great-aunt, and as she did not like to remark on any of the furnishings or bibelots in case she might seem to be appraising their value, she turned the conversation to her aunt's companion.

"Spenser? I cannot remember when she has not been with me. She came to me as a young woman, over twenty years ago, and she was lucky I took her in! There are too many people who remember that her mother was a Covington bastard, so there was small chance anyone would marry her. Well, she has been happy here, she tells me. But come! Spenser is of small interest to anyone, for although she means well, she is a very dull person, with no charm and little conversation, poor thing! Tell me, instead, who is suspected as the murderer!"

Caroline looked to Cecilia, and the girl said, "We have no idea, m'lady. It is frightening to think that there is such a person here among us. And truly it was decided that none of us should ever be alone, and when we are in our rooms that we lock our doors. For anyone could have done it, you know, anyone!"

"Except for Mr. Russell!" Lady Cecily said. "It was a shock to me to hear of it, and I have thought that perhaps I was wrong to invite you all here for an old woman's whim, but I never imagined that it would bring trouble to us all."

She looked sad and upset, and Caroline said, "So far, at least, we have escaped serious harm, even Alistair, and I suppose we must hope it will continue for the remainder of our visit."

"I have always enjoyed my wealth, but I am aware that the thought of gaining possession of a fortune can sometimes make even a normal person do things that are not in character," Lady Cecily remarked, looking at both the girls impartially as she spoke. "But I only wanted to be sure that my father's money should go to the best one of you. I shall see your brother this afternoon, Caroline, and then perhaps I will be able to make up my mind, and that might stop all this nonsense!" She nodded her head and added, "It is sooner than I would like, but perhaps it will be for the best."

The two girls spent the rest of the morning with their great-aunt. Caroline felt a certain admiration for the old lady in her outmoded wig and old-fashioned

135

gown, for she could tell from the way she twisted sometimes in her chair that she was in pain. When she asked if she could fetch anything for her to relieve her discomfort, Lady Cecily pointed to a bottle on her night stand, and when Caroline brought it over to her, she took a spoonful and then made a face.

"Horrible taste!" she said. "I much prefer spirits, but the doctor has forbidden me to touch them. Silly old woman, Dr. Ward! As if it made any difference to me now!"

Eventually Miss Spenser came in with a tray of lunch, and the two girls curtsied and excused themselves. Lady Cecily waved them away without speaking. She looked tired and old, Caroline thought as she nodded to Miss Spenser, standing by the door to see them out. The woman was dressed in her customary black gown, with her hair pulled back into that hideous bun as usual, but her expression was brighter. As she left the room, Caroline wondered idly if Miss Spenser fancied herself in love with the doctor, and then chuckled to herself for such flights of imagination.

"Whew!" Cecilia whispered. "Thank heavens that is over, and with any luck, she will not ask to see me again! Now I can tell Mama that I did everything she told me, and smiled and was charming, and still it did not answer!" She skipped a little on their way to the library, she was so relieved.

"But perhaps Lady Cecily will choose you, Cecy!" Caroline teased. "It is true that you were very charming, and she did say how pretty you are!"

Cecy stopped short. "I do not depend on it, for she also called me a pea-brain! But I do not care, Caro, for I intend to go to London and marry a very rich man, so there!"

They found the Danvers in the library, and Sylvia began at once to question them. What had Lady Cecily asked them, and how had they replied? Had she mentioned Roger, and had she thought to

136

point out to her great-nieces that they should emu-
late his example and marry? Caroline said absently
that no one had given Roger a thought, much less
spoken of him, and his wife frowned.

"And as for marrying, she as much as told Caro
she did not have to if she didn't want to! After all,
she is a spinster too!" Cecy said pertly, so relieved to
have the ordeal of the visit she had been dreading
over with, she became quite bold in her relief.

"I must say, Cecilia, that these snippety ways you
have fallen into do nothing to add to your consequence! Mind your tongue!" Lady Danvers told her.

"Well, I like that!" Cecy said, bouncing up and
down on the sofa. "I guess I can say what I want to,
can't I? Besides, Sylvia, you are only four years older
than I; this behaving as if you were a dowager
duchess does not become you either! Pooh!"

Roger bustled over from the window, where he
had been watching the snow that had begun to fall
again. "Now, ladies!" he said, rubbing his hands
together and peeking at his wife's rigid, disapproving face. "Let us all be happy and serene! No words,
mind! There must be no quarrels or disagreements,
for we would not want them to get back to Lady
Cecily, now, would we? We must all be one big
happy family together!"

Caroline stood up and excused herself in the silence
that followed. "I have a headache," she said when
Cecilia begged to go upstairs with her. "I must ask to
be alone for a while, Cecy. Please stay here with
Roger and Sylvia; I am sure I will be all right just
going up the stairs in broad daylight!"

But this she was not allowed to do. Roger escorted
her to the stairs, clutching her arm tightly, his little
fat face darting suspiciously from one side of the hall
to the other, which caused Crowell to so far forget
himself as to stare at m'lord in amazement. Neither
did Roger relax his vigil then, but remained at the
bottom of the flight until Caroline reached the door
to her room.

"I think I shall go quietly mad," she told herself as she went to her window, "if I have to remain here much longer! A fortune is not everything!"

Gregory was summoned to Lady Cecily's room after lunch, and Crowell announced that Mr. Russell had especially asked for his cousin Caroline to visit him as well. Both of these pronouncements were made before the whole company at the luncheon table, and Caroline flushed a little as all eyes turned her way.

"Do you wish my attendance, missy?" Mr. Covington-More asked. "I would be glad to go with you."

Caroline thanked him but said that would not be necessary, careful not to look in John's direction. He had appeared for the first time at luncheon, and seemed quiet and subdued, and oblivious to the general conversation.

"Well, I never!" Sylvia said, putting down her fork, her eyes wide with shock. "Go alone, to a man's bedroom, Cousin? Your poor mother would not believe such boldness!"

Caroline was stung to reply. "Do not be so silly, Sylvia, or so busy about my business, if you please! Alistair is my cousin, and he is very sick. The tone of your mind is disgusting!"

Lady Danvers bridled and turned bright pink, but Caroline did not notice, for she was rising from her chair and begging to be excused.

"I shall go at once! Thank you, Crowell, for your message!"

As she left the room, her head high, she heard Sylvia say, "I shall certainly have a spell if I am subjected to any more rudeness, and from spinsters, too! No one seems to have the least idea of my consequence! Furthermore, as the only married lady present, I feel it is my duty to set the moral standard of propriety that should be followed while we remain here. Besides, he is only her *second* cousin!"

"But since he is so sorely wounded, m'lady, I think Miss Covington's reputation is safe and we may all be calm. The man is hardly capable of lascivious behavior, at least right now!" Mr. Covington-More remarked.

Lady Danvers sniffed and turned away from his amused face, and Gregory spoke up, even though as the youngest of the house guests he had refrained from voicing his opinions before this. "I say!" he exclaimed. "It seems to me that bickering won't help us! Surely it would be more pleasant if we at least try to maintain a semblance of good will towards one another!" He looked to Lord St. Williams to reinforce this sentiment, but John's dark face was thunderous, and he remained a silent presence.

Roger, however, was quick to agree, and began to tell a long and boring story about someone he knew who had a terrible temper and what had happened to him as a result of it, and by the time he had concluded, everyone had forgotten what the quarrel had been about in the first place. Gregory was delighted to excuse himself to go to his great-aunt's room.

In the meantime, Caroline made her way to Alistair's room, and knocked softly. The door was opened by Mr. King, and she was glad to see that Alistair, wrapped in his dressing gown and propped up on several pillows, was looking much better than he had the last time she had seen him. His face had regained some color, and his eyes were bright.

"Thank you for coming, Cuz!" he said, waving her towards a chair near the bed. "I am finding it a bore to have to remain in bed, so I depend on you to tell me everything that has been happening below-stairs! That will be all, King; I shall ring when I need you."

Caroline took the chair he had indicated, as the valet bowed himself out.

"There, now we may have a comfortable coze," Alistair continued. "How kind of you to relieve my isolation and keep me *au courant!*"

"You must tell me at once when you become tired, Alistair," Caroline said, smiling at him and feeling better just to be away from the rest of the house party, and especially John St. Williams. "I will then go away immediately!"

"Do not fear; I slept most of the morning after Dr. Ward had changed the dressings," he replied. "He seems a competent surgeon; one must give thanks for that. I would not have been at all surprised to have had an elderly Scottish crone called in with all her herbs and potions! And Miss Spenser—poor thing—was very efficient as well, although I am sure she is not often summoned to the bedsides of men who have been shot!"

Now it was Caroline's turn to ask him if he had seen who fired the shot, but he admitted he had not, only that it had come from the back of the hall. He complimented her on her bravery in going down to recover the pistol, and added, "We three must stick together now, you, and I, and John, for we are the only three who could not have committed all these things!" He was surprised to see her blushing and he looked at her more sharply. Was Cousin Caro looking conscious because he had mentioned John? Could it be that she was developing a *tendre* there? How very amusing if it were so!

"I must admit that I am puzzled by John's behavior," he said, determined to find out all he could, for Alistair was a man who thrived on gossip and intrigue. "He is certainly not so fond of *me* that my being shot would throw him into depression, but he has looked so angry and black for such a time!"

Caroline nodded in agreement, but she did not speak.

"I think it all began when I asked you to remain with me in the breakfast room; do you remember, Cuz? Can it be that he is jealous? Every time he saw us together, he frowned!"

Caroline tried to look amused. "I am sure you are wrong there, Alistair. After all, we barely know each other! And I must tell you that he was convinced that I was the murderer, when he caught me

140

with the pistol, and nothing I told him, not even giving my word, could change his mind. So you see, your theory will not work; surely a man who was attracted to me, as you put it, would not behave in such a way!"

Alistair noted her eyes, sparkling with anger, and the determined set of her mouth, and adroitly changed the subject.

"Of course you must be right! But tell me, who else has seen Lady Cecily, and what was the result of their visits?"

Caroline was glad they had stopped talking of Lord St. Williams, and told him as much as she knew. He smiled when she mentioned that Cecilia had insisted on her company that morning, and what Lady Danvers had said afterwards, and she also told him how Sylvia had frowned on Caroline's coming to his room alone, which made him laugh out loud, and then frown as the movement brought him pain.

"You are hurting; I am so sorry!" Caroline exclaimed. "I promise I will not mention another amusing thing!"

Alistair waved away this comment. "But that, of course, is why I asked you to come, and not any of the others," he said when he had caught his breath. "There is no one here, with the exception of you and John, who is in the least amusing! And since John has turned so solemn and uncommunicative, I wanted to have your opinion of the situation. Come, Cuz, tell me what you think will happen next."

Caroline frowned a little. "I have no idea! I have thought and thought, but who is doing these things, and why, remains a mystery. John—I mean Lord St. Williams—did say that you might have been shot because Lady Cecily liked you so well. It is enough for me to hope that she has formed a fervent dislike for me!

"Gregory is with her now," she added, "but he is so young and careless with money, I am sure she would never choose him as her heir, even if he is the only male here with the Covington name! But I wished I had told him to keep his own counsel about the visit!"

She thought Alistair looked thoughtful at her words, and wondered about it.

"Sometimes I think it would have been better if none of us had come," she added, getting up and wandering over to the window. "I am sure I will never have a fortune to dispense, but if I ever should, I will remember this time, and quietly name my heir as soon as possible."

"Money is always a problem!" Alistair agreed. "If you don't have any, you are in trouble; and if you have a great deal, like Lady Cecily, you have another kind of predicament. But I can see how she could not withstand pitting us all against each other. I should most assuredly do the same!"

Caroline turned back to him. "Even after all that has happened, Cuz?" she asked, not really believing him.

"Of course! I am not very nice, Caroline!" he said, looking at her frankly. "Did you think I was? How sad to have to disillusion you! I imagine Great-Aunt Cecily is much the same as I, and could not resist the fun of it. After all, no one is going to shoot or poison her! You remember how carefully she told us that if anything happened to her, not one of us would inherit?"

"Yes, I do! But I refuse to believe you, Alistair, when you speak about yourself so. I shall certainly go on thinking you a true gentleman!"

"So I should hope, my girl! I did not say I was not a gentleman!" he replied, looking so indignant that Caroline had to laugh as she came back to the bed and took her seat again.

And it was thus that John St. Williams found them, laughing together, when he came into the room. If they had thought his expression dark before, it was positively thunderous now.

"I am sorry to interrupt your amusing tête-à-tête, cousins, but Mr. King tells me it is time for your draught, Alistair," he said, his voice cold. Caroline rose from her chair at once, and Alistair could not resist reaching for her hand and kissing it lightly. "Come back again soon, dear Caro!" he said, a wicked gleam in his eye. "It does me such good to see your lovely face!"

Caroline withdrew her hand, thinking that perhaps he had assessed his character correctly after all. He seemed determined to make trouble, only because it amused him. None of her thoughts showed in her face though as she said, "Of course, Alistair, any time you wish!" She nodded distantly to St. Williams and left the two men together.

That evening, at the dinner table, Gregory found himself the center of attention, for he had remained with Lady Cecily until well after teatime. As always, Lady Danvers was especially interested in what he had talked about with his great-aunt, and even though Caroline tried to catch his eye so that she might frown and shake her head, hoping he would hold his tongue, her brother ignored her.

"Why, she's a great gun!" Gregory enthused, helping himself to more chicken. "I never thought to like her so well! Some of the stories she told me of things that happened to her when she was young, you would not believe. Did you know that her father took her to France and Italy for the Grand Tour, disguised as a boy? He wanted her to travel and see the world, and knew he could not take her as a girl. She had fencing lessons, learned all about pistols and marksmanship, and several other things besides; and she said no one ever suspected she was not young Lord Covington!"

"How very unusual!" Lady Danvers said. "No wonder she is so eccentric in her old age!"

"Did she like you as well, Gregory?" Cecilia asked. Caroline wished she might throttle the girl, and her brother too, as he replied, "She claimed she did!

Smiled at me, and said I was a proper young 'un! I told her tales about my special cronies and she laughed 'till she cried at some of our escapades!"

He sounded so proud of himself, that Caroline could barely conceal a startled exclamation, and she looked around the table carefully, to note everyone's expressions. Mr. Covington-More looked disapproving and a little bored, Cecy was smiling and nodding her head, Sylvia Danvers was sniffing and indignant, and Roger did not seem to have noticed anything but his wife's temper. John St. Williams' face was stern and set, and as she looked his way, he caught her eye and shook his head, both eyebrows rising at Gregory's impetuosity. For a moment, Caroline felt a surge of happiness that their thoughts were so similar and he understood what she was feeling, until she remembered the previous evening and lowered her eyes. How very sad it was that she and her cousin should think so much alike one moment, and be so far apart the next!

She was glad when Sylvia gave the signal for the ladies to adjourn, and was careful not to look his way again.

CHAPTER 8

WHEN GREGORY COVINGTON went up to his room that evening at eleven with the other guests, he was careful to lock his door behind him. His sister had reminded him to do it, as they were all preparing to retire, and although he thought she was behaving like a typically frightened woman, he decided to humor her. Besides, he reminded himself, he had no desire to end up like Cousin Alistair—or worse! He stretched after he had placed his candle on the dresser, and yawned, even though he was not at all tired. Gregory was fast becoming heartily bored; with the storm, this house, the other guests, and most of all, with his enforced inactivity. He was a young man used to a great deal of physical exertion, and a little genteel conversation, lengthy dinners, and being cooped up in a tumbling-down castle on the northern shores with a group of older people was not very amusing. He wished he might go back to London, and that as soon as possible.

Taking off his evening coat and slinging it carelessly over a chair, he prepared to remove his boots, thinking longingly of his valet. As he sat down on the bed to pull them off, he noticed a note that had been placed on his pillow and reached for it, feeling a thrill of excitement. The note was short, and written in no hand he had ever seen before, and it told him that if he wished to discover who was bent on destroying all of Lady Cecily's guests, he should go at midnight to the shed in the garden, where he would find the evidence he needed to uncover the culprit.

Gregory knew that he should on no account do so; he was not foolish, and he was well aware of the danger, and the fact that the night was black and cold, but he could not resist shrugging into his coat again, absent-mindedly putting the note into his pocket as he did so. His heart was pounding with excitement. He knew he was strong and well able to take care of himself—why, he had never been bested in a mill—and he would be careful to approach the shed cautiously, checking to be sure he was alone. He waited until it was midnight, impatiently pacing his bedroom until the hour was right, and then he put on his greatcoat and hat. He wished he had a pistol, but he had neglected to bring one north with him, so that omission could not be helped.

He let himself out of his room only after checking the hallway carefully. There was not a sound, and nothing moved, so he made his way to the stairs, carrying his candle and trying to tread softly so he would not wake the others. What a coup it would be if he could deliver the guilty person tomorrow, this feat accomplished by his own intelligence and efforts. How Caroline would exclaim over him, and Cecy applaud him! And Great-Aunt Cecily as well, he thought, grinning to himself. It would be such a relief to her to have the murderer apprehended that she might very well make him her sole heir. Gregory's mind was already busy planning a tremendous party with some of the proceeds, as well as the new team and perch phaeton he would now be able to purchase, as he let himself out the front door, after extinguishing his candle and taking it with him. He was glad he had his Pocket Luminary with him and did not have to rely on flint and steel.

146

The night was very dark and cold, and it was snowing lightly again. He shivered a little and turned up the collar of his coat. He should have brought gloves and a muffler, but he did not intend to remain in the shed for long, and he was too impatient to return to his room to fetch them.

He made his way slowly and with some difficulty through the neglected garden, at first struggling through the drifts that had formed from the wind, and he was relieved when he reached the shelter of the first hedge, for the snow was not so deep there. Ruefully he could feel the cold damp right through his breeches where he had gone down on his knees in one drift that was deeper than the others, and he could not help thinking of his warm bed with longing.

It took him several minutes to locate the path that led to the gardener's shed, and for a moment he stood very still to peer at it through the falling snow. It was dark and seemed to be deserted, but still he waited, his hands thrust deep into his pockets for warmth. At last, several minutes later, when nothing had moved or made a sound, he edged cautiously forward, trying to keep as close to the hedge as possible so as not to present too much of himself as a target, and stopping often to listen and stare about him.

When he reached the shed, the door was slightly ajar, and he stood back and pulled it open, quickly stepping to one side. His heart was pounding in earnest as he waited for the shot he had been almost positive would come, but nothing happened, and after the echoes of the door as it had crashed against the outer wall had ceased, there was no sound at all except for the incessant rumbling of the breakers and the moaning of the wind. Feeling a little foolish, he went up to the door and peered inside. It was so black he realized that he would have to light his candle if he were to see anything at all. He stepped over the threshold and, putting the candle on a rough bench that he had stumbled into, he prepared to light it, now that he was sheltered from the wind.

And then, with a suddenness that startled him and caused him to swing around in haste, the door crashed shut behind him, and even as he rushed to open it, he heard a heavy bar come down and lock into place with cold finality. He put his shoulder to the door and pushed with all his might, but it did not move an inch.

Feeling sick at his predicament, he made his way back to the bench and his candle, and after he had it lit, he felt much better. He held it up and stared around. The shed, which was made of the same stones as the house, was small and had no windows. On three sides were some crude shelves filled with odds and ends; a broken keg, some jars of nails, a few old gunny sacks, and some broken tools. Outside of the bench there was no furniture at all. He noticed bitterly that there was also no evidence of the murderer's identity. He was trapped by his own reckless folly, and with nothing to show for it!

He sank down on the bench and for the first time noticed how very cold it was. The damp air of the unused stone shed seemed even icier than when he had been exposed to the wind and the snow outside. He stared about him in dismay. His candle was almost half burned; when it finally went out he would be left alone here in the dark. For a moment, he fought a rising tide of panic, a feeling he had not had since he was ten years old and caught on the river in a sinking punt.

He got to his feet in a hurry and, waving his arms about and clapping his hands to restore warmth, he began to pace the narrow confines of the shed. Four paces one way, and four the other.

He knew he would not freeze as long as he kept moving, and he told himself that there were any number of ways he could escape from the shed long before the candle went out. First he inspected the contents of the shelves more carefully. The broken, rusty tools crumbled and snapped in his hands when he tried to use them to force the door, and he threw them away in disgust. Next, he managed to break up the keg and, putting the pieces against the base of the door with some strips torn from the gunny sacks, he attempted to start a fire. He had only one sulphur-tipped wooden splint left in the bottle when the fire finally caught, and for a moment he congratulated himself on his ingenuity, sure that he would soon be back in the house and warm in bed. But then, as the smoke from his small fire began to fill the shed, he started to cough and gasp. Quickly he stamped it out, for he knew if he did not, he would suffocate long before the door burned down sufficiently to let him escape.

A little more desperate now, he got down on his hands and knees and tried to make an air hole in the hard, frozen dirt that comprised the floor of the shed, under the heavy door. The tools were worthless, so he scratched at the dirt with the nails. After what seemed a very long time, he succeeded in making a small space—perhaps an inch high—and he was relieved when the lingering smoke began to escape. He knew it was of no use to call for help. He was a long way from the house, and everyone was asleep.

All this while he had kept an eye on the candle, and when there was only a little bit of it left, he took the gunny sacks off the shelves and put them next to him on the bench. He would wrap up in them if necessary, to keep warm. So far he had been so busy he had been able to ignore the cold, but now, sinking back down on the bench and staring at the stub of candle that was all that was left, he could feel how cold his extremities were becoming. He stamped his booted feet hard and tucked his hands under his armpits, feeling very sorry for himself. It was a long, long time to morning, and he knew he might not be missed until lunchtime at least.

He wondered what time it was; surely he had been here for hours! He had left the house at midnight, and it had taken him a long time to reach the shed and check it out, and with all the escapes he had tried, it must be at least two in the morning! Sadly, he realized he was probably miscalculating, and even if it were two, he had at least ten more hours to sit here, trying to keep from freezing to death, which of course the murderer fully expected him to do! And if the temperature dropped any further or the wind rose to a higher pitch, he would be in serious trouble long before anyone thought to search for him. And who could say how long it might be before they looked in the unused shed? Suddenly he grinned, remembering the note. As soon as Caro spotted that in his room, she would come and let him out. Then he groaned out loud and drew the note from the inside pocket of his coat, realizing he had taken the only clue to his whereabouts with him. He smote his forehead with one cold hand. Had anyone ever been so stupid?

For a moment, he wished he were not a man known for his courage and daring, for he felt very close to tears. Swallowing the lump in his throat, he determined that no matter what, he would *not* freeze to death, for he would spend the night telling himself stories, singing all the old songs he knew, and planning an adventure that would have Tony and Gerald and Percy stunned in admiration for his ingenuity. And whenever he felt cold or sleepy, he would make himself get up and jump up and down, swinging his arms and shouting to keep up his spirits. He wondered if the murderer would come back with a gun, to make sure that he died. After all, he or she could not be positive that Gregory might not remain alive through his own efforts. His handsome face turned grim as he considered this possibility, and then the candle sputtered and went out, and he was left alone in the cold and the dark.

Caroline slept late the following morning, and when Wentworth came in to open the curtains, she saw that it was still snowing. The maid put some more coal on the fire, remarking as she did so that it was a bitter-cold morning, and the chill went right through a body! For a moment, Caroline snuggled back down between the blankets, but soon she was out of bed and wrapped in a warm dressing gown to sip her hot chocolate while Wentworth laid out a morning gown and a warm shawl, chattering as she did so.

Caroline had known her maid since she was a little girl, and she was very glad to have her here with her in Scotland. Unlike Molly, Cecilia's maid, Wentworth never got flustered or excited, and even the events that had occurred here, she took calmly. Caroline wondered if she wished they might go home, but she knew Wentworth would never say. Instead, she talked about an altercation in the kitchen that morning between the cook and one of the maids. Caroline listened with half an ear. It was plain that Miss Wentworth, lady's maid from Falconfield, felt vastly superior to any of Lady Cecily's servants. In her mind's eye, Caroline could see just how the woman would make her exalted position plain, below stairs.

The maid brushed her hair a long time before she twisted it into a chignon, low on Caroline's neck, and handed her her shawl. She asked if Miss Caro had any special requests for her, for if she did not, she thought she might do the laundry and some mending.

Caroline approved her plans and went downstairs. She greeted Crowell as he came out of Lady Cecily's room bearing a tray, and nodded to the elderly footman who was crossing the hall with some coal for the library fire.

As she went into the dining room, she was disturbed to see that there was only one other occupant. John St. Williams rose and bowed, his dark eyes intent on her face. Caroline hoped she was not blushing as she said good morning and went to the sideboard for her breakfast. Now, why does he have to be here? she wondered, praying that Gregory or

151

Cecy or even the Danvers would follow her shortly, for she had no desire to sit here alone with m'lord, involved in a travesty of casual conversation.

None of these thoughts showed on her face, however, as she took her seat, and nodded when St. Williams asked her if she wanted some coffee.

"Thank you, m'lord," she said as he poured it for her from the heavy, slightly tarnished silver urn. She began to eat her scones and ham without another word, and John St. Williams returned to his own seat and the remains of his breakfast.

For a moment there was silence in the room, and then he said, in a tight, strained voice, "Caroline! Miss Covington, I mean . . ."

Caroline looked up to see that he was leaning towards her, his dark face serious and one hand stretched towards her in supplication, and her eyebrows rose. "Yes, m'lord?" she asked him in an even voice, wondering if he could hear the pounding of her heart from his place across the table.

"My dear Caroline, I must ask you once again to forgive me! I am very sorry that I suspected you, but Caro, what would *you* have thought if you had caught me with the pistol that shot Alistair? And if I told the same tale that you did, would you not suspect me still, even if I gave you my word that I was telling the truth? Come, Caro, admit that you would have behaved just as I did! This situation has become intolerable, with you avoiding me and never speaking if you can help it, and now Alistair . . ."

He stopped, as if he wished he had not said that.

"What has Alistair to do with anything, m'lord?"

He had the grace to flush a little. "I should not have mentioned him, of course. But Caro, can you not forgive me and call me 'John' again?"

Caroline looked into those dark eyes, with their pleading expression. For a moment she almost relented, but then she remembered how hurt she had been at his suspicions, how he had not trusted her to tell him the truth, how he had been going to lock her in

152

her room until the law could arrive, and how he had been fully prepared to give her up to the local justice as a potential murderer, and her expression hardened.

"I am afraid I cannot, m'lord!" she said, putting down her coffee cup so he would not notice how her hand had begun to shake.

He sighed and ran one hand through his hair in that now-familiar gesture. "Very well!" he said grimly, and Caro knew he would not ask her forgiveness again, and felt a stirring of regret. "However," he went on, in an impersonal tone, "I would remind you that of everyone in this house, I am the only one, besides yourself and Alistair, who could not be the culprit, and I must ask you to come to me if you discover anything, or have any suspicions at all, even if you would rather not talk to me! This affair is still dangerous; I am afraid that whoever is guilty has not given up his mad plan!"

Caroline nodded. "Of course! I . . . I was very upset last evening when Gregory insisted on bragging so about his conquest of Lady Cecily, and her affection for him; I saw you agreed with me. How I would like to have shaken him for being so careless!"

"It is true we must keep an eye on him," Lord St. Williams said, and then Cecilia and the Danvers came in together, and there was no chance for further private conversation.

As soon as she could, Caroline rose and excused herself. She did not feel comfortable in the same room with St. Williams, not after what had just transpired between them. She went into the hall, wondering what to do that morning. Of course, she could write some letters in the hopes that the post would be able to go before long, or she could work on her tapestry, or search the library for a book to read. As she crossed the hall, after deciding on this final course, she wondered where her brother was. He was generally an early riser in the country, but it had been plain that she and Lord St. Williams had been the first ones down, from all the clean place settings at the table.

Frowning a little, she shrugged and would have gone on to the library except that she remembered m'lord saying they should keep an eye on Gregory and, turning, she went up the stairs. She knocked on his door and waited, calling out his name, but there was no answer, so she tried the door. To her surprise, it opened at once. Furious, she stepped inside, prepared to give him a piece of her mind for not locking it, as she had told him. The fire had gone out, and she went to the window to fling back the curtains, and as the light filled the room, she saw that his bed had not been slept in. She put both hands to her mouth in horror. Where was he? What had happened?

Without pausing to think, she flew back down the stairs and across the hall into the dining room.

Sylvia Danvers was holding forth at great length, impartially lecturing both her husband and Cecilia, who was looking exceedingly stubborn, but Caroline did not hesitate.

"Lord St. Williams!" she broke in, causing Sylvia's jaw to drop. "I must speak to you at once, if you please!" she continued, as Lady Danvers exclaimed, "How dare you interrupt me, Caroline? Such rudeness, such wanton behavior! I am afraid your dear mother would blush for you if she were here! Why, I have never . . ."

But Caroline did not hear any more, for St. Williams had risen from his chair when he first caught sight of her pale face and agitated expression and, taking her arm in his, was leading her swiftly from the room. He paused only to close the doors behind them, and what Sylvia Danvers had been about to say was lost forever.

"Come in here!" he said, quickly crossing the hall and taking her into the back salon, with its dust-sheeted furniture. "Now, what is it, Caro?"

"I am so very frightened!" she whispered. "I went up to see why Gregory had not come down to breakfast, and he is not in his room! Furthermore, his bed has not been slept in! Where can he be, oh, where can he be?"

The tears began to fall, and she felt a faintness coming over her, and St. Williams, who seemed to know how close she was to giving way, took both her hands tightly in his and stared down at her as if to give her some of his strength.

"Control yourself, Caro!" he said harshly. "Hysteria will not help Gregory! Come, take me to his room; he may have left some clue to his whereabouts."

Now that she had told him, and with a course of action to follow, Caroline felt calmer. When they reached Gregory's room, he stared for a moment at the smooth counterpane of the bed and frowned, one hand rubbing his chin, before he said, "He came up to bed with the rest of us, at eleven. I remember, because he said something to me about hoping the snow would stop so we might get outside today. He was obviously restless, being kept in by the inclement weather."

"Yes, that is true," she agreed in a little voice. "I told him to lock his door, for I was afraid for him after his conversation at the table . . ." She paused and swallowed before she went on. "He promised to do so! And that was the last time I saw him, as he went into his room, laughing at me for my concern!"

St. Williams seemed deep in thought. "His bedroom candle is missing. I recall that Gregory always took the candle with the pewter holder. It is strange, is it not, how we all take the same one each night? Lady Danvers prefers the silver holder, and you the china one with the blue flowers . . ."

Breaking off, he went to the wardrobe and threw open the door. "Look through Gregory's clothes, Caro, and see if anything is missing while I go down and organize a search of the house."

He was gone in an instant, and Caroline eagerly ran her hands through Gregory's coats and waistcoats and breeches. When Lord St. Williams came back a few minutes later, she was able to tell him that her brother's greatcoat was gone, as well as the clothes he had been wearing last evening.

"So he did not undress for bed," John remarked. "And the greatcoat implies that he meant to go outside."

Caroline sank down on the other side of the bed, her blue eyes dark with worry. "Outside? In this weather, in the middle of the night?"

"He took his candle," m'lord reminded her. "I checked the table downstairs where the bedroom candles are kept, and it is not there. Crowell says he has not seen it either. But the front door was bolted, and so were the French doors in the back salon, as well as the kitchens. That implies that he never left the house; the servants are searching it now, room by room."

Caroline could hear for herself the bustle and excited chatter that wafted up the stairs from the hall below, the slamming of doors, and the calls from one servant to the other. "Not here!" "The green room is empty!" "Not in the servants' rooms!"

She began to pace the room, her hands tightly clasped before her, and St. Williams watched her from the doorway. Finally he said gently, "Come downstairs, Caro! There is nothing we can do until every part of the house has been investigated!"

Obediently, she went with him and did not protest when he took her back to the dining room and poured her another cup of coffee.

"Drink it!" he commanded, and she did so even though it was hard to swallow, she was so upset.

Cecy and Lady Danvers were exclaiming and questioning her, but she did not hear them; nor did she hear Lord St. Williams order them to be quiet, for Caro could not attend to them right now. Lord Danvers took exception to this slight to his wife and would have blustered, but John quelled him a single fierce look before he turned his attention back to Caroline's white face. When Mr. Covington-More came in and was appraised of the situation, his ugly face showed his concern, but Caroline did not notice that either.

156

Greg! she was thinking to herself. Where are you? As children they had been so close they had often known what the other was thinking, and she concentrated on her brother now, as if somehow he might be trying to tell her his whereabouts. It seemed a very long time before Crowell came to the dining-room door and announced that the house had been searched from the attics to the cellars, and Mr. Covington had not been found anywhere, for after all, Rockledge was a very large old stone pile, with many nooks and crannies and cupboards and unused rooms. As the old butler stood there, awaiting further orders, Caroline suddenly remembered the priest's hole and asked him about it. He admitted that no one had thought to look there. It took only a moment for Lord St. Williams to investigate, and when he came back into the room, Caroline's eyes flew to his face and she knew at once he had been unsuccessful.

"Nothing!" he said bitterly as he came in. "Gregory is not in the house, so we were right, Caro. He took his greatcoat because he meant to go out."

"But . . . the locked doors!" she exclaimed.

Suddenly she knew who had locked the doors, after Gregory left the house, and her face grew so ashen that St. Williams started to go to her in alarm. She raised her hand. "I am all right, m'lord. This is no time for fainting spells, as you yourself pointed out. We must search the grounds and the stables at once!"

Cecy interrupted her. "But he could not be out *there*, dear Caro! It is so very cold!"

Her voice died away when John St. Williams sent her a murderous look as he rose to leave. "Mr. Covington-More, I would appreciate your help organizing the servants. What a pity we had fresh snow last night, covering all footsteps!"

As the two men left the room, they met Dr. Ward at the door. He immediately offered to help in the search, but m'lord took him to one side and spoke to him in low tones. As if from a great distance, Caroline wondered what they were saying, but then they were gone, and she could not see the doctor hurry up to Gregory's room to order the fire made up immediately and more blankets brought. He had little hope of it, but if the boy was alive, his services would be needed here at the house when he was found, and it was just as well to be prepared. But he felt it was futile; it had been well below freezing last night, with a fierce wind as well, and if the boy had not found shelter, he had almost certainly frozen to death hours ago. He shook his head sadly and, coming upon Miss Spenser outside Mr. Russell's room, he told her of the problem.

"Dear me!" she exclaimed, her eyes wide. "Surely there is little chance he might have survived, but I shall help you prepare his room, Doctor. How very distressing!"

She went away to fetch some warm quilts and to order the fire made up and water heated for the stone bottles that would be placed in Gregory's bed, after agreeing with the doctor that perhaps it would be better not to tell Lady Cecily what had happened, just yet.

In the dining room, Caroline began her pacing again, and finally Sylvia Danvers said, in quite the kindest voice anyone had ever heard her use, "Do sit down, Caro! You are wearing yourself out to no purpose, and when Gregory is found you will have no strength left to help him!"

"When he is found . . ." Caro repeated. "But I cannot remain here, tamely waiting!"

She ran from the room to fetch her fur-lined cloak and hood and boots so she might join in the search, before anyone could stop her.

In the meantime, Mr. Covington-More had taken some men towards the stables and barns, and John St. Williams, with two footmen, was searching the drive and the front of the house and cursing the fresh white snow that so thoroughly covered any clues that might have helped them.

Even though there were no tracks leading towards the main road, he sent one of the footmen off in that direction with orders to search the deserted gatehouse. Suddenly, he stopped and turned back to the house, remembering the gardener's shed. Located as it was, deep in the garden and completely apart from any other structure, it would not have been thought of for some time, but he remembered it now because that was where he had had the old bulldog's body placed until the doctor could get a chance to examine it.

With the remaining footman close on his heels, he pushed his way through the drifts until he reached the hedges surrounding the garden. There he found, as Gregory had, that the going was easier. He was very cold now, and the footman was shivering and holding the collar of his livery close to his neck, and John felt bleak despair. Whatever chance was there that the boy was still alive if *they* were both so chilled after just a few minutes outdoors, and engaged in vigorous exercise as well?

When he reached the path leading to the shed, he saw it was securely bolted from the outside, and very, very still. "Gregory!" he shouted, hurrying down the path, but there was no reply.

"Here, man!" he ordered the footman. "Lift that bar away!"

The footman hastened to obey, and in a moment, Lord St. Williams was across the threshold. At first he was sure there was no one within, but then he saw the figure on the bench, curled into a tight ball and leaning against the wall, wrapped in gunny sacks.

With an oath he sprang forward. "Gregory!" he exclaimed as the footman drew back in horror, sure they had discovered a corpse.

John took up one cold hand from beneath the sacks and felt for the pulse. The boy was blue with cold, but he could feel a faint, thready beat and thanked God he had been in time.

Without turning his head he ordered, "Get back to the house as fast as you can and tell the doctor we have found Mr. Covington. Then hurry back here with blankets. I do not want him exposed to the outside air until he is more warmly wrapped."

The footman disappeared, and John stripped off his own coat and covered Gregory with it.

Caroline was standing on the front steps, wondering in which direction to start her search, when the footman hurried up. Recognizing the poor young man's sister, he told her the good news, and with a glad cry she rushed off to the shed.

John, who was chafing the boy's hands and trying to bring him back to consciousness, was surprised when the door was thrown open, for he had never expected such quick action on the part of the footman, but even before she reached his side, he knew the new arrival had to be Caroline. The delicate scent of the lily-of-the-valley perfume she always wore and that he had come to identify with her reached his nostrils, and he said, "Help me to try and rouse him, Caro! We must bring him around before it is too late!"

Caroline was quickly beside him, shaking her brother and talking to him in a loud voice. By the time the footman came back with another servant and several blankets, Gregory was murmuring, "Cold . . . so cold . . . so dark!"

He relapsed into unconsciousness again, but John was relieved as he helped the servants to wrap him in the blankets before they carried him up to the house, as fast as they could go.

The hall seemed full of people, but St. Williams, with Caroline right beside him, did not pause as he hurried the men up the stairs to Gregory's room, where he knew Dr. Ward would be waiting.

At the door, he motioned the men inside, and turned to face her when she would have joined them.

"Go and take off your cloak, Caro!" he said. "This is men's work now! We will undress him and put him to bed, and until the doctor has had a chance to examine him, you will only be very much in the way. I will come the instant I can to tell you how he does."

With this she had to be content, but she did not go downstairs to join the others, but stayed in her room, a little way down the hall, with the door open so she might hear what was going on. She heard Miss Spenser sharply order a maid to bring more hot water, she heard the doctor's soft voice answering John's questions, and she watched more coal being brought, and additional hot water bottles, and she wished with all her heart that there was something she could do to help. When John came to her room, she was standing before the fire, tears of relief streaming down her face. Blindly, she turned to him, holding out her hands in supplication.

"Is he . . . will he be all right, m'lord?" she asked in broken accents.

St. Williams made one move to go to her and comfort her, and then he clenched his fists tightly and remained by the door. Caroline wondered why his voice sounded so strange when he answered.

"The doctor assures me of his complete recovery, although there is still some danger of frostbite, which must be watched. Gregory was able himself to tell us a little before he dropped off again. A normal sleep!" he added, as she started. "He kept himself alive all night by staying awake—doing exercises and talking to himself. If he had not, Dr. Ward said he would most certainly have died of exposure. But come and sit with him, as I know you are longing to do. He will want to see you when he wakes, and I will arrange to have some hot food sent up for you both."

"I do not know how I am to thank you, m'lord!" she said over her shoulder as she hurried down the hall to her brother's room. John St. Williams' mouth twisted wryly when he heard her thank the doctor, in much the same tone of voice, before she bent over Gregory to kiss his forehead softly, and smooth back the brown curls that lay tumbled there. Gregory mumbled a little and slept on, oblivious to everything, which the doctor assured her was the very best cure for him after his close brush with death.

Caroline was not seen downstairs again that day. Trays went up to her and her brother, as well as to Alistair Russell, whom John had visited to tell the news. The rest of the company ate their dinner in a subdued mood, everyone thinking of Gregory's close call.

After dinner, when Lady Danvers and Cecilia had gone to the library and the three men who were left, sat around the dining room table with the decanter of port, Lord St. Williams excused himself and went back upstairs to knock softly on Gregory's door. He was pleased that Caroline asked who was there before she unlocked the door, and when he stepped inside, he saw that although she was pale and looked tired, her expression was happy.

"He is sleeping again! But he ate a good dinner!" She smiled up at St. Williams, shaking his hand and leading him towards the window, where they could converse in normal tones.

"I do not know, m'lord," she began in a halting way as she stared out the window so she did not have to look at him, "how we are ever to thank you, Gregory and I! If you had not remembered the shed, he would most certainly have died!" Her voice shook, and although her face was averted, he saw a tear slide down her cheek. "Dr. Ward said it was a very near thing indeed; another hour at the most . . . and if it had not been for you . . ."

He gritted his teeth. "There is no need to thank me anymore, Caroline!" he said, staying away from her only by the strongest test of his willpower. "Anyone would have done the same. I only remembered the shed because that was where I had the

162

servants put Lady Cecily's dog after he was poisoned. I wanted the doctor to look at him."

He stopped, and for a moment there was a strained silence between them, and then Caroline said in a low, bitter voice, "I am so ashamed of myself! I began by suspecting *you*, and then, after you caught me in the most compromising position and behaved as anyone would, I was unable to forgive your actions. What must you think of me, m'lord?"

She turned towards him at last, her hands outstretched, and much too sorely tested, Lord St. Williams gave up the struggle and took her in his arms. He stared down at her dear face, the blue eyes swimming with tears and pleading to be forgiven, and then he bent his head and kissed her. After only the tiniest hesitation, she was kissing him back, her arms stealing around his neck to hold him close.

Gregory Covington turned over in bed and awoke. For a moment, he stared through his half-closed eyes, but then he yawned and stretched and, closing his eyes again, dropped off to sleep. I must be dreaming, he thought in his last second of consciousness, for what would Caro and Lord St. Williams be doing here in my room, kissing each other?

Over by the window, John finally raised his head, and Caroline opened her eyes and looked up at him, blushing at the fervor of her response. She was surprised to see him frowning, and quickly he drew away from her, his arms falling to his sides, and his eyes troubled.

"John?" she whispered. "What . . . what is it?"

He buried his face in his hands for a moment, and then he looked directly at her, his face stern.

"No, Caro! It will not do; not this way!"

She could see his hands clenched into fists and hear his agitated breathing, and she was speechless with shock. For a very long moment there was silence between them, and then he said, his voice harsh with emotion, "I must ask you to forgive me once again. That was hardly the action of a gentle-

163

man, to take advantage of you while you were so distraught! No!" Holding up a deterring hand when she would have spoken: "Please do not speak! Think about what I have said, and I will pray that you can find it in your heart to not only forgive me, but to forget what has just occurred between us. I can assure you, on my honor, that it will not happen again!"

He bowed and went swiftly to the door, while Caroline stared after him. When he had opened the door, he turned back, and she felt a surge of hope that he might return and explain what he had just said, but he only looked at her without a smile and remarked, "Be sure and lock the door after me, Cousin. I bid you good night!"

The door closed swiftly, leaving a bewildered young lady with a very heavy heart.

CHAPTER 9

NEITHER LORD ST. WILLIAMS nor Caroline Covington spent a very restful night. After he had left her with her brother, John made himself go back downstairs to rejoin the others in the library. He did not even see Mr. Covington-More's frown of disapproval as he poured himself a large brandy, and retired to a chair somewhat apart from the others to drink it, his solemn face carefully composed. Neither did he hear Cecilia's nervous chatter or Sylvia's incessant speculations about the events of the day. When Roger had to speak to him twice, he shook himself out of his revery to find everyone staring at him.

"I am sorry, cousins, I was thinking of something else. Yes, Roger, to answer your question, Gregory is much improved. He is, after all, a strong and healthy young man, and I expect there will be trouble if anyone tries to keep him tied to an invalid bed tomorrow! Is Dr. Ward with Lady Cecily? And has anyone heard what the lady thinks about the excitement we have had this day?"

Mr. Covington-More said he had called on the lady before dinner, and that although she was distressed at Gregory's misadventure, she was so relieved at his being rescued in time that she had asked the doctor to dine with her and Miss Spenser in her room. By the time he had finished this explanation it was obvious that John had retreated into his thoughts again, and Mr. Covington-More wondered what on earth was the matter with the man, while Cecy pouted at being ignored by the only good-looking man left to her as long as Alistair and Gregory kept to their rooms.

John St. Williams did not go up with the others when the hall clock chimed eleven, but said good night at the door of the library.

"Is this wise?" Lady Danvers asked. "Surely you would be safer upstairs, locked in your room, Cousin, than alone here in the library!"

John thanked her for her concern but said he did not wish to retire just yet, and when she would have continued to remonstrate with him, he bowed and closed the library door behind him, leaving the lady in mid-sentence.

"Well! Such rudeness!" she exclaimed as Roger led her to the stairs. "Has everyone lost all sense of civility?"

"Leave the man alone!" Mr. Covington-More growled. "It's plain to see he has something on his mind. Nattering at 'im won't help!"

Lady Danvers sent him a haughty look for presuming to advise her and, taking her bedroom candle from her husband's hand, made her way upstairs, followed closely by Cecilia and Roger. Mr. Covington-More sent a speculative look back at the closed library door, and then, shaking his head, followed the others.

John stood before the fire, grateful to be alone at last, and stared down at the coals. Finally he groaned and lowered his head to his hands, where they rested on the mantel. What he had just done, in Gregory Covington's room, was the most difficult thing he had ever had to do in all his thirty-two years. He knew now how much he loved Caro; the memory of her kiss would be with him always, but he had meant it when he said it would not do. He wanted no bride who came to him out of gratitude! When he remembered her unsmiling face at the breakfast table, her angry eyes and set jaw, and how she had said she would never be able to forgive him, he realized that that was the true state of her mind, and what she was feeling for him now was only a sense of obligation because he had saved her brother's life. And she had been vulnerable, for the day had been so difficult for her, so full of worries and fears and agitation. When he had put his arms around her and kissed her, she had responded because she was tired and feeling a weakness and a need for comforting that he knew she would despise as soon as she had had some rest. And for him to press her, when she was so distraught, was most unfair, and she could not help but come to resent it. He might love her with all his heart, but he knew she did not return that love, even though he could easily have made her promise to marry him, after that one searing kiss. His eyes grew bleak as he resolved that the course he had chosen was the only honorable way to behave, and that no matter how much pain it brought him, he would continue to act honorably.

He groaned again. To think he had been so immune to love all these years, so casual and uncaring! And now he knew he would never again be free of it or able to forget her.

Upstairs, Caroline sat by her brother's bed, waiting for Wentworth to relieve her. The maid had insisted on taking over her vigil at midnight so Miss Caro could get some sleep. As if I will be able to after what has happened, she thought, watching Gregory's deep breathing and peaceful expression. She envied him his oblivion.

But still she did not understand! Why had John said what he had? Surely he had wanted to kiss her; she could not have been mistaken by the passion he had shown. Of course, she admitted to herself, I know very little about it, never having been kissed that

167

way before! Maybe it meant nothing at all to him, maybe he was just taking advantage of me; how can I say? She colored up as she remembered how she had put her arms around his neck and kissed him back so eagerly. Putting her hands to her hot cheeks she thought, "What can he think of me? So wanton . . . and so immodest!"

That must be it. The way she had responded had given him a disgust of her! No gentleman, she was sure, wanted a wife lacking in both self-control and decorum; why, it was as bad as if she had tied her garter in public! She wondered how she was ever to face him again, and she wished with all her heart that she and her brother were even now back at Falconfield and she had never met Lord St. Williams, all six feet four inches of him, with his crisp, dark hair and intent, disturbing eyes, and the wry way he had of smiling when he was amused, and his strong hands, and . . .

She got up from her chair abruptly and for several minutes busied herself straightening the already neat room.

When Miss Wentworth finally scratched on the door, she was more composed, for she had decided that the only thing she could possibly do was to follow John's advice. If he asked her, she would say that of course she had forgiven him, and forgotten the incident as well, and she would say it lightly, in an indifferent voice, as if the whole subject bored her tremendously, so that he would be instantly relieved. And then she would avoid him as much as possible until they were able to go home.

After a whispered consultation with her maid, she marched off to bed, her head high and her chin firm with her resolve. It was a long time before she was able to get to sleep, however, and she was horrified at the time when her maid finally came to wake her the next morning.

"How is Gregory, Wentworth?" she asked as she

sprang out of bed to put on the warm robe the maid was holding out for her.

"He is fine, Miss Caro! M'lord St. Williams sent his own valet to tend to him, and Gregory—er, Mr. Covington, told me to go away so he could be shaved!"

She sniffed, and Caroline hid a smile. She could see that Miss Wentworth, who had known Gregory since he was a little boy and still did not consider him very grown up, had not taken kindly to being banished in favor of a strange manservant.

"He *says*," she added, "that he will not stay in bed, and insists on getting dressed! I told him he was to do no such thing until the doctor had examined him and given his permission. Men! Bah!"

"Did he agree?" Caroline asked, sipping her chocolate.

"Of course!" Miss Wentworth said, poking at the fire. "I had only to tell him I would not leave the room until I had his promise."

By the time Caroline was dressed and had gone to knock on her brother's door, the doctor had been to see him, and she found him not only dressed, but sitting in a chair by the window, tucking into a large breakfast. As Buttles, m'lord's valet, bowed himself out, he grinned at her and waved a heavily laden fork in greeting.

"Come and sit down, Caro! There is plenty for both of us, and an extra place setting as well!"

After she had kissed the top of his head, Caroline drew up a straight chair and sat down opposite him. "I see I shall have to make haste, before you eat it all!" she said, taking some eggs and a scone from the covered dishes on the tray between them.

"I admit I am ravenous! Perhaps there is something about almost freezing to death that increases the appetite," he replied, pouring her a cup of coffee.

"Gregory!" she said, suddenly remembering. "Have you any idea who locked you in the shed? And why, my dear, idiotic brother, did you go out there in the middle of the night? Surely it was very dangerous!"

169

Gregory blushed a little, for he had been thinking the whole thing over, and he realized that his impetuous actions had indeed been very foolish. Without speaking, he drew the note that had been left in his room from his pocket and handed it across the table to her, and Caroline stopped eating to read it carefully.

"I do not know whose hand this is," she mused. "I wonder if we could somehow get samples of everyone's writing . . ."

"I don't think that would help, for it is obviously disguised. See how awkwardly the letters are formed, almost as if the person printed it with the left hand?"

"But Gregory—promising the solution to the mystery, and in the shed, too! And ordering you to come at midnight! Weren't you the least little bit suspicious?"

Her brother admitted that he had been, but when he told her what he had done, and how sure he had been that he would be able to defend himself, Caro, although aghast at his daring, saw how impossible it had been for any twenty-one-year-old with an ounce of spunk to ignore such a challenge. When he had finished his tale, she asked again if he had seen anything that would give him a clue to the identity of the murderer.

"Not a thing!" He frowned. "I had my back turned to the door, for I was trying to light my candle, when it was slammed shut behind me, and the bar dropped into place before I could force it open."

"Could it have been possible for a woman to do that?" she asked.

"Somehow I assumed it was a man," Gregory said, "but the bar is not heavy; anyone could lift it, even you or Cecy."

"Thank you, my dear!" she replied, and then added before he could protest, "And of course, once again, we were all separated, alone in our rooms, supposedly in bed, so it could have been anyone at Rockledge!"

She rose and began to pace the room, her breakfast forgotten. "I am so frightened, Gregory! This person, whoever it is, is very, very clever! And we have no idea if he or she will try again, now that the first scheme did not work!"

"But no one has tried to shoot Alistair again!" Gregory reminded her, his face pale, for he had not thought he might still be in danger.

"But that is because he is kept in bed, locked in his room!" his sister pointed out. "He does not see anyone but the doctor, Miss Spenser, his valet, and Lord St. Williams, and once, he asked to see me. Oh please, do not go downstairs today, Gregory. It is not safe! I wish we had never come to Rockledge; no fortune is worth what we have been through!"

Gregory thought she sounded very bitter, and wondered at it, even as he promised her he would keep to his room at least until lunchtime, and then always be careful to remain in company. Caroline thanked him for calming her fears and suggested a game of cards to pass the time. She knew it was useless to suggest a good book or a morning spent writing letters, where her brother was concerned.

She had lost an enormous sum of fictional guineas by the time Buttles knocked on the door and announced that luncheon was being served and that he would be glad to escort them both to the dining room.

"Thank you!" Caroline said with her warm smile. "I shall go with my brother and I am sure that will be sufficient, although we both appreciate all your help, Buttles!"

Gregory added his thanks and the two Covingtons went down to the dining room arm in arm. Caroline was suddenly nervous at the prospect of seeing John St. Williams again, although she need not have worried about any awkwardness, for he ignored her completely, after one quick searching look at her face. She did not even notice, since she was greeting Cecilia North at the time.

Gregory found himself in the pleasurable position of being lionized by everyone throughout the meal, and was begged to tell the story of his adventure once again, to Cecy's exclamations of horror, Lady Danvers' sniffs, and her husband's prodding questions. Only Lord St. Williams did not speak, nor did Mr. Covington-More, but when there was a lull, that gentleman remarked, "Stupid thing to do, boy! Especially after everything that has happened!"

Gregory blushed as he nodded his agreement, and then Lady Danvers began to read him a lecture on prudence, patience, and perspicacity. Caroline could see her brother's color rising and his expression hardening as Sylvia went on and on. She almost intervened after the lady openly accused him of trying to steal a march on the rest of them, so as to get into Lady Cecily's good graces even more by his impetuous actions. But as Caroline was about to speak, Lord St. Williams said in his deep, commanding voice, "I think we all know, m'lady, that it was nothing more than boyish carelessness. And now, may I suggest we forget the whole thing? I begin to find these constant references to the incident boring and repetitive. Shall we talk of something—anything—else?"

His voice was so casually uninterested that Caroline longed to hit him, but Gregory was relieved and sent him a grateful smile. Being the center of attention had soured somewhat during Lady Danvers' lecture, and he was happy when Mr. Covington-More and m'lord began to discuss the weather and the state of the roads.

As they were all rising from the table, Crowell announced that Lady Cecily wished them to come at once to her room, and added that even Mr. Russell would be present, for the doctor had had him carried down by the footmen and placed on a chaise longue.

Lady Danvers' eyes narrowed as she smoothed her morning cap and straightened her gown, and Caroline could see she thought it a golden opportunity to

172

undo any harm that her husband might have committed by blundering when he had been alone with his great-aunt. Cecilia came to Caroline's side and whispered, "Now what do you suppose she wants? I had so hoped I would not have to see her again until I went to bid her good-bye and thank her for her *wonderful* hospitality!"

"Shall we go and see, Cuz?" Caroline asked as Gregory offered them each an arm.

Once again the house guests followed Crowell's slow, measured footsteps along the hall to the drawing room. When he had announced them and they stepped inside the overly warm, crowded room, they saw that in addition to Alistair, lying on the chaise, Dr. Ward was also present, as well as Miss Spenser, in her usual position beside her mistress. Lady Cecily stood before the fireplace, leaning on her silver-headed cane and watching them as they filed in. Her expression was unreadable, but Dr. Ward was frowning, Alistair was looking at each one of them intently, and Miss Spenser was wringing her hands and looking more frightened and mouselike than ever.

Lady Cecily did not speak; she pointed her bejeweled hand at the chairs placed near her, and her guests moved to take their seats.

"Dear Caro!" Alistair called to her, his eyes sparkling with mischief, "do come and sit beside me! It seems such an age since your last delightful visit!"

Caroline went to a chair near him and asked how he did, missing the malicious smile he sent John St. Williams, who had gone to lounge against the table, as he had done the first evening they had all assembled here.

"Come, sit down!" Lady Cecily commanded. "I am gratified at your prompt attendance, dear relatives! I would not have seen you all together again, except there is something we must discuss. Dr. Ward thinks I should summon the law to join our little party, after what nearly happened to young Covington."

She paused, and then, with an expression of warm

173

concern on her face, she asked how Gregory was feeling. Caroline flinched, wishing the lady would not be so partial, for look what had happened the last time she had made so much of Gregory!

Gregory said he was fine, bright as a trivet, in top form, and none the worse for his adventure, m'lady, I do assure you!

"But next time ... who can say what will happen?" she asked, turning her attention to the others again. "This ... this person, who has so far been most inept, is gaining experience, and might easily have improved his or her skills to the point where there will be a successful conclusion next time!"

Cecy whimpered, and Lady Cecily nodded to her as she made her way to the wing chair, as if she were suddenly too tired to stand anymore. Miss Spenser hovered over her until she was told, in no uncertain terms, to cut line and make herself scarce! The poor woman flushed and stole a look at the doctor before she went to stand behind the lady's chair.

"Yes, you are right to be afraid in this instance, Cecilia!" Lady Cecily continued. "All of you should be frightened!"

"I rather think I shall ask to be excused from such paltry behavior, m'lady," Alistair drawled in his light baritone, and as everyone's eyes turned towards him, he drew his right hand from beneath the light blanket that covered him and showed the company the dueling pistol he was holding. "It is loaded, of course, and it never leaves my hand except when I am safely locked in my room," he said, waving it gently and impartially in everyone's direction.

"Put that away, man!" Mr. Covington-More said harshly. "You are frightening the ladies!"

"I beg your pardon, ladies," Alistair retorted, "but there is one among us that I do most sincerely wish to frighten! Take care, whoever you are, for I am an excellent shot!" His voice was as cold as ice and quietly menacing, and Caroline shivered a little. "I find I take exception to being shot at; why, the whole

174

experience has made me quite cross!" he continued, "and when I think of the irreparable damage to my new coat from Stulz, I can only say that that alone would be enough for me not to hesitate in the slightest if I felt I was being threatened again!"

Lady Cecily waved her hand. "Enough, Alistair! I quite agree with your preventive measures, but enough. As I see it, there are only four people in this room who could not be the one who is so bent on destroying the others: Alistair, Gregory, Dr. Ward, and myself! Everyone else is suspect, each and every one of you!"

Her keen eyes under their bushy brows swept over the guests. "Is it John St. Williams? Cecilia? Caroline? Covington-More? Or Tweedledum or Tweedledee?"

Caroline almost spoke up, but in glancing at John St. Williams, she saw him shake his head almost imperceptibly. For some reason he did not want her to mention how the gun had disappeared while they were together, thereby exonerating them both. She settled back in her chair, bending her head meekly.

"I must point out to you, m'lady," Lady Danvers said pleasantly but firmly, as if she were going along with some irrational whim of the old lady, "that neither Roger nor I can be considered as a suspect. You forget, dear Lady Cecily, that I was also supposed to be a victim!"

She sat back smiling in triumph, until Lady Cecily remarked, "But you could have poisoned the comfit yourself, to draw off suspicion, for you did not even taste it, but let it drop where Excalibur could find it. As for Lord Danvers, there have been many husbands who did away with their wives—some of them with even less provocation than he has had to bear, poor man!"

Lady Danvers flushed an angry purple, and she gasped. Her husband leaned towards her, whisper-

175

ing in a perfectly audible voice that dearest Sylvia was not to listen to such awful talk; why, of course he adored his darling, sweetest wife, 'pon his word, he did, and to say otherwise was to lie! Lady Danvers took out her salts and handkerchief and waved his fervent expressions of devotion aside. Such a remark from an elderly, sick old lady only reinforced her own notions that the woman was senile, and therefore incapable of writing a valid will. She was not at all vanquished by this little setback, for she nodded her head to the others, tapping her forehead as she did so when Lady Cecily turned aside for a moment to speak to Miss Spenser, who then left the room. Alistair leaned forward on his chaise and breathed to Caroline, "If only this were not so terribly dangerous, I would have to admit I have not been so diverted for years!"

Caroline nodded, but he noticed that her face was pale and she did not seem to be in her usual spirits. He hoped she would recover them soon, for otherwise she would be as boring as the rest of the company. Surely her brother's misadventure had not overset her mind to this extent! He looked at his cousin and found John St. Williams was also pale and frowning. He wondered idly if there could be a connection between the two.

"M'lady!" Dr. Ward said, coming forward a little from his place. "I must repeat what I said to you this morning! I think it would be wise to summon the justice of Rockledge. As you yourself just said, this person only has to succeed once, and there will be tragedy here!"

"No, sir!" Lady Cecily said strongly, banging her cane on the floor for emphasis. "There will be no minions of the law at Rockledge, prowling around and cutting up all my peace! Why, the scandal of it, the law . . . here! The Covingtons have never had anything to do with 'em; I'll not start now!"

"But if there is murder done?" the doctor pressed

her. "Then you would have no choice! Surely you cannot wish your relatives to die?"

Lady Cecily opened her mouth to reply and closed it thoughtfully, as her dark eyes darted around the assembled company.

"I quite agree, m'lady!" Alistair remarked. "So much better *not* to say what you had in mind, eh?"

Lady Cecily laughed, a hearty cackle. "I do so like you, Alistair! You are no better than you should be, but at least you are honest! Very well, for the sake of peace I will hold my tongue. But to return to the subject we were discussing; let us put our heads together and think hard, and perhaps we may discover the identity of this mysterious would-be murderer!"

John St. Williams spoke for the first time. "Although it is not impossible, can we assume that it could not be one of the servants, at least for now, and leave them out of our deliberations?"

Lady Cecily nodded and then she called, "Spenser! Where are you, woman? You're as slow as an old horse on its way to the knackers!" Miss Spenser hurried back into the room with quill and paper and ink.

"Take that place at the table, and write down what I tell you!" Lady Cecily ordered her companion.

Sylvia Danvers leaned forward expectantly, clutching her salts. Was Lady Cecily about to draw up her will? How fortunate everyone was present, and the doctor as well, for he would be able to testify to the lady's incompetence and senility!

"Make two columns, Spenser," came her next order, dashing Lady Danvers' hopes. "In the first put these names: Alistair Russell, Gregory Covington, Matthew Ward, and Cecily Covington. In the other column, list John St. Williams, Cecilia North, Caroline Covington, Lord and Lady Danvers, and Covington-More." She waited impatiently until the scratching of the quill became still.

177

"Now, write this down: poisoned comfit and Lady Danvers, the shooting of Alistair Russell, and locking Gregory Covington in the gardener's shed to freeze."

She turned to her guests. "Think, all of you! Who had the opportunity, the wits, and the nerve to attempt all these crimes?"

"Perhaps it would be wise if we could decide first *why* all these things have been done," John St. Williams suggested, and when Lady Cecily nodded her head and motioned for him to continue, he said, "I have no idea who poisoned the comfit; it does not seem to fit the other crimes. You will remember, m'lady, that both Alistair and Gregory were attacked shortly after their visits to you, and they both made a great deal of how much you seemed to like them; Gregory from his innocence, and Alistair from his love of mischief. You must pardon my analysis of your character, Cuz!" he added, bowing to a completely unconcerned and amused Mr. Russell. "I have thought that the murderer wanted to do away with them because they were clearly your favorites as the heir to your fortune. But why kill Lady Danvers? Even if you liked her, she only inherits through her husband, not directly. Why not, therefore, kill him instead of her?"

"Perhaps that mishap has nothing to do with the others," Alistair remarked into the silence that followed his cousin's commentary. "Or perhaps it was as Lady Danvers maintained at first. The dog got into some poison on his walk that Miss Spenser did not notice, and there was no poisoned comfit at all."

"But how could that be?" Mr. Covington-More asked. "No one puts down poison for the rats out in the frozen grounds, and surely it was impossible for the dog to get into the poison in the gardener's shed!"

178

Alistair raised one white hand. "But stay! There is another solution! Did *you* poison the dog, Miss Spenser?"

The companion gasped, and her face turned ashen, and Dr. Ward got up and went to her aid as her mouth worked helplessly and the tears came into her eyes.

"I . . . I . . . of course not!" she finally got out, twisting the quill in her hands until it snapped. "What . . . what a terrible thing to say!"

"But Miss Spenser," Dr. Ward said as he patted her hand, "you must be calm. It is entirely possible that, out of the kindness of your heart, you felt the animal had suffered long enough. You have heard me so many times suggesting to Lady Cecily that she have the dog put down. Anyone could see he was in almost constant pain!"

"I did not . . . Lady Cecily has always been most adamant on that point, Doctor," she whispered. "You know she would never permit it!"

"And you, of course, did everything she wanted at all times, eh?" Alistair asked, as Lady Cecily snapped, "She had better—or else!"

"You are all forgetting that it could have been a former servant or a small boy bent on mischief," Dr. Ward added, "that put the poison where the dog would find it. Lady Cecily has her enemies—er, I mean . . ."

"No need to pull your punches, Doctor!" Lady Cecily snapped again. "I have never cared to be queen of the firth!"

"Come, let us move on!" John said, getting up to pace the floor. "Perhaps we should forget the poisoned comfit for now, since it does not seem to fit with either Alistair's shooting or Gregory's being left to freeze, and might have a perfectly logical explanation."

"And what about the eye in the library?" Cecilia spoke up, overcoming her fear of her great-aunt at last. "You are all forgetting that, and it was so horrible!" She shuddered, and Lady Cecily leaned forward, grasping her cane.

"What's this, miss? An eye? In the library? Whatever are you talking about?"

Caroline was stunned. Was it possible that the lady had not been told about someone using the priest's hole to spy on the guests? Somehow she had thought that John, or Miss Spenser, or someone, would have mentioned it. Now, as Gregory and Cecilia related the incident, she stared at them in bewilderment.

"I do not understand!" she said finally. "If you were all, each and every one of you, in the library, who could it have been?"

"Naturally, we assumed it was you, yourself, m'lady," Alistair said in his light voice. "And what could be more natural, after all? There is an entrance to the priest's hole right here in your drawing room, and how very revealing it would be if you could hear us talking when we did not know you were listening. Sort of thing I would do myself; perfectly understandable, I assure you! You must not think we mind!"

"That's very kind of you, Alistair!" Lady Cecily said. "Perhaps I might have spied on you, but I did not!"

"You did not?" Lady Danvers asked, her tone incredulous; and her husband said hastily, in a soothing tone, "Of course she did not! The lady's notions of propriety are much too nice. Told you all along it had to be a servant; sort of thing they get up to, y'know, spying on their betters!"

"But why?" John St. Williams asked.

"Perhaps it was someone who does not have all his wits," Lord Danvers supplied, pleased to be able to show his great-aunt his intelligent grasp of the situation. "Sort of thing someone who doesn't have much in his cockloft might find amusin'!"

"I do not employ idiots!" Lady Cecily said, glaring at him.

Lord Danvers quickly retreated, saying he had not meant, of course he understood, he knew she would never, and other sentiments of like nature, until Sylvia pulled his coattails, and in a fierce aside told him to be quiet, for he was just making things worse.

"Never mind that!" Lady Cecily said, waving her cane. "Does it really matter who it was? I see no connection between someone spying on you, and the attempted murders, but I say this to you: such things must stop! I never meant these things to happen, when I summoned you all here; indeed, I would not have done so if I had known that one of you wanted my fortune all to yourself so badly that you would kill to get it!"

"If it were only that easy, m'lady," John St. Williams said. "But let us admit it is unlikely to happen, just because you give an order. One does not order a murderer to reform and expect obedience. No, m'lady, not even for you!"

He paused, and Lady Cecily nodded her head slowly in defeat.

"What I suggest is that we all be very much on our guard. That no one goes anywhere alone, that we all meet at specified times and remain together either in the library or the dining room or the hall. That there will be no wandering off alone to investigate—" and here his eyes swept briefly over Caroline before he continued, "and that as soon as the roads are passable, we leave Rockledge. I know you planned for us to wriggle on the end of your pin a while longer, m'lady, but you must see that it will not do, not now!"

"You are right, John," she said. "I beg you, Dr. Ward, to remain with us as well. I have a great regard for your wisdom, and perhaps between the two of us, we can solve this mystery."

The doctor nodded his gray head, but he did not seem at all pleased with the prospect of an extended stay, or the lady's compliment.

"And there is also the fact that you will be on hand if there should be any further—ah, mishaps!" Alistair added. "Allow me to beg the pleasure of your company as well, sir! I have seldom been more fervent in my pleading, you may believe me!"

Caroline could see that Lady Cecily was tired, for she was sitting slumped over in her chair, one hand shading her eyes. She looked to the doctor and nodded her head in Lady Cecily's direction, and he rose at once.

"Come, m'lady! As your doctor, I insist you rest now, and that the others withdraw. This has been very upsetting for you, and it has tired you."

For once the old lady did not demur, as the guests rose to take their leave and Miss Spenser summoned the footmen to carry Alistair back to his room.

"Yes, I am tired," she muttered, and then said, in a stronger voice, "Spenser! Bring me the paper you have been writing; I wish to study it later!"

As Caroline followed the others from the drawing room, she heard the lady chastising her companion.

"What a terrible hand you write, Spenser! How am I ever to decipher these chicken tracks? Why, this is even worse than you generally produce!"

Caroline could only feel pity for the poor lady, and wondered how she was able to stand being Lady Cecily's companion when she was so constantly abused and belittled, but then Cecy began whispering to her as they moved to the library, and she put Miss Spenser from her mind. She, after all, had a larger problem on her mind. How was she going to stand being cooped up with John St. Williams in the same room most of the days and evenings? Perhaps, she thought as she went to the window seat and the book she had left there, I shall come down with infectious influenza or a putrid throat and have to remain in my room with only the faithful Wentworth in attendance, until the day comes when we can leave here at last! But she knew she would never resort to this ploy, for then she would miss all the excitement, the conversations and speculations, and possibly the unmasking of the murderer as well.

CHAPTER 10

DR. WARD WAS called to Lady Cecily's room again late that afternoon. She had had a long nap and, much refreshed, had spent some time studying the list of suspects that Miss Spenser had copied out. When her companion answered the bell, she was told to bring the doctor to the drawing room and order tea for the three of them.

"Now that Matthew Ward is coming, I am sure you will find it impossible to tear yourself away, eh, Spenser?" Lady Cecily laughed, shaking a finger at her. "Silly thing! I know what is in your mind, you know, but it will not do. The doctor is not the marrying kind, and he does not have the slightest idea of your doglike devotion to him!"

"I . . . I *beg* your ladyship!" Spenser said in a pained, frightened voice. "Please do not speak of such a thing to the doctor! It is untrue and so embarrassing to me, and you know I would never leave you while you have need of me!"

Lady Cecily stared at her companion, as plain as ever in the inevitable black dress and her severe hairdo, and the mortified gray eyes behind her large spectacles. There were two red patches on her thin cheeks and such an agonized expression on her face that the old lady had the grace to be ashamed of herself. She watched Spenser's hands endlessly twisting her handkerchief and said, "I was but teasing you, woman! Have you no sense of humor at all? Of course I would not dream of telling the doctor! Now, go and fetch him!"

A few minutes later Matthew Ward came in and took a seat across from Lady Cecily before the fire, while Miss Spenser bustled about, directing Crowell and the footman as to where to put the tea tray.

"Pour out, if you please, Spenser!" Lady Cecily said as the servants left the room. She tapped the paper before her and stared at the list of suspects before she said, "I wanted to ask you especially, Doctor, now that we are alone, if you have any suspicions as to who might be the culprit. After all, you came late on the scene, and as a stranger, might have seen something the rest of the family has missed."

Dr. Ward took the cup that Miss Spenser was holding out to him, and smiled his thanks before he spoke.

"I wish I could help, m'lady," he said, "but no obvious name leaps to mind. And yet . . . I cannot help but suspect Mr. Covington-More. He never says very much, but I have noticed how carefully he watches the others, with a most amused smirk on his face, as if he knew something that they did not."

Lady Covington waved her hand. "He probably just feels uncomfortable to be here among all the legitimate Covingtons, and I am sure he has been treated badly by some of them during his stay. I know Alistair Russell could never resist twitting him, and Lady Danvers has no doubt put him in his place time without number, horrible woman that she is!"

"Perhaps he hates them because they are legitimate?" the doctor asked. "It cannot be easy, knowing you are a bastard through no fault of your own, and that all the others are considered superior to you because of their birth."

Lady Cecily stole a glance at Miss Spenser, now sitting quietly to one side, sipping her tea with a painful flush on her face as she listened to the conversation.

"Then, too, he is an uneducated man," he continued, "and for all we know, might need the money desperately!"

Lady Cecily interrupted him by laughing out loud in delight.

"Now, there you are well off the mark, Doctor! Covington-More has more money of his own than I have to dispense in my will; I daresay more than any of the Covingtons put together! He is an industrialist and an inventor, with manufactories in several cities. Can it be you have never heard of the More loom, or the More reaper? He has made a fortune for himself, bastard or not. No, the only reason he might be guilty is because he hates all the rest because of their legality. I have spoken to him many times and have seen no sign of any such hate. I have no doubt he is probably just amused at the machinations of the others, or at least he was until these incidents began! He knows he will never inherit, for I have told him so. I may have suggested it to the others, but of course my father's fortune would never go to a bastard. Now what is the matter with you, Spenser?"

Her companion had put her cup down on the table and was coughing into her handkerchief. In a moment, she wiped her eyes and said in her hesitant voice, "Your pardon, m'lady! I must have swallowed the wrong way!"

"Do me the kindness to remain still!" Lady Cecily snapped. "Unless, that is, you have something to contribute? Perhaps you have an idea who is doing all these things?" she added sarcastically.

"Oh no, m'lady!" Miss Spenser breathed.

"I suppose it was too much to ask, for you to have a thought in your head, Spenser, for a sillier widgeon I have never seen!" Lady Cecily told her "Pass the doctor the plate of cakes· it is all you are good for!"

Matthew Ward frowned at her rudeness, for although he agreed that Miss Spenser was a silly woman, he could not help but feel sorry for her. Over the months he had seen how Lady Cecily treated her, and although he knew she was considered lucky to have her position at all, Lady Cecily's temperament made her job very difficult. To be constantly ridiculed and put down was enough to make anyone timid and silent and unsure of himself.

Thinking to take the lady's mind off her hapless companion, he spoke up again. "But if it is not Mr. Covington-More, who can it be?"

"I myself have always liked Alistair Russell as the villain," Lady Cecily said. "Or I did until he was shot, that is. They say he is wealthy, but I have a suspicion that things have not gone well for him lately, and the Covington fortune might be only too welcome. Besides, I consider him quite capable of destroying his fellow men—and women—if he stood to gain by it. Now, however, he is out of the lists!"

She sounded so regretful to lose her favorite suspect that Dr. Ward could not restrain a little smile. "How about Lady Danvers, then?" he asked, nodding as Miss Spenser offered him another cup of tea.

"It would be so satisfying if she were the one!" Lady Cecily enthused. "But can you picture her, Doctor, firing at Alistair or luring Gregory to the shed at midnight? She is greedy enough for the inheritance to try anything, but unless she is in cahoots with her husband, it is just not possible. They share a room; how could he not know of her nefarious activities? Roger Danvers does not have the intelligence to plan or carry out such schemes, being the most boring, idiotic man I have ever met. He is so stupid that even if his wife were doing them with his connivance, he could not keep the secret. No, not the Danvers, either one of them!"

In the silence that followed, Dr. Ward said, "But

187

you cannot suspect Miss North; she is so young, so shy, and so frightened of you, m'lady, from what you have told me. And that leaves only Lord St. Williams or the Covingtons. Well, well!"

"Lord St. Williams," Lady Cecily mused aloud. "Yes, John is capable of it, and so, I think, might Caroline Covington be. Her brother, no. Murder is not his way. On second thought, it cannot be Caroline either. I like her! Surely I could not have so misjudged her character!"

"So that leaves only Lord St. Williams!" the doctor said.

"Yes, it must be he, but for what reason I have no idea. He is very rich; it cannot be for the money, unless he, like Alistair, has fallen on hard times. These young rakes are all alike—women and gambling and wasting their substance!"

Lady Cecily put her cup back on the tray and folded her hands in her lap. For a moment she stared up at the portrait of her father over the mantel, and then she nodded a little. "I can tell *you*, Dr. Ward, although I do not think it wise to tell my guests, that I have made up my mind who is to inherit."

The doctor looked interested, and even Miss Spenser stopped fussing over the tea tray to listen more closely.

"I shall leave all the money to the Covingtons!" the old lady declared. "Besides bearing the name, young Gregory is a man after my own heart: bright, daring, and charming! Of course the money will be held in trust and he will only be able to enjoy the income, for although I may like him, I am more than two and ten, and I see he would squander it in a se'en month if he had his hands on the capital!" She chuckled until she had to wipe her eyes. "And a high old time he would have doing it, too, young devil!"

"If I may ask—why his sister as well, m'lady?" the doctor asked, curious as to her reason.

"I suspect that Miss Covington has decided to remain Miss Covington, and since she has no desire to marry, may very well need the money to live in the first style of elegance. I did not need to marry, and if the girl wishes to follow my example, she should have the means. It is very difficult for a penniless spinster in this man's world we live in, Doctor. Besides, I like her. She is intelligent, calm, and steadfast—all excellent qualities the Covingtons have never boasted before—she deserves it!" She laughed again. "Of course, with the Covington inheritance behind her, she may find it very difficult to keep to the single state. She will be besieged with offers!"

She stood up, clutching her cane, and Miss Spenser rushed to help her until she should have her balance, but Lady Cecily waved her away to fetch Crowell to remove the tea tray. When she was gone, and as Dr. Ward was bowing and taking his leave, his patient said, "I think I will join you all for dinner this evening, Dr. Ward. I am feeling restless! Now, remember, not a word about my decision to the others! I will tell them when I am good and ready."

The doctor went away after promising he would not breathe a word, and, meeting Miss Spenser in the hall, asked her to accompany him to Mr. Russell's room so he might change the man's dressings. Miss Spenser was only too happy to do so, and so she missed the very unusual sight of Lady Cecily telling her butler that she would dine with the family this evening. Crowell's eyebrows rose after he left her room. This was a new come-out indeed, for Lady Cecily had not left the drawing room for over three years. He went to the kitchen at once to confer with the cook, shaking his head and mumbling as he did so. All these changes and alarums! It was more than a man of his years should be asked to cope with: first a houseful of guests, with their many demands, then poisoned dogs, and gentlemen getting shot in his hall, and finding themselves locked out in the cold, and he didn't know what all! He'd be glad to see the back of them, even if they were all Covingtons!

The afternoon had been just as long as Caroline Covington had suspected it might be. The book she had been holding on her lap as a defense, only occasionally remembering to turn the pages, had not held her interest, not with Lord St. Williams so near to her as he played chess with her brother. She noticed unhappily that he rarely looked her way, except to answer some of Cecy's artless chatter. Cecy was flirting with John, and her cousin Gregory as well, for all she was working so diligently on her embroidery. After one particularly leading remark, accompanied as it was by a delicate blush, Lady Danvers closed her book of sermons with a snap.

"This is most unbecoming—most forward of you, Cecilia! Your behavior is such that any decent woman must blush for you, and you are not to excuse yourself by pointing out the gentlemen are relatives. That will not wash, my girl! Strive for a more retiring and modest nature, if you please!"

Cecilia tossed her head and frowned. If she had not been so very bored, she might have held her tongue, for she could no more help flirting when there were handsome gentlemen present than she could stop breathing.

"I do not have to listen to you, Sylvia, for you are not my mother, no, nor even a relative, except by marriage! I shall do as I please!"

"It would pain me very much indeed," Lady Danvers replied, her round face red from being contradicted, "if I should have to write to your mother. Then she would know there was no chance for you to be named the heiress, behaving as you have done. That would make her very cross, would it not?"

Cecy bridled but held her tongue, for she would not have put it past Lady Danvers to do just as she threatened, if only to make mischief.

"Oh, do be quiet, both of you!" Caroline exclaimed, rising to pace the library. She had not missed the look of amusement on John's face for Cecy's antics.

190

"You are squabbling like fishwives! Aren't things bad enough without that?"

Lord Danvers rose from his chair and shook a fat hand in admonition. "Now, now!" he said, turning from one angry face to the other. "Birds in their little nests agree, you know! Let us have decorum of conduct such as will bring sweet harmony and a family closeness!"

The ladies continued to look mutinous in spite of this noble sentiment. Mr. Covington-More looked up from the desk, where he had been writing letters, and snorted, Gregory looked amazed, and Lord St. Williams said dryly, "The only little birds that I have ever observed in their nests, Roger, were all busy trying to annihilate their siblings, in the hopes of getting a larger share of the next worm. Hardly an appropriate simile, do you think?"

"But he doesn't think, now, does he?" asked Covington-More in a quiet, uninterested voice.

Just then the first dressing-bell rang, and the company of little birds was only too happy to leave this particular nest and go up to their rooms to dress for dinner.

No one noticed that John St. Williams did not mount the stairs with the others, but stood quietly to one side of the hall until they had all reached the second floor. Only then did he go and tap softly on Lady Cecily's door. He found the lady alone, resting before the ordeal of eating dinner with her relatives, and he spent so many minutes closeted with her that he had to run lightly up the stairs and hurriedly change into his evening clothes so as not to be late.

In the meantime, Caroline had summoned her maid, deciding she would wear her dark-brown velvet gown again. She thought perhaps it would cheer her up, for she knew it was becoming, even without the extravagant compliment Alistair Russell had given her when she wore it before. After Wentworth had hooked it up and shaken out the creamy lace ruffles at the shoulders, Caroline took her pearls from her jewelry case and asked the maid to be especially careful of her hairdo tonight. Miss Wentworth looked searchingly at Miss Caro's face, wondering about her motives. She had seldom seen the girl more unhappy; why, if it were anybody else but Miss Caro, set down anywhere else but this horrible Scottish castle, she would have suspected the girl was in love. Shaking her head a little at her fancies, she proceeded to curl and arrange her soft brown hair. Caroline was still not ready when Cecy knocked on the door, but fortunately Gregory came along just then and offered to escort his cousin downstairs. The second bell had gone before Caroline was ready, and she hurried downstairs, accompanied by her maid, who insisted on seeing her safely bestowed with the others.

To her complete surprise, Caro found her great-aunt standing in the hall, leaning on John St. Williams' arm and giving a series of angry orders to the various servants who had gathered there.

"Crowell, have this fire built up at once! It is freezing here in the hall! Whatever were you thinking of to allow such a puny blaze? You know my father always insisted on a roaring fire here on cold winter evenings. And you, there, Dolly! Bring more candles! How can anyone see anything in such gloom?"

The butler and footmen hurried to their tasks and the maids bustled about, as Lady Cecily's guests stood dumbfounded. The old lady allowed John to lead her to a seat by the fire.

"I have been informed by the cook that there will be a slight delay," she announced next, "and if dinner is anything like the disorder I have found here in the hall, I can well understand it! Why did none of you mention the conditions prevailing outside my room?"

"Perhaps, m'lady," John St. Williams said, smiling down at her from his position before the fire, so darkly handsome in his well-cut evening clothes, no one would have guessed how quickly he had dressed, "it was because we assumed that life here at Rockledge was always like this. Small or nonexistent fires, poor skimpy meals, few candles, and dusty, neglected rooms."

Lady Cecily bridled and looked so angry that Cecy tried to disappear behind Caroline's skirts, but then she drew a deep breath and smiled up at him.

"Dear boy! So naughty of you, *especially*, not to have told me! Spenser!"

Her companion hurried forward, wringing her hands in her inevitable way and looking very distressed.

"This is your doing, Spenser! I shall deal with you later!"

"Yes, m'lady," poor Miss Spenser breathed, hanging her head.

At last Crowell announced dinner, and Lord Danvers, prompted by his wife's firm hand at his back, hurried forward to beg the honor of leading his great-aunt in to dinner.

"Certainly not!" she snapped, raising one bejeweled finger and beckoning to John. "Dear St. Williams will take me in; he is much the best of you, and I feel so safe on his strong arm!"

Lady Danvers frowned, Lord Danvers bowed and retreated, and the rest looked amazed at this sudden affection that seemed to have sprung up between Lady Cecily and her oldest great-nephew. Caroline and Gregory exchanged glances as John bent his head and whispered something to the old lady, and she laughed out loud and rapped his knuckles with her fan. They walked slowly to the dining room, followed by the other guests, with a blushing but unhappy Miss Spenser on the doctor's arm bringing up the rear.

The table was set very differently from other evenings, and Caroline could not restrain a gasp at the amount of crystal and plate that was laid out. Several large candelabra were set at intervals on the table, and the centerpiece was a vast silver bowl decorated by cupids and flowers. Instead of merely the elderly footman with the sniff, there were three others in attendance, as well as Crowell to serve them.

Caroline heard Covington-More chuckle as he surveyed the table while Lady Cecily took her place at the head, still smiling up at John.

"You must take the place of honor opposite me, John!" she commanded. "The rest of you sort yourselves out as you wish. We will not stand on ceremony."

By dint of another well-placed shove, Lord Danvers took the seat to Lady Cecily's right. Next to him Gregory had placed Cecilia, leaving Lady Danvers to take the chair next to Lord St. Williams. Lady Cecily told Caroline to sit at her left, after one glare at the hapless Lord Danvers, as if she was determined to have some intelligent conversation during dinner. Dr. Ward was next to Caro, with Miss Spenser beside him, then came Covington-More to St. Williams' right.

The dinner that was served was vastly different from anything they had been treated to before during their stay at Rockledge. When Lord Danvers enthused over the huge roast of venison and the pigeon pie and rhapsodized about the enormous platter of lobster fritters and a delicious cream soup, Lady Cecily looked amazed.

"But of course! I do not keep a French chef, but Mrs. Stewart is a good, plain cook! John, do try the haggis! If you have anything of Scotland about you, you must eat haggis! Crowell, more wine for Lord St. Williams!"

Caroline stole a glance down the table to where John was nobly helping himself to the haggis, which she had never had the courage to try after learning its ingredients. Now, why was great-aunt making such a fuss over him? she wondered, waving away a second helping of turkey in a brown sauce. She thought there was an air of quiet but positive determination about John this evening, and pondered over it. She could see from Sylvia Danvers' frown, even as she concentrated on her heaped-up plate, that she was not the only one to notice.

Cecy was whispering to Gregory, and she could hear Covington-More attempting a conversation with Miss Spenser, so she turned to the doctor and asked him when he thought the roads would be clear enough to travel.

"Well, Miss Covington," he said, his eyes twinkling a little as he replied, "now that the storm is over, I should think by the end of the week. You must be anxious to return to your homes, in the south. Scotland is not the most salubrious place in February, even without the excitements we have been treated to. The first winter I spent here, I was sure I was never to see green grass again, or ever have the wind stop howling. We do have a few pleasant days in summer—somehow, they seem all the more beautiful for being so rare!"

Crowell offered the doctor more wine, and Caroline took a moment to observe Lady Cecily on her other hand. She was wearing another outdated gown; this one a blue satin over a lace petticoat and huge hoops. On her head was her powdered wig, complete with dangling curls and, this evening, embellished with jeweled combs and feathers. Her neck and arms and fingers were covered with jewels, and they sparkled in the light of the many candles. Caroline smiled to herself. Her great-aunt was surely a most eccentric and unusual old lady, but she admired her nonetheless. There was an air of gallantry about her, a willingness to face whatever life brought to her without whimpering or regret, even though she made it very clear that she wanted her own way in everything and would brook no interference with her wishes. Suddenly, Caro felt she was being stared at, and she turned to survey the table. In doing so, she caught John St. Williams, his dark eyes intent on her face and his wineglass forgotten in his hand. Her eyes widened, but she made herself nod distantly to him before she turned again to Dr. Ward in some confusion. She had never seen such a look on his face before, so concentrated and serious, as if he were trying to memorize her features or tell her something that was in his mind. She shook herself mentally. Surely this was merest fancy, for John had made it very clear in what light he regarded her.

After the last course and the several removes that accompanied it had been served, Lady Cecily rapped on her goblet to gain everyone's attention. Motioning to Crowell, who immediately left the room, she waited until there was complete silence.

"My *dear* relatives!" she said sarcastically, staring at each and every one in turn. "I have a very important announcement to make, for just before dinner I decided which one of you will inherit the Covington fortune!"

She paused and smiled at their astonished looks and exclamations; even Dr. Ward was staring at her, for hadn't the lady told him only a little while before that she had no intention of announcing the heirs? Lady Danvers leaned forward in her chair, her little eyes greedy in excitement, and the remains of her dinner forgotten. Across from her Covington-More smiled to himself as Gregory and Cecy exchanged eager glances, and Lord Danvers wiped his perspiring face with his napkin. Miss Spenser shrank back in her seat, one hand over her mouth, and Caro wondered why the lady had chosen this particular moment for her announcement. Whoever the heir was, he or she would certainly become the primary target for the murderer!

Crowell and footmen came back into the dining room, bearing champagne and some beautiful old cut-crystal glasses, and Lady Cecily motioned them to serve it. When this had been accomplished, to the subdued whispers of the guests, Lady Cecily tapped her glass again and said triumphantly, "I give you my heir: milord John St. Williams!"

She drank her champagne, and in the excitement that followed, no one noticed the doctor's questioning look or Lady Cecily's almost imperceptible shake of the head. Gregory was congratulating John, and Lord Danvers was nervously pleating his napkin as he peeked down the table at his wife. He was so very afraid that dear Sylvia was about to treat the company to one of her spells! And so it appeared she might, for her face had turned very pale as her mouth worked, trying to get some words out. Covington-More never took his eyes off her, a now-huge grin on his face. Cecy pouted a little even as she said how happy she was for her cousin, and Caroline turned back to John St. Williams to find him studying each of the company in turn.

"But . . . but," Lady Danvers finally sputtered, "why? He has no need for the money; why, he is rich as Golden Ball already!"

"There is that, of course," Lady Cecily said, nodding to Crowell to refill her glass, and ignoring the doctor's sudden frown. "But he is the oldest among you, and certainly has shown the most sense. Besides, he is a man, and I have been impressed with his character and intelligence. I chose him because I felt the Covington inheritance would be safest in his hands. But come, drink up! This is an evening for celebration!"

She turned to Caroline and whispered, "If looks could kill, dear John would come into his new wealth this minute! Do observe Sylvia Danvers, my dear. I have not been so amused in years."

Caro took one look at the lady in question, her face now purple with indignation, and tried not to smile.

"But ma'am, why did you announce the heir tonight?" she asked in a quiet aside meant only for Lady Cecily's ears. "Surely it will be very dangerous for Lord St. Williams!"

Lady Cecily gave her a shrewd glance. "As you

say. But now that you will all be making preparations to leave Rockledge, I could not resist. You're a good gel, Caro; do not worry! St. Williams is very capable of defending himself!"

It would be safe to say that the dinner party concluded in a somewhat somber mood. John had very little to say for himself, after he had stood and thanked Lady Cecily and proposed a toast to her continued good health.

Before she gave the signal for the ladies to withdraw, she asked the gentlemen to join them in the drawing room after port, and announced that Alistair Russell, who had dined in his room, would be carried down to join them. Two footmen, one on either side, helped her to her feet and assisted her from the dining room, followed by the ever-hovering Miss Spenser, and Caroline, Cecilia, and Sylvia Danvers, who still looked distinctly unwell.

Caroline thought she had never seen such an air of excitement and delight as rested on her great-aunt's face, and realized that, of everyone present, she was the only person who was enjoying herself to the fullest. As she walked down the hall in her wake, she wondered what other surprises the lady had up her sleeve for the evening.

CHAPTER 11

THE LADIES DISCOVERED Alistair already established on the chaise in the drawing room. Lady Cecily greeted him and then went slowly to the wing chair near the fireplace, directing one of the footmen to serve him some port. "For," she said with a smile, "in spite of being forced to endure only our female company, you shall not be denied your wine, sir!" Alistair thanked her, and Caroline noticed that he took up the glass with his left hand. So Alistair had not abandoned his pistol! For some reason it made her feel better as she went to ask him how he did. Ever since Lady Cecily's surprising announcement, she had not been able to shake off a mounting sense of unease.

As she took a seat near the chaise, she also restrained a momentary feeling of regret that Gregory had not been named the heir. Her father, although possessed of a comfortable fortune, was hardly as wealthy as Lord St. Williams, or even Alistair and the Danvers. Gregory would come into a modest inheritance, while her portion could only be called respectable, but being a fair-minded person, she acknowledged that her great aunt had the right to dispose of her wealth any way she wanted, and no one could have counted on being the recipient of her bounty. And, she admitted as she took the cup of tea that Miss Spenser was handing her, she had to agree with Lady Cecily's assessment of the man. He *was* the best among them in her eyes too, and certainly more sensible and mature than her gay young brother.

"Spenser!" Lady Cecily ordered. "Have Crowell bring up the last bottle of Napoleon brandy from the cellars! I regret I cannot offer it to anyone but John, for there is very little left, but I wish him to taste it on this very important evening."

At this, Alistair Russell's eyebrows rose, and Caroline told him in an undertone what had occurred in the dining room. His face grew pale and he frowned, but when he saw her looking at him so curiously, he essayed a light laugh.

"So, to the wealthiest go the spoils, eh? The world is most unfair, do you not agree, Cuz? I myself would have been delighted to have been named the heir, but since it is not to be, I shall have to struggle on with what is left of my fortune, until I can find a wealthy heiress. What a shame you are not such an one, my dear, for we have dealt extremely well with one another, and if I have to marry someone, I might wish it were you. At least you have some conversation!"

He sighed and looked so glum that Caroline laughed at him. "But I have heard it said, sir, that all heiresses are beautiful!" she could not resist pointing out.

"And beauty is in the eye of the beholder, and handsome is as handsome does, and money cannot buy happiness!" he intoned, shaking his head. "I know all those old chestnuts, Caroline, and not a one of 'em are true! In my experience, the heiresses that I have known have all been distressingly ugly; squint-eyed, obese, with shrill voices and red hands! Well, I daresay I shall become accustomed!"

Caroline laughed again as she pictured her elegant relative beside just such a vision as he painted, and promised him she would be on the lookout for as handsome an heiress as she could find, to whom she would praise Mr. Russell in the most glowing terms, at the same time sending him an urgent express to come immediately.

Alistair grinned at her. "And how was dinner, Cuz? Lord, I wish I might have been there to see the fun! Did La Danvers cut up royally? I can see from her expression that she is not best pleased with the results of her stay at Rockledge."

Caroline saw that Sylvia, although supposedly attending to a conversation between Lady Cecily and Cecy North, had not contributed a word. Her lips were compressed in a thin, disapproving line, and her little eyes were cold. As she watched her, she saw Crowell come in behind Miss Spenser, bearing an old bottle of brandy on a silver tray. He brought it to Lady Cecily and presented it reverently.

"Yes, that's the one! Put it over there on the drinks table, Crowell, but somewhat apart from the others. That is ambrosia, and not for mere mortals!"

Crowell obeyed and, after adding more coals to the already blazing fire, bowed himself out, and Miss Spenser went to stand behind Lady Cecily's chair, as was her custom.

"Caro? I asked you a question! It does seem to me that you might be more attentive to the wounded. Life has not been very amusing for me, you know, lying on my bed of pain all alone, and now that I discover that John is to be the lucky heir, I am quite cut up! Come, tell me of the dinner and everyone's reactions, and cheer me up!"

Obediently, Caroline amused him with a quick account of the party, not forgetting to mention the lavish food accompanied by no less than four different wines, and the elaborate table decor, as well as their great-aunt's unholy delight in the mischief she had stirred up. Alistair was still laughing at her description of Lady Danvers' alarming changes of facial color, when the other gentlemen came in.

Gregory, who had been speaking to John, was surprised at the ferocious frown that came over the latter's face as they entered the room together, and wondered what he had said to bring such a look to his cousin's face.

"Ah, there you are!" Lady Cecily exclaimed. "Come in and join us; I have always hated that custom that requires the ladies to leave the gentlemen after dinner. I am sure that women miss the most interesting conversations, and all the best jokes, for it seems to me that men save the good parts for when they are alone together. So unfair!"

Lord Danvers hurried to his wife's side and, taking the seat beside her, bent over to whisper in her ear. Lady Danvers did not appear to attend to him, or even to notice when he took her hand in his and patted it gently as he spoke. For a moment there was some confusion as the men took their seats or wandered over to the drinks table for liqueurs. Lady Cecily ordered Spenser to bring her a glass of port.

"I know, Doctor, I know, but you must permit me to indulge this evening. It is only once that one names one's heir, after all. John, my dear, I have had what is left of the last bottle of the good brandy my father laid down years ago brought up from the cellars especially for you. You will find it there on the table. Now, Dr. Ward, not a word!"

The doctor subsided, shaking his head, as John inspected the old bottle with much the same reverence Crowell had shown, and then he poured a generous measure into a snifter that stood nearby. He began to turn the glass slowly in his hands to warm it, raising it to inhale the aroma, and then lifted the snifter to Lady Cecily in thanks. Still holding it, he strolled over to ask Alistair about his health. All the company listened while Alistair said he was gaining strength every day. "I know you are anxious to return to town, John, but do not desert me, I beg of you! I am sure I shall be able to drive within the week, isn't that right, Doctor?"

Dr. Ward nodded his head and agreed Mr. Russell was healing well, as Miss Spenser brought Lady Cecily her port. Conversation grew general, and Caroline, staring into the glowing flames of the fireplace, thought to herself that although this appeared to be an ordinary evening with everyone comfortably replete after a magnificent dinner, in reality there was an undertone that made her shiver a little. She shook her head at Gregory when he asked her if she wanted any wine, and frowned at him when he went to refill his glass. All those wines at dinner, then champagne, then port, and now heaven knew what he was drinking. Gregory would be sorry tomorrow!

John St. Williams was lounging against the center table, still holding the snifter of old brandy in both hands, when for some reason Caroline's glance was drawn to Miss Spenser. The woman was again standing behind Lady Cecily's chair, but now Caroline saw that she was leaning forward eagerly, her eyes wide with excitement as she stared at Lord St. Williams. Her mouth was slightly open and she was clutching the top of the wing chair so tightly that her knuckles were white. Caroline turned swiftly just as John raised the snifter to his lips.

"NO, do not drink it, John!" she exclaimed, rising from her seat to go to him. "I fear it is poisoned, my dear!"

St. Williams put the snifter down on a table and sent her a warm although startled glance. "I suspected it was, Caro," he said in his deep voice, "for I only pretended to drink. How did you guess?"

Caroline hesitated. It was only a suspicion she had, with not a single bit of evidence, and if Miss Spenser had not looked so strange, she might never have spoken. But how could she accuse her? It was so unbelievable that she should be the guilty one! She saw that John was now staring past her at Lady Cecily's companion, his gaze intent and somber, and she looked behind her furtively, and gasped. The woman had moved away from the chair and was leveling a pistol at the company, every one of whom appeared frozen with horror.

"Do . . . do not move!" she commanded, her voice high and cracking with nerves. "Mr. Russell! Throw the gun that you are holding under the blanket, on the floor behind you!" Alistair hesitated, and she brought her pistol to bear on his heart. "Do as I say or I will shoot, and this time I shall do more than wound you!"

Alistair took one quick look at the lady's gray eyes, shining with fanatic intent behind her thick glasses, and obeyed, his pistol skittering away across the rug.

"SPENSER?" Lady Cecily asked, in a faint, disbelieving voice. "So, it was you after all?"

"Yes, m'lady!" she replied, her eyes darting around the group to be sure no one moved. "A stupid, silly widgeon, as you have called me so often, fit only to pass the plates and pour the tea! I planned it all, and *I* carried it out!"

"But why? I do not understand!" the old lady asked in bewilderment.

Her companion laughed, a shrill, bitter travesty of humor. Some of her hair had escaped the tight bun and was straggling around her face, which was mottled in red blotches on her thin cheeks. She was panting in her excitement, and her hurried breathing was perfectly audible in the stunned silence of the room. Now she nodded her head and laughed again, and Caroline, who had never heard anything that sounded so demented, so mad, could not restrain a shiver of fear.

And then Miss Spenser screamed suddenly, "Because the Covington inheritance is rightfully mine! Do you hear me, it is MINE? What right had all these others to come here after so many years of neglect and calmly take it from me? Eating and drinking so much, and burning candles and coal without counting the cost! All these years I have been so very frugal, for when you died, Rockledge would belong to me! Oh, I was upset when you said your father's money would never go to a bastard, but then I remembered that I am of legal birth; it was my mother who was illegitimate, and she was your father's daughter and your half sister as well, my *grand* lady! Of course the money is mine! None of the rest of you were going to have it, not if I had to kill every one of you!"

Her voice had risen to a shriek, and Caroline stole a look at John St. Williams. He was staring at Miss Spenser, his eyes narrowed and intent, and his body was so tense that Caroline knew he was only waiting for the right time to try and disarm the woman. Oh, do not attempt it, my dear, she prayed silently, for she is quite mad, and will not hesitate to shoot! Her gaze went over the others in the room.

Cecilia had fallen back in her chair as if in a faint, Lord and Lady Danvers sat close together, clutching each other's hands and looking like a parody of the nursery rhyme pair Lady Cecily had compared them to, and Alistair and Gregory appeared to be as frozen as a still-life painting. Even Mr. Covington-More's mouth hung open in shock.

"My dear Miss Spenser, you are distraught!" came the calm voice of Dr. Ward as the echoes of that shriek died away into silence. "Come, give me the pistol and let me help you."

Miss Spenser smiled at him, a coquettish simper that was somehow ridiculous on her faded, wrinkled face. "Of course, *you* would want to help me, Matthew," she said softly in a coy, girlish voice. "You know very well that after *she* dies, and Rockledge and all the money are mine, that we can be married at last! How long we have waited, my dearest Matthew, but it will not be long now, I promise you!"

The doctor stared at her, and the hand he had been holding out for the pistol dropped to his lap.

"Marry? Marry you?" he asked in complete incredulity. "Of course I will not marry you; wherever did you get such an idea?"

For a moment Miss Spenser frowned, but then she tossed her head and smiled at him again, while behind her thick glasses, her eyes glittered. "Oh, it is like you to pretend, sir, but I have known all along of your feelings for me, even though you tried to hide them! Those tender smiles, the way you took my hand and always asked so carefully after my health! In the beginning, I could not really believe it, for it was like a dream come true—all those years that I slaved away here alone, caring for that horrible old woman, but now my reward—and yours, too, my darling—is at hand! Why should I allow strangers to take away my money? I earned it, and I have waited so patiently for such a long time! After twenty-seven years of devotion and hard work, I was to sit quietly and watch it left to another? Never!"

For a moment there was a stunned silence, and then Alistair said, smiting his forehead with his good hand, "Of course! You remember the day I was shot, John, I told you that although I could not recall then, it seemed to me that I did know who had pulled the trigger? Just now, when she turned towards the fire, and the light glinted off her glasses, I remembered seeing that same flash of light just before the shot was fired!"

"Yes, and if you hadn't turned away slightly, the bullet would have found your heart!" Miss Spenser said in a rapid, hating voice. "The smart London fop, so beautifully dressed and so very amusing to Lady Cecily! You were to be the first, since I had failed to kill Lady Danvers!"

"But why—why did you try to kill me?" Sylvia Danvers asked in a quavering whisper.

"You, Lady Greedy-Grab? I saw you the first afternoon, as I took you over the house, eyeing all the valuable antiques and silver. I saw from the way you handled the old gold salver that you coveted it! That was my Grandfather Covington's salver! And you are not even a relation! But I knew you would steal as many things as you could, even if your husband was not named the heir! So I had to kill you so that not one single thing that belongs to Rockledge should be taken away. It is all mine—everything here!"

Sylvia Danvers sank back against her chair as Miss Spenser laughed at her and pointed the pistol in her direction. Caroline, who was afraid she might fire, she was so incensed by Lady Danvers' greed, spoke up in what she hoped was a normal tone of voice.

"And did you lure my brother to the gardener's shed and leave him to freeze to death because Lady Cecily liked him so much?"

"Of course! He was becoming such a little pet of her ladyship's!" Miss Spenser agreed, nodding her head violently, so that more hair escaped from her bun. She smiled at Caroline, and her voice became almost conversational. "That did not work either—I have had very bad luck, when you come to think of it; so unfair!—but my plan this evening was sure to dispose of him, and you too, Miss Covington, you too! I went to fetch more of the poison from my room this afternoon after I heard Lady Cecily telling my dear Matthew that she was determined to leave all her money to you and your brother. When or why she changed her mind I do not know, but after her announcement at dinner, it was a simple matter to change the victim and put the poison in the brandy meant only for Lord St. Williams. When Crowell brought the bottle up from the wine cellar, I told him to go and fetch another glass, for the snifter he had put on the tray was dirty. His eyesight is such that he could not tell whether I was speaking the truth or not, and while he went back to his pantry to get it, I put all the poison in the bottle and recorked it. You have had a narrow escape, Miss Covington, both you and your handsome scamp of a brother! And you must admit that for a stupid, silly widgeon, I have been very clever, have I not?"

She giggled and looked to Dr. Ward as if for approval, and Caroline, remembering how she had handed her a cup of tea, and how she had drunk it down, shuddered. How easy it would have been for Miss Spenser to poison her, puttering around the tea tray as she always did!

Lady Cecily, who had been sitting upright in the wing chair, listening intently, now spoke. "Not as clever as you suppose, Spenser, and thank heavens you did not succeed! I never intended to leave you Rockledge and the inheritance, never! And now I shall have to summon the law and charge you with all these crimes!" Her old voice was strong, and so controlled and determined, that Spenser turned towards her.

"What can you mean, m'lady? Until all these others came, you know you were planning to leave the money to me! Why, I have always counted on it! It is just that these London society people have turned your head, but when they are gone, you will come to your senses again! Matthew, *you* knew she meant the money for me, did you not? And I know you will help me convince her of my rightful claim, for then we can be married just as I have dreamed and planned . . ."

Dr. Ward shook his head. "I fear you have been suffering from a delusion, Miss Spenser. Lady Cecily never mentioned any such plan to me, and as for marrying you, that is not possible! It was only ordinary kindness that made me inquire for your health; I fear you have been imagining a warmer regard."

"But . . . but you love me, dear Matthew, I know you do!" Her voice cracked again, and in spite of her fears, Caroline felt sorry for the woman. Mad she surely was, but she had been building castles in the air all these years, imagining herself a great heiress and loved by Dr. Ward as well. How shattering to find out that none of it was true!

Miss Spenser began to weep, the heavy sobs racking her thin shoulders and chest. The gun she was holding fell to her side, and John St. Williams made a move as if he would try to take it from her.

"No, m'lord! Stay where you are!" Dr. Ward whispered, his eyes never leaving Miss Spenser's face, as he started to edge towards her.

"I cannot bear it, no, no, I cannot!" she cried out now in a despairing voice. "To think it was all for nothing, all of it! And I have worked so hard over the years, and made so many wonderful plans, and then when the money was almost within my grasp, it has been denied me! Oh, cruel, cruel!"

She reached up a shaking hand to wipe the tears from her face and, seeing the doctor and St. Williams moving towards her, crouched and raised her pistol again.

"Get back! Everyone stay exactly where you are!" Although her voice shook, it was firm with resolve again, and both men stopped. "You shall not send me to prison, Lady Cecily! There is still a way out for me!"

Suddenly, Caroline saw her glance at the snifter of poisoned brandy before she ran towards the table where it stood. Her intent to kill herself was obvious, and Caroline's hands flew to her breast in horror. But as Miss Spenser rushed by the wing chair, Lady Cecily thrust out her silver-headed cane and tripped her, and her companion went down in a heap of black skirts. Instantly, John was upon her, wresting the pistol from her grasp, the doctor close behind. At this last failure, the ending of her own life, all Miss Spenser's wits seemed to leave her, and she began to shriek at the top of her lungs, spewing out demented ravings and curses as she struggled with the two men trying to subdue her.

Caroline was glad they had been able to move; for herself, she felt frozen to the spot where she stood, and she noticed that none of the others had moved either. Miss Spenser was kicking and scratching now, never ceasing her vitriolic keening, when Mr. Covington-More took a hand. Waiting until her face was turned briefly towards him, he hit her sharply on the jaw with his fist, and immediately she sagged, unconscious, into Matthew Ward's arms.

"I suggest you take her away and tie and gag her, Doctor. In fact, I'll help you!" he said. "The woman is mad; she belongs in a lunatic asylum!"

Dr. Ward nodded, although his eyes were sad, and between them, they carried the unconscious woman out of the room. Everyone was silent until the sound of their footsteps died away.

"I really do think," Alistair said gently, as he shifted to a more comfortable position on the chaise and sighed, "that I shall be forced to leave this place whether my wounds are healed or not! One must think of one's nerves, after all!" The others stared at him, still speechless, as he bowed a little in Lady Cecily's direction. "My compliments, m'lady! That was surely an act of genius to trip the lady with your cane. I doubt if any of the rest of us would have thought so quickly or acted so decisively!"

Lady Cecily had sunk back against the squabs of her chair, the hand that was shielding her eyes shaking, but at his words, she raised her head and nodded.

"I must admit that I was so angry, Alistair, that I did not think of anything but stopping her!"

"Yes, it was very bad, all those planned murders; she is indeed insane!" he murmured.

"Well, yes, there is that too," Lady Cecily agreed, her voice gaining strength, "but at the time, what really made me cross was the fact that she had poisoned the very last bottle of Napoleon brandy!"

John St. Williams shook his head, but Caroline saw the tears on the old lady's cheeks and knew she was not so heedless of her companion's fate as she pretended.

"Would you like us to leave you now, m'lady?" she asked gently, going to kneel before her and offering her her own handkerchief. "This has been so very upsetting for you!"

"You're a good gel, Caro, I have always thought so!" Lady Cecily said, mopping her eyes and trying to smile. "But please do not go! I am so wrought up I would never be able to sleep. John, a glass of port, if you please, before Dr. Ward comes back and forbids it."

St. Williams moved to do her bidding, and Gregory, who all this time had been holding his glass perfectly still, gulped the contents suddenly, as if he had just remembered he had it. He joined John at the table, asking Alistair what he could get for him, in a solemn voice. Lady Cecily patted Caroline's cheek and suggested she see to Cecilia.

"I think she has fainted," she said. "And who can blame her?"

Caroline went to her cousin and was glad to see that, outside of her pallor and shallow breathing, she was conscious, for she had begun to wring her hands and moan a little. Lady Danvers stared straight ahead of her, her face still white and frozen, and her husband, his pale-blue eyes popping in amazement, tottered over to fetch her some brandy from the bottle he had used earlier, John St. Williams having moved the poisoned glass and bottle to the mantel, where they would be out of the way.

"I seem to have made the most frightful mull of things," Lady Cecily remarked after a sip of port. "M'father would be ashamed of me! But thank heavens you came to see me this afternoon, John, and convinced me that by naming Caro and Gregory as my heirs, I was putting their lives in danger!"

"And he, of course, was perfectly willing to brave that danger, if he could be named the Covington heir instead!" Lady Danvers bristled, speaking for the first time, her breast heaving in indignation at John's cleverness.

Lady Cecily sent her a look of complete dislike. "That was only play-acting for this evening! John was sure the murderer would make a move after I announced my heir, and was on his guard, which neither of the Covingtons would have been."

Caroline's eyes widened and went quickly to John's face, her color rising, and he grinned at her even as he shook his head.

"M'lady makes me seem foolishly courageous, but in truth there was little danger. After talking the situation over and pooling our knowledge, Lady Cecily and I devised the trap, using the Napoleon brandy as bait. You see, I was almost certain the culprit had to be Miss Spenser, although Lady Cecily could not believe it. Alistair had been shot, and Gregory's life attempted as well, and I knew it could not be Caroline, after the gun disappeared that night in the hall. That left only Cecilia, the Danvers, or Miss Spenser, and somehow I could not seriously believe either Cecy, Sylvia, or Roger were murderers; in any case, they could not have been the spy in the priest hole."

"Thank you," Lady Danvers said sarcastically, but her husband bowed in his ponderous way and in a serious voice thanked m'lord for his compliment.

Lord St. Williams continued as if he had not been interrupted. "Only Miss Spenser could have been the owner of that mysterious eye, and since she was so seldom in our company, the priest hole was the perfect means to keep abreast of our activities and conversations. But even knowing all that, we could not just accuse her without proof. Of course, neither Lady Cecily or myself had the slightest idea the woman expected to inherit, and was quite mad as well, or that she would have the pistol with her this evening, for I would not have placed you all in such jeopardy."

Everyone was silent for a moment, remembering that madness and what might have resulted from it, and then Cecy spoke up, her brow creased with thought. "But did you forget Mr. Covington-More?" she asked.

Lady Cecily explained the gentleman: his enor-

212

mous wealth and his complete acceptance of the fact he would never inherit, and soon everyone was exclaiming and talking over these extraordinary events, although in a subdued way, for death had been very close to all of them this evening.

Caroline put up her chin and went over to where John St. Williams was lounging against the center table, tall and dark and powerful-looking as he warmed a new snifter of brandy in his hands.

"It appears that I—and my brother as well—have reason to be grateful to you once again, m'lord!" she began, and was surprised to see the frown that crossed his features.

"Do me the kindness to stop being so everlastingly grateful to me, Caro!" he snapped, his teeth gritting as if his patience had worn thin. "I do not want you to be indebted to me!"

"Not . . . not want it?" she whispered, afraid the others might overhear this unusual conversation.

"It is the last thing I want from you, my girl!" he said, and then he sighed and folded his arms as if he had come to a sudden decision, and his brooding eyes never left her face. "Do you realize how impossible this situation is for me? How can I possibly propose to you if you feel under obligation to accept me because I have saved not only your own life, but Gregory's as well?" He ran his hand through his dark hair in that familiar, impatient gesture as Caroline paled. "But of course, there has been an additional impediment placed in my path now!" he mused with a rueful grin.

"Another impediment?" she asked, feeling the color coming and going in her cheeks, and wishing she had better control of her complexion, even as she wondered if she had really heard him correctly. John St. Williams propose? to *her?*

John laughed a little and sipped his brandy. "How very unlike you, my dear, to be so tongue-tied that you can only repeat my words back to me! What I meant was that now you are an heiress, you will have the whole world chasing you, beginning with my cousin Alistair, who even now is trying so hard to get your attention! So you might well begin to doubt me and think I was only determined to get my hands on the Covington fortune one way or the other. 'Ware fortune hunters, Caro!"

Caroline put her hands to her hot cheeks. "But you are so very wealthy already, John—and besides, you know very well that that night in Gregory's room, after you kissed me, why—why, you begged my pardon and were so very cold to me, and I thought—well, of course, what else was I to think? —I mean . . ."

Her voice died away, and John grinned down at her for the most tangled sentence he had ever heard in his life. "What a shame we are trapped in this crowded drawing room! I would dearly love to explain to you why I behaved as I did, and to repeat that kiss as well!"

He put his glass on the table and moved towards her, and Caroline retreated, for he looked so dangerous she was afraid he might forget himself and do just that.

"You must excuse me, m'lord," she said, feeling at a terrible disadvantage in this improbable conversation. John stared down into her confused blue eyes as if he wanted to see into her mind and soul or let her know what was in his.

"Very well, dear Caro," he said more quietly, "I will let Alistair have his chance, but you must believe me when I tell you that I love you with all my heart and have no intention of giving up my pursuit!"

Caroline swept him a shaky curtsy. "I wish you good fortune, sir!" she said demurely, glad to turn away and go to Alistair, and determined to ignore the sudden light that flashed in his dark eyes at her words.

CHAPTER 12

BUT JOHN ST. WILLIAMS' good fortune was not allowed to flourish unchecked in the days that followed.

The morning after the unmasking of the would-be murderer, everyone was relieved to discover that Dr. Ward had already taken Miss Spenser away; a calm and docile Miss Spenser, so Crowell told them, who behaved as if she were going on her wedding journey, even to throwing an imaginary bouquet from the gig as it drew away from the front steps, and waving her hands to the crowds of retainers and servants that only she could see.

Lord and Lady Danvers left later that day, taking Cecilia North with them, for Cecy was anxious to begin her preparations for the coming London season, and Lady Cecily had asked both Caroline and Gregory to remain at Rockledge a while longer. Gregory, dazed by his good fortune, quickly agreed. "Happy to stay as long as you like, m'lady!" he grinned expansively, and Caroline nodded as well, delighted that she was not to be separated from m'lord St. Williams quite yet, although she told herself it was only that she wished to see her great-aunt comfortable before she returned to Falconfield.

She had smiled openly when she saw Cecilia's

effusive leave-taking of her brother, and her wheedling a promise from him that he would not fail to call on her during the season. She could see that Cecy was not at all afraid to face her mother now, for although she had not been chosen as the Covington heiress, with the headway she had already made, she saw no reason why she should not become the heir's wife. Lady Danvers stiffened as Cecy kissed Gregory good-bye so warmly, blushing adorably as she did so, and Caroline could see that Cecy was soon to be treated to a lecture on the proper behavior of young misses of the haut ton, until they reached the English border at the very least. She was very glad she was not a member of *that* traveling party!

Sylvia Danvers' good-byes were brief and coldly formal, although Roger acted as if he had had the most pleasant sojourn possible in Scotland, and was still extolling the healthful benefits of the bracing salt air and extending his compliments to one and all when his wife pulled him into the coach.

Mr. Covington-More was not long behind them. He told Lady Cecily and the others that he had been away from his business too long as it was. As he took his leave, he pressed a Methodist tract into Gregory's hands, which the young man was astonished to discover was all about the evils of drink and loose living, and how difficult it was for a rich man to enter the gates of heaven.

"Something insane about a camel going through the eye of a needle, Caro!" he told them all that evening at dinner, "And what has that to say to anything, I should like to know? We have no camels in England, except possibly at the Royal Enclosure, and I am not such a flat that I would try to put one through the eye of a needle in any case! Such stuff!"

Lady Cecily laughed so hard that Caroline was afraid she would choke on her steak-and-kidney pie, and even Alistair and John were grinning at Gregory's indignant confusion.

Alistair had come downstairs unaided for the first

time, saying he felt much better and was ready to travel any time John chose. M'lord, careful not to look in Caroline's direction, replied that he would not dream of rushing his cousin; why, to start off too precipitously might well open his wound again, and he would never be able to forgive himself if that should happen!

Alistair was not best pleased with this decision. The evening of Miss Spenser's startling revelations, he had been quick to whisper to Caroline when she finally came to his side, "Dear Caro! How fortunate that you heard my proposal *before* I learned you would inherit! Now you—and the world—cannot accuse me of any mercenary intent! Say you will consider it, my dear, for I would find it so tedious to have to begin courting another lady not half so charming as yourself. In fact, it does not bear thinking of; I am sure to be bored!"

Caroline had laughed at him, but he had received no other encouragement. She was charming and polite, but she made it clear that not even saving him from his creditors could tempt her to marry him.

It seemed to John St. Williams that Caroline was deliberately avoiding him. When he came down to the hall in search of her, it was to find her disappearing into Lady Cecily's room and firmly closing the door behind her. If he smiled at her at the table, she lowered her eyes and began to speak to her brother, and if he ran her to earth in the library, she always seemed to be planning menus with the excellent housekeeper she had found to care for the household, or interviewing applicants for the now-vacant post of secretary-companion.

He was determined to bring matters to a head, and the afternoon Great-Aunt Cecily's solicitor arrived to draw up her new will, he was waiting for her in the hall. He had met Gregory there, dressed to take his sister for a walk, and by some clever maneuvering, had arranged to take his place. Gregory was perfectly happy to stroll down to the stables,

217

instead, and inspect his great-aunt's cattle. When Caroline came down in her warm cloak, she was startled to see John St. Williams waiting for her at the foot of the stairs, dressed in his greatcoat and tapping his gloves against one strong hand, his beaver set at a rakish angle over one eye.

"And where is my brother, m'lord?" she asked, feeling a little breathless as he tipped his hat and raised one eyebrow.

Caroline was in a quandary. She had indeed been trying to avoid John, not from any desire to be coy, but because she could not be sure he had meant what he had said that fateful evening in the drawing room. Besides, the depths of her own emotions frightened her, for she had never been in love and she had not known it would consume her this way. She was aware now that she loved John St. Williams completely and forever, for when he had been about to drink the poisoned brandy, her heart had all but stood still in agony that she might lose him. Surely such passion was not normal, and while she admitted she was helpless to restrain her feelings, she still found the whole situation terrifying. What if he kissed her again, and she disgusted him by responding as emotionally as she had before?

Now he took her hand and tucked it in his arm as he led her down the hall to where Crowell was waiting to open the front door for them.

"Gregory has excused himself," he said blandly. "It seems that there are some urgent letters that he must write, so I volunteered to take his place."

Caroline smiled in spite of herself. "What a whisker, m'lord! Gregory has never written an urgent letter in his life! Who would he write to? All his correspondents have given him up long ago, for he never sets pen to paper!"

She went down the front steps on St. Williams' arm, and he guided her around the circular drive without replying. She wondered why her heart was skipping beats and then racing so erratically, and hoped he might think her blushes resulted from the cold fresh air.

"Shall we stroll down the drive, as we did before, Caro?" he asked, his dark eyes smiling down at her.

She nodded, suddenly not trusting herself to speak. They walked on a little way in silence until they came to a bend in the drive, and then John stopped and glanced over his shoulder.

"Yes, we are out of sight! Now, my dear Caro, an answer, if you please!"

"An answer?" she asked, brushing back a brown curl that had escaped her hood.

"We will not start *that* again, you replying by repeating my words back to me!" he said, and then, as if he could wait no longer, he took her into his arms. He tipped up her chin with one gloved hand and bent his warm, firm lips to hers. Caroline concentrated on standing very stiff and still until she felt she could not bear it another moment. Fortunately, before she lost all her self-control, John raised his head and stared at her.

"What on earth is the matter with you?" he asked, his dark brows coming together in a ferocious frown as his hands tightened a little on her arms. "That was not the way you kissed me in Gregory's room!"

Caroline closed her eyes for a moment, for how could she possibly explain? But Lord St. Williams was not about to allow her to escape.

"Answer me!" he growled, shaking her a little for emphasis. "I cannot believe your feelings have changed so much; why, that was like kissing a marble statue! And all this time I have been dreaming of the warm, vibrant woman who returned my kiss so passionately that night! It has kept me awake more nights than I like to tell you, my dear. But stay!"

Suddenly he dropped his hands and, stepping back, said in a harsh voice, "Perhaps you have had second thoughts? Or perhaps I was right, and that kiss was only from gratitude?" He laughed bitterly. "In that

219

case, I shall endeavor to save you and all your family at each and every opportunity!"

Caroline could bear it no longer. "No, John! That is not why I behaved as I did! I was afraid that my kiss might give you a disgust of me; I knew I should not be so . . . so unrestrained! What gentleman wants a wife who is so wanton, so abandoned, so . . ."

But she was not allowed to finish her sentence, for John had taken the two steps back to her and lifted her off her feet to hold her clasped against his broad chest.

"Idiot!" he said fondly. "A DISGUST of you? Caro, you are all about in your head! If you really want to punish me, continue to kiss me the way you just did; why, I might just as well have kissed Lady Cecily's butler! You know very little about men if so you think. What I want is a repeat of your earlier performance, and that as often as possible!"

He bent his head again, and with a little sigh of relief, Caroline put her arms around his neck and fervently complied with the gentleman's request.

At last he set her back on her feet again, but he kept one strong arm around her to hold her close. "You must allow me to explain my actions in Gregory's room that night, dear Caro!" he said, his deep voice a little unsteady. "You see, I knew I was falling in love with you, but it was plain to me that the only emotion you felt for me was gratitude for saving Gregory's life. After all, you had told me earlier that you would never forgive me; I had to believe that that was the true state of your emotions towards me. And so, when I could not help myself and kissed you, I knew it was unfair to you."

"You might have asked me, John," Caroline interrupted, "instead of just kissing me, and then turning so cold and formal!"

"You will never know what that cost me, to behave so honorably, dear Caro, when all I wanted to do was repeat that kiss . . . like this!"

It took them a long time to reach the deserted

gatehouse and the road and begin to retrace their steps to Rockledge, for there were many such stops along the way.

As they came at last within sight of the house, John said with a fond grin, "At least I cannot be accused of fortune hunting! I know what you have done, my love, for Lady Cecily told me! Giving away some of your fortune to Alistair to settle his debts, as well as adding to Cecy's portion and insisting Lady Cecily leave enough money to keep Miss Spenser in comfort for the rest of her life. You are not a very astute business woman, I'm afraid, but it is like you to be so kind!"

Caroline blushed and hugged his arm. "Perhaps I knew that you, with all your vast wealth, would take care of me, John!"

"Be sure I will, my love—always!" he promised, a fond and serious look in his dark eyes.

As they gained the steps, he stopped and raised an eyebrow at her. "But how can this be, my love? I fear you have forgotten the Danvers, and that, of course, is a serious oversight! Having been so very generous to the others, of course you must remember them!"

Caroline swept him a curtsy, and as he drew her up and close to him again, she said with a laugh, "But I have remembered them! Lady Cecily agreed with me that the perfect legacy for Sylvia Danvers was Grandfather Covington's antique gold salver, since the lady coveted it so much!"

"Minx!" he murmured through his laughter, and then he pushed back the fur-lined hood and buried his face in her brown hair, whispering endearments all the while.

It was a very long time before Crowell was summoned to open the front door.

Let COVENTRY Give You
A Little Old-Fashioned Romance

☐ MISS KEATING'S TEMPTATION   50226 $1.50
    by Margaret SeBastian

☐ A FRIEND OF THE FAMILY   50227 $1.50
    by Denice Greenlea

☐ THE HEIRESS COMPANION   50228 $1.50
    by Madeleine Robins

☐ DELSIE   50232 $1.50
    by Joan Smith

☐ MISS MIRANDA'S MARRIAGE   50233 $1.50
    by Claire Lorel

☐ THE SUN WITH A FACE   50234 $1.50
    by Meriol Trevor

ROMANCE From Fawcett Books

☐ **A NECESSARY WOMAN**   04544 $2.75
by Helen Van Slyke
Mary Farr Morgan seemed to have everything—a handsome husband, successful career, good looks. She had everything except a man who could make her feel like a woman.

☐ **THIS ROUGH MAGIC**   24129 $2.50
by Mary Stewart
A pretty, young British actress goes to Corfu for a holiday, and finds herself tangled in a web of romance and violence.

☐ **THE SPRING OF THE TIGER**   24297 $2.75
by Victoria Holt
A tale of intrigue and love. A young woman goes to Ceylon and finds herself in a marriage of thwarted passion and danger.

☐ **POINCIANA**   24447 $3.25
by Phyllis A. Whitney
A spellbinding saga of love betrayed and of a woman trapped by the past. Set amidst the lush splendor of Palm Beach.

☐ **THE RICH ARE DIFFERENT**   24098 $2.95
by Susan Howatch
This is the story of a young Englishwoman whose life, loves and ambition become intertwined with the fate of a great American banking family.

CURRENT CREST BESTSELLERS